Contents

THE PLAYBOY'S SEDUCTION

Lucy Monroe

Award-winning and bestselling author Lucy Monroe sold her first book in September of 2002 to Mills & Boon® Modern™. That book represented a dream that had been burning in her heart for years...the dream to share her stories with readers who love romance as much as she does. Since then she has sold more than thirty books to three publishers and hit national bestsellers lists in the US and England, but what has touched her most deeply since selling that first book are the reader letters she receives. Her most important goal with every book is to touch a reader's heart and when she hears she's done that it makes every night spent writing into the wee hours of morning worth it. She started reading Mills & Boon® Modern™ very young and discovered a heroic type of man between the covers of those books...an honourable man, capable of faithfulness and sacrifice for the people he loves. Now married to what she terms her "alpha male at the end of a book", Lucy believes there is a lot more reality to the fantasy stories she writes than most people give credit for. She believes in happy endings that are really marvellous beginnings and that's why she writes them. She hopes her books help readers to believe a little too...just like romance did for her so many years ago. She really does love to hear from readers and responds to every e-mail. You can reach her by e-mailing lucymonroe@lucy-monroe.com.

Lucy says...

"Keep the romance alive in your relationship through communication. Love before anger. Expecting the best and giving the best. My mum gave me great advice when I got married and both my husband and I live by it to this day. She said that a good relationship is not fifty-fifty...it is both partners giving one hundred percent of themselves and that is what we try to do. It works!"

Find more wonderfully sexy stories featuring Lucy Monroe's trademark gorgeous heroes in *With Love: Royal Brides* – available now from M&B™!

THE PLAYBOY'S SEDUCTION

BETHANY rushed back toward the quaint but expensive café where she'd eaten lunch, hope, frustration and worry playing an out-of-sync symphony along her nerve endings.

She'd been in Rome three days. Beautiful, warm days during which she'd spent more time getting lost than sight seeing and not one of which had taken her a single step closer to her goal. The plan to come to Italy, meet a sexy man, have a week long fling and go home with the certainty she was not the passionless prude her ex-husband had accused her of being, had been crazy from the start. Her mother hadn't agreed of course, having come up with the plan to begin with. She'd also given Bethany the all-expenses paid trip to Rome along with a boatload of advice on improving her image and a strong recommendation to have a no-strings affair.

Coming from the rather conservative, shy woman who had

spent thirty years married to the same man, the suggestion would have been hilarious if it hadn't been so shocking.

Not wanting to hurt her mom's feelings, Bethany had taken the self-improvement advice. She'd spent a hundred dollars having her mousy brown hair shaped and high-lighted, another thirty on a "Belly Dancing in a Box" kit, and several nights using the castanets and tips included to try to get in touch with her more sensuous side. She wasn't sure how much good it had done, but she now knew how to roll her hips with the best of them. She'd also had her very first pedicure so her toenails looked good in sandals.

None of which appeared to have done a bit of good in making Bethany appear any less boring to the opposite sex than her ex had accused her of being.

Shoving open the door to the small café, she propelled herself inside and ran smack into a wall. She didn't remember there being a wall opposite the entrance when she'd been here earlier.

Dazed, she contemplated that oddity as the wall shifted and two warm hands came down on her shoulders. *"Scusi. Siete guisti?"*

She lifted her head, and met dark brown eyes in a face angels would envy. She'd never met anyone this gorgeous in her life. Not even her ex, Kurt, was a patch on this guy. He'd been pretty boy handsome, but this Italian Adonis was all masculine maturity. Not that he looked old, quite the opposite. He couldn't be more than thirty, but there was a wealth of sophisticated knowledge in his gaze she doubted she would have when she was ninety.

"I'm sorry. I mean, *perdonilo prego,*" she said, repeating one of the phrases she'd learned from the set of Italian tapes her mother had insisted she listen to on the plane ride over.

"You are English?" The sexy voice reached a place inside that hadn't been touched in two years of marital intimacy and it was all she could do not to shiver.

"American."

His hands squeezed her shoulders, but he did not push her away and she made no effort to move back.

"You have no need to apologize."

"I wasn't looking where I was going."

"For this, I am grateful." He smiled, the implication of his words and look of male appreciation in his eyes unmistakable.

An invisible vacuum sucked all the air from her immediate surroundings, leaving her light headed and incapable of response to his flirtatious comment.

"You are in a hurry?" he asked.

"I am?"

His smile grew, sending her heart rate into the stratosphere. "You came through the door very quickly."

"Oh, yes. I am, in a hurry that is... I forgot my purse here earlier and didn't realize it until I was at the subway station wanting to buy a ticket," she babbled.

His expression turned grave. "This is not good."

"No." But at the moment she couldn't quite remember why.

Someone said something behind him and he turned, his hands dropping from her shoulders. He apologized for blocking the exit and then slipped an arm around her waist as naturally as if they'd known each other for years, and used it to guide her away from the door. A couple walked past them. The woman, a glamorous brunette who resembled a young Sophia Loren, gave Bethany a look of speculation tinged with envy as she passed by. Considering the fact she was with a pretty fine specimen herself, the envy surprised Bethany.

But she didn't dwell on the strange look long. She couldn't, not with his hand still attached to her waist. Sparks of excitement shot from where his fingers rested against her ribcage to the rest of her body in an electric reaction she'd never experienced before. She'd read about instant sexual attraction, but she'd never felt it and nothing she'd come across in books came close to conveying the sensations zinging along her nerve endings right now. She could barely breathe and it was a safe bet her brain wasn't functioning properly.

That was probably why she still hadn't done anything about reclaiming her purse. "I need to..." Her voice trailed off as their gazes met again.

"I will ask about your bag."

"Thank you."

He took her with him, his hand firmly curled around her waist...and she let him.

The possibility he did not feel the overwhelming sexual chemistry dominating her senses tried to form as a solid thought in her head, but she rejected it. Something this powerful could not be one-sided. Could it?

The owner, a short, rather round man with a friendly air, produced her purse with a big smile and voluble Italian when her companion asked about it.

Handing her the pink and black bag barely bigger than a wallet, he admonished, "You should take better care, *signorina*." He shook his head. "What would have happened if I had not seen it sitting on the chair, I will not guess at."

"It would no doubt be gone by now," the man by her side replied.

She shot him a sideways glance, wondering if he thought she was some kind of idiot for leaving it behind, but his expression was serious, not condemning.

"I don't keep my passport or most of my money in it," she said in her own defense. "Just a few Euros, my driver's license for identification and a credit card."

"Look to see it is all there. Antonio may have seen your purse after someone else did."

She nodded and then did a quick rummage through the contents. She wasn't worried about the make up and other girly stuff she'd only taken to carrying since her arrival in Italy, but none of it appeared to have been disturbed either.

She looked up at the café owner and smiled. "It's all here."

He nodded, puffing his chest out. "I see it almost the moment you get up from your table and put it behind my counter."

"Thank you." She took some money out to give Antonio as a thank you, but he waved it away.

"No, *signorina*. It is my pleasure to help such a beautiful woman."

She laughed, shaking her head at his typical Italian exaggeration. "Well, thank you, anyway."

"You do not believe him?"

"That it is his pleasure to help? I don't doubt it. He seems like a very nice man." And she smiled again at the proprietor. "You've really saved me a lot of hassle. Thanks."

"Ah, so it is the part about your beauty you discount?" her knight errant asked teasingly.

She shrugged, the feel of her arm brushing his torso as she did so temporarily waylaying the synapses connecting her brain to her mouth so she had to remember what he'd asked before she could answer him.

CHAPTER TWO

"I'M HARDLY Miss America material, but then few women are."

Was she fishing for compliments? Andre stepped back from her and let his gaze travel slowly up her body from her feet to the top of her head. "I would not mind seeing you dressed in an evening gown. It is part of the pageant, yes?" He brushed his chin with his thumb and forefinger, looking at her with a connoisseur's eye. "Or perhaps in a swim suit..."

"What?"

Andre almost laughed out loud at the comic look of disbelief on the lovely woman's face. He didn't, of course. She already looked ready to bolt. Shy uncertainty radiated off of her and a little used urge to protect roared to the forefront of his consciousness like a storm wave crashing over the bow of a ship.

"I'm sure this could be arranged if you asked her to dinner. Take her someplace very nice and she can dress up for you. Then maybe tomorrow, you will take her out of the city, someplace nice to bathe." Antonio's heavy-handed suggestion brought the sensual heat of Andre's thoughts to boiling point.

Her flirty sundress revealed the sort of curves that fueled his nighttime fantasies. The thought of seeing them in a skimpy bikini while they swam was enough to make his trousers fit extremely tight in places.

"But I... That's not necessary. You shouldn't..." She sounded like she was strangling on her own tongue trying to get the words out.

"Antonio, you are embarrassing her," Andre admonished the older man.

"Do not be stupid." His father's oldest friend made a sound of disgust. "The young. I am helping you out here. Can you not see that? In my youth, I would not have needed an old man to suggest I ask such a pretty girl out. You just ask your father."

Before Andre could reply, she was tearing herself from his side and moving away, a phony smile pasted on her face. "I'd better be going."

"You have plans?" He moved toward her, swallowing the small distance she'd put between their bodies, craving even such innocent intimacy on a level that shocked him. "You are meeting someone?"

"Uh...no," she admitted, her gray eyes wide. "I don't have plans exactly, but I wanted to try to see the Forums. If finding them is anything like finding the Sistine Chapel, I'll probably get lost again. You'd think it would be impossible, wouldn't you? I mean, I bet everyone in Rome knows where they are, but I've already managed to get on the wrong bus twice."

She started edging back toward the door, her expression pained. "If I don't leave now, I won't make it before they stop giving tours."

He reached out and grabbed her arm before she could run into the occupied table behind her. "Be careful."

She looked behind her, saw the table and then back at him, her face going pink. "I didn't realize... Uh, thank you."

He reeled her back in, not understanding this need he had to touch, but willing to feed it. "You wish to see the Forums?"

"Yes." She sighed, the blush on her cheeks intensifying. "There's so much I want to see, but I've spent hours every day trying to find things. I guess I sound like an idiot."

She sounded and looked like a woman who should not be on her own in such a large city.

"It is a big city. Getting lost is easy."

"I bet you never do."

"Of course not." Then he grinned. "But I do have the advantage of knowing the city quite well even though I do not live here."

He waited to see if she would take the bait and ask him for directions, or even better, to show her the way to the Forums.

"I could live here for years and still get lost, I'm afraid. Kurt used to say I could turn around in a bathroom and forget which direction to go when I came out."

"Who is this Kurt?" The idea of another man in her life bothered him more than it should considering he did not yet even know her name.

"My ex-husband."

"Ah. A man foolish enough to let you go can have no opinions worth remembering."

She laughed and shook her head as she had earlier when

Antonio had called her beautiful. "My mother says the same thing."

"She is a smart woman."

"Yes. She wouldn't get lost trying to find Rome's biggest attractions. She thought I should take a tour." A frown marred the sweet lines of her face. "Maybe I should have."

"This I do not believe. Had you come with a group, I should not have met you."

"Oh..." She stared at him as if trying to comprehend his words.

Since his English was excellent, he didn't think the problem was translation.

"I will take you to the Forums."

Her eyes lit up and then turned troubled as she flicked a glance at Antonio. "But..."

"It is alright, *signorina*. This is Andre di Rinaldi. He is a good man. I have known his father since we were boys on the same football team. He comes often to Rome on business and visits this old man."

She did not look appreciably reassured. "I did not tell you about me getting lost in hopes you would offer to take me yourself," she blurted out.

"But why not? Have you no wiles, child?" Antonio asked, sounding scandalized and amused at the same time while his eyes told Andre this woman was something special.

He had already figured that one out for himself. "I would not have offered if I had not wished to take you."

"Are you sure you have the time?" she asked.

"I have no appointments today. This is not usual for me. It must be Providence."

She stared at him for several seconds, chewing her bottom lip, her eyes cloudy with uncertainty. He waited, not wanting to pressure her, but knowing if she turned him down he would probably go to ridiculous lengths to discover where she was staying and engineer another meeting. He'd never felt this compulsion to be with a woman and as much as he liked her, he didn't like feeling so little control over his own desires. There was also a small part of him, the cynical man who had been raised in wealth and to expect people to try to take advantage of him, that wondered if any woman could be as sincere as she appeared.

He allowed none of these conflicting emotions to show on his face, however.

With a short little sigh, she put her hand out in the small space between them. "My name is Bethany Dayton and I would be very grateful if you would help me find the Forums without getting lost again."

Giving into the urge that had been riding him since she'd first propelled herself into his arms, he pulled her body flush with his and bent down to kiss both her cheeks. Her skin was soft and she smelled of spring flowers and warm sunshine.

She hung, suspended in his arms, making no effort to be released, her lips parted as if waiting for a much more intimate kiss and it took all his self-control not to give it to her.

"It is good to meet you Bethany."

Bethany couldn't string two syllables together to make a reply after he'd all but kissed her.

Well, he *had* kissed her, but not on the mouth. Who knew that lips touching cheeks could cause such unsettling reactions in her feminine places? It was a good thing her dress was made of opaque fabric or the stinging tightness of her nipples would be more than a minor physical discomfort. It would be downright embarrassing.

CHAPTER THREE

BETHANY concentrated on getting her physical reactions under control as Andre said goodbye to the café owner. It didn't help that as he led her from the restaurant, he kept her hand clasped in his.

He stopped beside a black car, slung low to the ground. It was some kind of sports car and looked expensive. It also looked too small for such a tall man to get inside. However, after leaning over her to buckle her into the passenger seat, making her breathing pattern resemble that of a marathon runner on his last mile, he had no problem sliding into the driver's seat. Unlike the taxi ride from the airport to her hotel when she'd spent the entire time cringing at how close they got to other cars, she barely noticed the traffic. She was too busy soaking in every detail about him.

She couldn't quite believe she was here with him, not only because he was a virtual stranger, but because he was the kind of man that made women swoon.

He turned and smiled at her. "You are watching me."

"Does it bother you?"

"To have a beautiful woman look at me? You are talking about an Italian male here." He grinned. "Of course I like it, even if it makes driving difficult."

"It bothers you to have people watch you drive?"

"Having *you* look at me takes my attention from where it should be. It puts thoughts in my head not related to the other cars on the road."

"Like what?" she asked before having a sudden revelation about what he could mean and wished she'd kept her mouth shut.

She could feel her face flame as his laughter filled the car.

"Do you really wish me to answer this question?"

"Uh...no."

His expression was all confident, sexy male. "Perhaps we can discuss it over dinner tonight."

"You want to have dinner with me?"

"Sì, carina."

Pretty one. She liked that. Warmth curled around her heart even as heat pooled deep in her belly at the thought of what he might want to discuss. "I'd like that."

* * *

He took her to an expensive restaurant just as his friend had suggested. It gave her an excuse to wear the ridiculously expensive, ruby red dress her mom had talked her into buying the week before she'd flown to Rome. It hit mid-thigh, which was not her usual length, but the look of blatant male appreciation in his eyes when she walked into the lobby of her hotel made her glad she'd gone for daring rather than drab.

However, at the table in an exclusive hotel dining room twenty minutes later, she had to struggle not to squirm as the clingy fabric barely covered everything important when she sat down. The fact her now bare thighs were covered by the tablecloth did nothing to increase her comfort because the expression in Andre's eyes said he knew her predicament and had x-ray vision to see the results.

He'd been like that all day, teasing her and reminding her of feminine sensuality. The hours they'd spent at the Forums had been incredible. Not only had he gotten her there without getting lost, but then he'd given her a personal tour of several monuments, showing an unexpected knowledge of Roman history that enthralled her.

"You are doing it again, Bethany."

"Doing what?"

"Staring at me."

She started and flushed with embarrassment. She had been. He was just so gorgeous and in his business suit, he looked like some kind of tycoon—not a guy she'd met in his father's friend's café.

"I can't help it," she admitted.

He smiled, making her heart do crazy things while the thighs that felt so exposed quivered.

"You are very forthright."

"Because I admit I like looking at you?" She didn't have the sophistication to play male-female games the way her ex-husband had done and Andre was so clearly expecting.

"You do not do the hard-to-get thing. I like this."

"I'm not very good at playing anything."

"I do not believe that." The wicked twinkle in his dark eyes let her know exactly what he was referring to and it had nothing to do with psychological games.

"You're right. I can play some things." She smiled mischievously as his dark eyes heated with desire.

"I am glad to hear this."

She smiled and fluttered her eyelashes in an obvious parody of a vamp. "Actually, I've been told I'm very good with my mouth."

His jaw dropped in shock and she had to hold back a shout of laughter as she leaned forward and whispered conspiratorially, "I play the tuba."

His laughter drew the attention of the other guests and a censorious glance from the head waiter. He shook his head, his eyes still glowing with humor. *"The tuba?"*

"I had to lift weights to stay in shape for marching band, but I was at a distinct advantage during cold weather. My instrument acted as a wind barrier."

"Do you still do weight training?"

"Actually, yes. I enjoy it. See?" She lifted her arm and flexed her muscles. She wasn't anything like the professional women body builders, but she was toned.

He lifted his hand and ran a finger slowly along her bicep. "I do see and it's lovely."

She gasped as feelings fizzed through her, making her toned muscles turn to jelly.

His brow rose quizzically.

"I can't believe the way I respond to your simplest touch," she admitted.

Smiling lazily, his finger trailed to her shoulder and slipped under the spaghetti strap as her arm dropped. "No touch between a man and woman who are attracted to each other is simple."

She liked the attracted to each other part. "I guess so, but this is a little overwhelming. My *whole body* is reacting to what should be a casual caress, for goodness' sake."

"I have noticed this." His dark gaze lowered to her breasts where she knew hard points had formed under the clinging material of her dress. "And I delight in it."

The self-satisfaction in his voice combined with his all too knowing expression made her feel vulnerable, which in turn made her angry. This trip had not been about her becoming receptive to yet another sexy, experienced man. She was on a mission to reinforce her own sense of feminine power.

It was all very well to say *they* were attracted, but she was the one whose desire was on display for the world to see. Pulling away from his touch, she crossed her arms protectively over her chest and tried to draw her defenses around her.

The smile slipped off Andre's face to be replaced by an almost fierce expression. "Do you think it is only one-sided, this powerful response? I could not stand right now to save my life."

Her gaze flicked questioningly toward where the table hid his lower body from her sight.

"Exactly," he said grimly. "If your body is susceptible to this thing between us, so is mine. I am not a hormonal adolescent any longer to be excited by the mere brush of my finger against a woman's bare skin."

Yet he had been.

CHAPTER FOUR

"IT IS NOT something you should fear, *carina,* for I am at its mercy as well."

"*It?*"

"This sexual need that is so strong it drowns out all logic and reason. Do you think I make it a habit to pick up strange women and spend the day with them, no matter how beautiful?"

"I don't know. You said it yourself. We're strangers."

"I assure you, I do not. No more than you would normally have dinner with a man you had never met before today."

"How do you know?"

He stared at her, his brown eyes seeing too much. *"I know."*

Her mind balked at the belief that a man as incredible as the one sitting across the table from her could be as affected by her as Andre claimed to be, but her heart beat with the necessity for his words to be true.

"This kind of thing is impossible. I don't believe in love at first sight." Especially after her disastrous marriage, which had been the result of a whirlwind courtship.

"Deep, abiding love between two people must grow." The words agreed with her, but his tone and expression questioned both their assertions.

"Yes," she stressed. "Like a plant. It takes lots of water, sunshine and healthy soil to make a flower bloom. Real love can't just happen in an instant."

"But there are plants that grow in a day. They are unique, extremely rare, but no less real than their more conventional counterparts."

"What are you saying?"

"I do not know, but this thing that is between us—we cannot dismiss it as nothing."

"No, we can't do that." Her voice was husky because the emotions coursing through her tightened her throat and made it hard to breathe.

He reached out once again, this time taking both her wrists in his grip and tugged. "Do not hide from me."

She resisted, her mind at war with her heart and her body until she saw in his face a mirror of the need and conflicting feelings raging in her. She let him pull her hands toward him across the small table.

His thumbs caressed her inner wrists while his eyes remained locked on her face. "It is physical, Bethany, but that is not all it is."

And she believed him because she felt it too. "I know."

They danced after dinner, her body pressed tightly to his. She could feel the affect their closeness had on him, but he made no move to take her someplace more private.

They talked in quiet murmurs. She told him why she'd come to Italy, about her short, but awful marriage and subsequent divorce. He told her about his older brother and a woman who loved him. He spoke so glowingly of this Gianna that Bethany began to stiffen in his arms.

He rubbed her back soothingly, while holding her with tensile strength against him. "I have no desire for Gianna. She is like a sister to me, I think to Rico also, but she feels differently."

"You wish he did too?"

"He's engaged to a mercenary bitch the whole family is hoping he'll have enough sense not to marry. Gianna would be a vast improvement."

"Mercenary?"

"She wants only what his money can buy her and the status he can give to her. She has no love in her heart."

"Your brother must be pretty well off."

"My father has gone into semi-retirement. Rico is the president of the Rinaldi Bank."

There were Rinaldi Banks all over Italy. "Do you mean he manages one of the branches?"

"My family own the banks."

This time she managed to jerk out of his arms. *"You own a bank?"*

"I own shares in the bank, as do my father and brother and several cousins." He grabbed her and pulled her back into his arms. "Relax, Bethany. It is no big deal."

"You don't run the bank?"

"No."

She breathed a sigh of relief and relaxed against him.

"I am Chairman of the Board. My brother and I run it together."

Before she could go tense again, his lips landed against the base of her throat and started doing amazing things to her equilibrium. "What I am does not matter so much, does it?"

"Your lifestyle must be so far removed from mine, we might as well live on separate planets. I bet you eat in places like this all the time. I don't. In fact, I've never ordered off a menu without prices before. I drive a Ford Escort and take myself out for a latte when I want to celebrate. You probably keep a bottle of expensive champagne chilling in your office for that kind of thing."

He stopped trying to dance and stared down at her, his expression so serious, she could not make herself look away. "Yes, I grew up around wealth and I've seen what it does to people. My brother's fiancée is typical in our set and that is not the kind of woman I want to spend my time with."

"There are nice rich women."

"Yes, my mother is one of them, but I've never met a woman like you, Bethany and I don't care if you dance topless for a living, I want to be with you."

"I work in a title insurance company."

"Good. My mother might have had a problem with the topless dancing part."

He'd told her a lot about his parents and she realized they weren't all that different from her own. They cared about their children and from the things he'd said, she could see his mother doing the same kind of crazy things her mom did to make her children happy. "Your family sounds wonderful."

"They are." The love he felt for them made his voice rich with feeling and another big chunk came crashing down from the defensive wall around her heart.

They danced until the music changed to something with a faster beat and then Andre paid for their dinner and took her for a walk. Not many stars could be seen in the night sky. The light pollution around Rome was too great, but it was incredibly romantic nonetheless, or maybe it was her companion that was so romantic.

"So, you came to Rome with the intention of having a hot affair?"

Her hand twisted nervously in his. "It sounds terrible when you say it out loud."

"No, merely interesting."

She didn't ask what he meant by that. He'd spent the entire day and evening showing her he wanted her and how much. The only question was whether or not she could go through with it. She hadn't expected to become emotionally involved, not in such a short time and the risk of intensifying that emotion with lovemaking scared her.

"I'm not sure I was thinking straight when I told my mom I'd give it a try."

"But you are thinking straight now and you want me, Bethany."

She didn't answer, silence her only defense against the truth.

He stopped her and pulled her around to face him. Looking down into her eyes, he asked, "Do you want me?"

"Yes."

"Do you want to wait?" Andre asked the question, unsure what he would do if she said yes.

"You haven't even kissed me." Her soft gray eyes mirrored bemusement.

Did she think he had to kiss her to know he wanted her? "If I start, I may not be able to stop."

"Really?"

"Really."

"Are you usually so lacking in control?"

"You know I am not."

"Yes. You told me."

And she had believed him. He liked knowing that.

She licked her lips, her chest rising and falling with short shallow breaths. "I want you to kiss me."

CHAPTER FIVE

ANDRE could not believe Bethany had said yes to the kiss after he had made clear the probability it would lead to much more. "Let me take you back to your hotel."

"All right."

"Do you know what you are inviting?" Did he?

He never did crazy things like this, but he knew she told the truth. About everything. She'd only been with one man, her ex-husband—the bastard stupid enough to cheat on her and then let her go. The only risk they would take in making love was pregnancy and he fully intended to use condoms. He was besotted, not stupid.

"I know," she whispered.

"Then let us go."

Her hotel room was not the luxury she was sure he was used to, but he said nothing as he followed her inside, the intensity of his desire surrounding her. The double bed dominated the smallish room, or perhaps it only felt that way because what she planned to do there consumed her thoughts.

She dropped her purse on the dresser and turned toward him, need that was much more than merely physical beating a sharp tattoo in her breast. "Do you want anything?"

He locked his hands on her waist and pulled her unresisting body flush with his own. "Only you, *carina.*"

Then he lowered his head until their mouths met. Skyrockets went off at the first touch of his lips against hers. She pressed her hands against the rock-like wall of his chest, enthralled by the heat emanating through his shirt. It called to her on a wholly elemental level. His smell, his taste, his very essence captivated her senses, telling her primitive mind he belonged to her and always had, long before she had met him.

No reticence belonged in this coming together and her body

seemed to know it from the top of her head that felt ready to explode with desire to her fingers busy undoing buttons on his shirt to her toes curled in her spiked heels. Everything about him was right for her. Everything about her was right for him. How she knew this, she could not fathom, but she knew. This was no one-night stand or the beginning of a short fling that would end with her return to the States. This was something far more.

His tongue pressed against her lips and she parted them without hesitation. He possessed her mouth with a sensuality that left her dazed and shaking as she leaned against him, unable to stand on her own.

Perfect. She'd never experienced anything so perfect.

His hands moved from her waist to her bottom and he touched her, squeezing her, caressing her, making her crazy with want before moving lower. Skilled fingers found their way under her skirt to the highly sensitive flesh along the backs of her thighs and up her buttocks. It felt so good, *incredible.*

She moaned, finally getting her own hands inside his shirt. The hair covering his chest was an unknown to her. Kurt had kept his chest shaved, but she loved the rich textures of Andre's skin and hair, the way he felt so much like a man. She could touch him like this forever.

Impossibly, he deepened the kiss while using his hold on her bottom to press her into the heat of him, making her supremely aware of his arousal. The way he moved his body against her, the masculine groans coming from low in his chest, the strength of his fingers against her bottom—they all bespoke of tenuous control and she wanted to push him over the edge.

The knowledge she could excite him like this turned her on as nothing else could have. She was no passionless prude with this man.

He pulled her bottom a little higher and without conscious thought, she separated her legs so she could wrap them around his waist. He made his approval of her move known with the flexing of his hips and guttural sounds of pleasure. His mouth tore from hers and he said a bunch of words in Italian, most of which she did not understand, but the words *beautiful* and *perfect* were in there.

"I want you, Andre."

"*Sì*. You shall have me."

Their clothes disappeared from their bodies as frantic movement accompanied impassioned pleas from both of them. By the time they fell together naked to the bed, she was ready to expire from the almost painful desire wracking her body.

She arched her hips up. "Take me now, Andre. *Now.*"

He fumbled with a condom and then he was doing as she'd demanded, filling her body with one swift, powerful thrust. Silken tissues stretched to their limit as she sought to accommodate a lover unlike any other. Her muscles went rigid with tension from the effort.

"You can take me, *mi amorino*. We are made for each other."

"Yes," she hissed as her feminine flesh relaxed and contracted around him, pulling him further inside until he touched her womb.

They made love, fast and furiously, climaxing together with so much power she lost touch with reality for several seconds. When she became more wholly aware he was kissing her all over her face, whispering words of approval and admiration against her skin.

She caught his lips with her own and it started all over again, the touching and pleasuring, but this time he kept the pace slow, bringing her to one more climax before once again taking her on a journey to the stars with him.

They got very little sleep that night and spent the next day together, in and out of bed. Two glorious days went by during which they were inseparable. He had his things moved to her hotel room and then proceeded to show her Rome as she had only dreamed of seeing it. On the third day, he had a bank meeting he had to attend. It was to be followed by a dinner and drinks after.

"I cannot get out of it, *carina,* but I will send a car for you so you can accompany me to the dinner."

After two days being made love to and told she was the most

beautiful woman in the world, there was little room for nerves in the face of meeting his associates. "I'll be ready."

"Wear the pink dress. It is perfect on you."

He'd taken her shopping the day before and insisted on buying her whatever caught her eye. She had balked at first, but he'd been adamant, telling her it gave him far more pleasure than it gave her.

"I'm sorry, Signor di Rinaldi, but there is an urgent call for you. From New York. A family matter... "

Andre looked up at the young man whose hushed voice had stopped the conversation around the conference table. The only family in New York at the moment was his older brother. His parents were on an extended cruise to celebrate their anniversary.

"I will take it in the manager's office."

Ten minutes later he put the phone down, disbelief warring with cold fear inside him. Rico was in a coma in a New York hospital.

Andre rapped out instructions to his assistant. He would need a take-off slot at the airport, his jet ready and fueled and some clothes from Bethany's hotel room. He called her, but she was still out sightseeing.

He'd hung up before he realized he should have left a message. It could be his last chance to talk to her for many hours. He wanted nothing more than to take her with him, but she was not carrying a cell phone and he could not wait for her to arrive back at the hotel. Every hour could count in seeing his brother alive.

CHAPTER SIX

WHILE ANDRE was busy with his meetings, Bethany visited the Vatican, but she spent more time thinking than sight seeing.

Today was her last official day in Rome, but she and Andre had not discussed the future. She wasn't even sure if he knew she was scheduled to fly out tomorrow.

She hadn't wanted to think about it, but now she could think of nothing else. Would he ask her to stay? Would he invite her to come back? Would he come to the U.S. if she invited him to visit?

She knew that if he asked, she would chuck her job and stay. It was impossible. It was crazy, but she'd fallen in love and it was a deeper, more consuming emotion than anything she'd felt for her ex-husband. The thought of leaving Andre made her feel like someone was trying to rip a hole in her chest. She had no desire to find out what it would feel like to actually go.

But for all the wonderful things he'd said to her, he'd never once implied their relationship was permanent. He had not said he loved her, though he called her his little love frequently. Was that simply the Italian way, or did he mean the endearment in a literal sense? If his only interest had been in enjoying a brief affair while he conducted his business in Rome, she could hardly stay on, clinging to a relationship that was not there.

She could barely believe she'd fallen in love with him and if the emotions roiling through her weren't so powerful, she wouldn't. It was a huge jump to believing the same might have happened to him, no matter how mutual their attraction. Things felt real with him. Permanent. More real than anything she had ever known, but feelings weren't fact and she was terrified hers were the only ones engaged.

She was so lost in thought; she was late getting to the room and only had a few minutes to dress before Andre's car was scheduled to arrive for her.

She frantically rushed around getting ready, which was why she did not notice the emptiness of the hotel room until she went to grab a pair of hose from the drawer. No male socks reclined in neat stacks beside the few pairs of hose she'd brought with her to Rome. She opened another drawer, unable to comprehend the meaning of the missing socks. His swim shorts were gone too.

She looked around the room, taking in details that had escaped her earlier. His suitcase was gone. Everything of his was gone. She searched for a note, but did not see one, called the front desk, but there was no message.

The fact his car did not show up for her at the appointed time was almost anti-climactic. Andre had left her. The tenuous hold she had on her heart snapped and it fell to shatter in a million pieces around her.

Fatigue burning his eyes, Andre rubbed them with his thumb and forefinger. He'd been flying for eight hours and anticipated touching down in New York in less than one. He could only hope he would find his brother alive when he reached the hospital. He'd spent the flight trying to work, knowing the responsibility of the bank would lie heavily on his shoulders for a while, even if his brother came out of the coma. His thoughts wouldn't stay focused though. Memories of his brother and growing up together in Milan spun through his mind, forcing out the less emotive numbers and business proposals printed on the pages in front of him. Rico had to live.

Andre went straight to the hospital from the airport. A call from his cell phone on the way there confirmed that his brother was indeed alive, though still in a coma. When he reached the hospital, he learned from the nurse that Gianna had been sitting by Rico's bedside for hours without eating or drinking anything. Andre brought sustenance to her, knowing Rico would be furious if Andre allowed her to become sick in her vigil watching over him. He refused to contemplate the possibility that his older brother would not come out of the coma now that his condition had stabilized.

Once he'd spoken to the doctors and taken care of Gianna, it was too late to call Rome. Bethany would be sleeping, but he could not wait to call first thing in the morning her time. He desperately wanted to hear her voice, to tell her about his brother and find the comfort he knew would be waiting for him in her tender heart.

Needing a shower and a change of clothes, he went to the hotel his assistant had checked him into. It wasn't until he was looking for something to wear after the reviving shower that his sleep deprived brain latched onto the fact that all of his clothes had been moved from the hotel.

Porca miseria! Bethany would think he had left her without a word. What had his assistant been thinking? Had the man even thought to leave a message? Andre called only to discover he had not. A furious glance at the clock revealed it was still the middle of the night over there. He could not yet call her and Gianna needed him to share her vigil beside Rico's bed. He returned to the hospital, counting the hours until he could talk to Bethany. He called at midnight, thinking she might still be asleep, but willing to take the chance.

Punch drunk from lack of sleep, he reeled in shock when he was told Bethany had checked out. Had she gone because she'd been hurt? He hated the thought, but could not dismiss it.

He realized he didn't even know when she was scheduled to return home or where her home was. She'd told him about her former marriage, about her family and even her job, but she'd mentioned the town of her origin only once and had never told him what state she lived in. As impossible as it was to believe, they had spent only a few short days together, not long enough to learn everything important. He had not asked for contact information because he had had no intention of letting her leave Italy or him. And *damn it*, he was sure she had not wanted to go. Now he had to find her.

Bethany finished checking the loan documents for her next appointment and set the neat pile of papers to be signed in the center of her desk. She'd been back from Rome for over a week, but she still wasn't adjusted to her old routine. Just when she wanted nothing more than to lose herself in work, her concentration was shot.

The abrupt ending to her relationship with Andre had been playing havoc with her emotions since the moment she realized he wasn't coming back to the hotel. She'd barely slept that night, not at all on the plane and when she'd arrived home, her stubborn heart had insisted she try to contact him. She'd called his bank in Milan, where he said he lived most of the year. The receptionist hadn't been willing to put her call through to his private voice mail. When Bethany asked to leave a message, she was informed Andre had flown to New York and was not expected to return for some time.

Obviously something had come up business-wise, but the way he'd left without a word made it clear *she* meant nothing to him. She'd been so sure it was more than mind blowing sex; that they were meant to be together. She'd been wrong.

It was over.

CHAPTER SEVEN

BETHANY swiped at angry tears, refusing to allow the emotional pain burgeoning inside her to take over. She should have learned from her first marriage that gorgeous playboy types couldn't be trusted. She was telling herself that she was better off without him and having a miserable time believing it when the front receptionist buzzed to say Bethany's next appointment had arrived.

She took a deep breath and prepared to meet the young couple buying their first home. She'd gotten more than pain from her time with Andre, she reminded herself. She'd learned she was capable of incredible passion. So, she'd accomplished what she set out to do with her trip to Italy. If it had come at a price she had not been prepared to pay, she had no choice but to soldier on and accept the bad with the good.

It was late in the day when the phone on her desk rang. She picked it up. "Bethany Hayden speaking."

"Bethany."

No. It wasn't possible, not after a week of complete silence. "Andre?"

"Sì. Bethany, it is so good to hear your voice."

Right. She wasn't falling for any of his practiced lines this time. "Are you still in New York?"

"You know about my trip?"

"The receptionist at your bank told me when I called trying to find you."

"This is good. I am surprised. Our policy of confidentiality is strict, but I am very glad she ignored it in this instance. When my assistant took all my things without leaving a note, I was sure you would be hurt. How could you think anything but the worst in such a scenario?"

"You're right. How could I?"

"But now you understand."

Apparently he hadn't figured out yet that understanding and accepting were not the same things. She'd understood her husband's serial infidelity—Kurt had been a man incapable of faithfulness—but she had not accepted it. "Why did you bother tracking me down?"

"Surely you know. I wish you to join me in New York."

"I don't think so."

"I will send my jet for you. You need not worry about procuring an airline ticket."

"I'm not coming to New York in your plane or anyone else's."

"You refuse to come? At all?" He sounded shocked by her denial, bewildered even.

As well he might be. Apparently, he thought she was a real push over. She may have been once, but she was through being stupid and she'd had an entire week shoring up her defenses. Even so, the sound of his voice was detrimental to her recovery and she had to cut this call short. That or she was going to do something unforgivably idiotic, like agree to be his convenient mistress and offer to fly to New York as soon as his jet could arrive.

"Look, Andre, it was fun while it lasted, but it's over now. I'm not interested in having a repeat of Rome."

"You do not wish to continue our relationship?"

She wouldn't call it a relationship, not with him looking for nothing more than uncommitted sex and walking away whenever he wanted. "No, I don't."

"Bethany, I could not help leaving you. I was needed here."

"I'm sure you were." He was an important man, but she couldn't stand being with him if she wasn't as essential to him as he was to her.

"I had thought you would understand." His voice had grown husky with tiredness, as if the conversation had taken his last bit of energy.

He must be working very hard.

She squashed the thought that bordered on concern and said, "You were wrong."

"I see that."

"Was there anything else?"

"No, nothing else."

The phone clicked in her ear as tears burned a path down her cheeks.

Andre hung up the phone, a sense of desolation destroying the joy he had felt upon discovering the extremely expensive international detective agency he had hired had found Bethany. Even his relief Rico had woken from his coma was muted by his despair at learning he had been wrong about Bethany, that he had lost her. She'd told him she was looking for confirmation of her feminine power. He'd given it to her and now she wanted nothing to do with him.

How could he have been so mistaken about a woman? Could her compassion truly be so lacking?

After days without adequate sleep, he did not have the mental energy to grapple with the problem. He had enough to worry about without allowing his personal emotions to take precedence. Rico had woken paralyzed from the waist down. The doctors were hopeful he would walk again, Gianna was certain of it, but Andre's optimism was tempered by concern for his brother he did his best to hide.

Andre could not afford to dwell on his loss or it would cripple him, leaving him useless to both his brother and the bank he had to run while Rico tried to get better.

Bethany picked up the magazine in the doctor's office while she waited to be called in to hear her test results. She knew what the doctor would say, however. Her body's symptoms were unmistakable and home pregnancy tests were 98% accurate nowadays. She was carrying Andre's baby.

He had used a condom each and every time they made love, but he'd still managed to plant his child inside her. All birth control had a risk factor, but she'd thought a condom had to break before it didn't work. Remembering some of the ways he'd pleasured her, she could maybe see how it had happened, but how would Andre react to hearing he was going to be a father? For she had to tell him, and a tiny part of her rejoiced at the excuse to see him again.

She stared unseeingly at the magazine in her lap, her feelings a conflagration inside her. She'd spent five weeks wondering if she'd been more of a fool to trust Andre in the first place or to refuse to see him again and hear why he'd left her without a word. The longer she'd thought about it, the more convinced she became that it was the latter.

She'd given up too quickly on their relationship and it had

taken her several days to face the fact that she'd done so out of fear rather than necessity. She'd been afraid of the over-whelming feelings she had for Andre. Kurt had hurt her so much, but she hadn't felt one tenth the emotional connection to him that she'd felt to Andre after their first night together.

She sighed and went to flip the magazine shut when a face on the page caught her attention. It looked like Andre, but it wasn't. Was it? The caption read, Banking Tycoon Rico di Rinaldo Rocks the Financial Community When an Accident Leaves him Paralyzed. The article said he'd been hit by a car while preventing a mugging and spent five days in a coma. The date of his accident was the same one Andre had left her.

Nausea made her stomach cramp as she read about the man's fight for his life, his paralysis and the necessity of his younger brother taking on additional duties with the bank while Rico went through physical therapy. Andre had needed her and she had refused to go to him. She jumped up and rushed to the bathroom, making it just in time to be sick in the sink.

CHAPTER EIGHT

BETHANY'S nerves were like shattered glass as she walked up to the receptionist desk in the main branch of the Rinaldi bank. She'd checked into a hotel after the long flight over, but she'd taken minimal time to freshen up before taking a taxi to the financial district in Milan.

She could not believe she was back in Italy. When she left Rome seven weeks before, she'd been hurting so much, she had thought she never wanted to come back. She was hurting now, but not for herself. Compassion for Andre and what he must have gone through tormented her.

She had come to apologize and tell him she was pregnant with his child. What he did after that would be his call. She had to see him, but she was terrified he would reject her as coldly as she had dismissed him.

When she gave the receptionist her name, the other woman looked at her with speculation as she rang Andre's assistant. She spoke in rapid Italian and then hung up the phone. "Signor Mercado will be here shortly to escort you to Signor di Rinaldi's office."

Bethany couldn't believe how easy it was to get through this time when before, the woman hadn't even been willing to give her Andre's voicemail. Maybe it was a different receptionist.

A young man wearing a business suit and a grim expression touched her shoulder less than five minutes later. "Miss Hayden?"

"Yes."

"Signor di Rinaldi said he would see you in his office."

"He knows I'm here?"

"Yes." Now, even the man's tone was grim. "Follow me, please."

She did, her heart beating her to death on the long elevator ride to the top floor. Andre was on the phone when she was led into his office, a huge room beautifully decorated with dark woods and classic artwork on the walls. She bit her lip, looking around. His life was so far removed from hers and yet they had connected as if none of the trappings mattered. Would he remember that, or only her fear-induced cruelty?

He hung the phone up and stood. "Bethany. Has your mother bought you another trip to Italy?"

She shook her head, her thirsty heart drinking in the sight of him with great gulps. "I came because I had to see you."

"The last time we spoke, you made it clear you did not wish to see me again."

"I was wrong." Her throat closed on tears she couldn't bear to shed in front of him and she had to breathe deeply for several seconds before she could talk again without exposing him to the burden of her pain. "I'm so sorry. I was stupid and I'll understand if you never want to see me again, but I love you and I need you and I'll spend the rest of my life making up for letting you down if you'll just give me one more chance."

His expression rock-like, he didn't say anything.

"I didn't know," she explained in a choking voice, "about your brother. I thought you'd gone to New York on business and left me behind without a word. When you told me your assistant hadn't left a note, I thought I wasn't important enough for you to deal with personally. It hurt." She paused, gathering her thoughts, trying not to go off on a tangent. "I know if I'd trusted you then, I could have avoided a lot of pain for both of us, but you already had such a hold on my heart. I thought if I saw you again, gave you a bigger one, you could destroy me with what I thought was your indifference."

She searched his face for a clue to what he was thinking, but he didn't so much as blink. "Andre?"

His jaw tautened, but he didn't say anything and she dropped her head in despair. How could she tell him about the baby now? Maybe she should just write to him. It wasn't exactly news he was going to rejoice in and she wasn't sure she could deal with seeing the horror in his expression when he realized she carried his child. She turned to go.

"You did not know about Rico?"

She stopped halfway across the carpet. "No."

"It was in the papers." He was right behind her now, though she hadn't heard him move.

"I don't read the papers."

"When did you find out?"

"Three days ago."

"You came very quickly."

"But still too late."

His hand cupped her shoulder and he turned her toward him. "Too late for what?"

She looked up at him, her love almost suffocating her with its strength. "To be there for you when you needed me."

"I always need you."

She couldn't have heard right.

"You said you loved me." His eyes bore into hers as if testing the truth of the words.

Unable to believe she was allowed to touch him, her hands came up to clutch at his shirt. "I do love you, so much it scares me."

"And this fear made you turn me away?"

She couldn't fight the tears any longer. Relief and hope flowed through her in too powerful a wave. "Yes."

"We had little time together, not enough to cement what we meant to each other."

She swallowed and nodded, unable to speak past the lump of emotion choking her.

"I love you also, mi amorino."

"Even after I rejected you?"

His lips answered her and she'd been so starved for the feel of him that she went up in flames with that one kiss. She discovered he had a small apartment accessible through the back of his office when he took her there and made love to her with a hungry desperation that mirrored her own.

She snuggled into his warm, hard body afterward, so happy she was almost sick with it. He had forgiven her. He loved her. He would be happy about the baby. She was sure of it.

"This time we marry as soon as possible. No more misunderstandings."

"I would like that very much, but there is something I have to tell you." She brushed his hairy chest, her fingers tingling with joy at the ability to do so.

He tilted her chin upward. "You are nervous. What is it?"

She swallowed. What if he didn't trust her like she hadn't trusted him? What if he thought the baby wasn't his? What if he thought she'd done it on purpose? Refusing to let the terrifying possibilities intimidate her, she took a deep breath. "I'm pregnant."

He went so still, she wasn't sure he was even breathing. "Prego?"

"I'm carrying your child."

"This is why you came back to me?"

She couldn't tell what he was thinking, but she shook her head. "No. I mean, yes." She didn't want to lie to him, even by omission. "I was planning to come when I realized I was pregnant, but once I found out about your brother, nothing could have kept me away even if I hadn't been. In fact, if I'd known how to get a hold of you in New York, I doubt I could have stayed away regardless. I needed you, Andre, and it was killing me by inches to stay away."

"The separation, it was killing me also." He looked down at her still flat stomach and touched it with reverence. "Mi bambino rests here."

"Are you glad?"

He looked at her and the joy shining in his dark eyes was so intense it brought tears to her own. "Can you doubt it?"

"I love you, Andre. Always."

"I love you, my Bethany, until they lay me in my grave."

They were married in a small, secret ceremony a week later, but when Andre's family found out about it, his mother insisted they have a double blessing with Rico and his wife, Gianna. Signora di Rinaldi even sent all the way to Greece for a mantilla that matched Gianna's for Bethany to wear. Bethany's parents flew over for the ceremony and the celebration lasted late into the night after both brides announced their pregnancies.

Gianna and Bethany agreed the di Rinaldi men made excellent husbands because they were so easy to love and so very good at loving in return.

* * * * *

ONE ENCHANTED CHRISTMAS EVENING

Heidi Rice ★

Heidi Rice was born and bred and still lives in London, England. She has two boys who love to bicker, a wonderful husband who, luckily for everyone, has a huge amount of patience, and a supportive and ever-growing British/French/Irish/American family. As much as Heidi adores 'the Big Smoke', she also loves America and every two years or so she and her best friend leave hubby and kids behind and Thelma and Louise it across the States for a couple of weeks (although they always leave out the driving off a cliff bit). Some of their favourite haunts include Monument Valley, the Nantahala Forest in North Carolina, St Michael's in Maryland, Marfa in Texas and New Orleans. Heidi's been a film buff since her early teens and a romance junkie for almost as long. She indulged her first love by being a film reviewer for the last ten years. Then two years ago she decided to spice up her life by writing romance. Discovering the fantastic sisterhood of romance writers (both published and unpublished) in Britain and America made it a wild and wonderful journey to her first Mills & Boon® novel, *Bedded by a Bad Boy,* and she's looking forward to many more to come.

Heidi says…

"The most romantic place I've ever travelled to would be New York in 1994, the World Cup Final match between Ireland and Italy. We got married the next day in New York City Hall (and Ireland won!)."

Don't miss Heidi's fabulous new Modern Heat™,
Public Affair, Secretly Expecting – **coming next month!**

ONE ENCHANTED CHRISTMAS EVENING

'In my office, Serena.'

Serena Jacobs' fingers jerked on her keyboard at the curt command that boomed from her desktop intercom. She shot the machine a withering look and heard the sharp click as it shut off.

Typical! No *please*. No *thank you*. Not even the courtesy of waiting for her reply. Yet more proof that Jack Strider, her new boss of two weeks, had fewer manners than Sammy.

The thought of her five-year-old son had Serena taking two deep breaths as she picked up her notepad. *Calm down*. Christmas was less than a week away, and Sammy's kids' club fees were going up in January. She couldn't afford to lose this job.

'Sounds like the Hunk wants more coffee.' Her colleague Tracy winked from the desk opposite, her Santa earrings bobbing.

'He's not a hunk,' Serena snapped.

'Rubbish.' Tracey snorted out an incredulous laugh.

'Dreamy blue eyes, jet-black hair, a tight, squeezable butt and that master-of-industry act all wrapped in six-feet-three of toned, designer-clad muscle. A woman would have to be dead not to classify that guy as a hunk.'

Ignoring Tracy, and the ridiculous little leap under her breastbone at the thought of those designer-clad muscles, Serena forced a tight smile onto her face and walked into Strider's office, busy chanelling goodwill to all men.

The smile lasted about five seconds. The goodwill not much longer.

'I certainly will *not* pose as your fiancée.'

Jack Strider's eyebrow winged up at the outraged shout from his prim PA. A bright flush stained her cheeks and enmity flashed in her sea-green eyes.

Well, well, well. The ice maiden had thawed out. In fact, she was practically on fire.

'It's only for one night,' he said, surprised he was having to argue the point. Women didn't usually object to spending an evening with him. And up till now Serena Jacobs had been the picture of cool, calm efficiency. A little too cool and calm for his liking.

He tried to deny the prickle of awareness that had been bugging him ever since he'd set eyes on the woman, but the truth was she fascinated him.

She was slim—petite, even—but he suspected she had some interesting curves under the plain skirt and blouse sets she habitually wore, and her dark red hair looked thick and shiny even tied back in an eye-watering bun.

He was dying to find out what secrets lay beneath that buttoned-down façade.

Unfortunately, he had one important rule. He didn't flirt with women who worked for him—which had added a large dose of frustration to the fascination.

'We need to secure this deal with Mannix Media,' he said

gruffly, annoyed at getting sidetracked by the enigma of his pretty PA yet again. 'Old man Mannix doesn't consider bachelors a good risk. I need a fiancée for the Winter Ball tonight.' His gaze flicked over her. 'You fit the bill.'

He saw her stiffen and felt a twinge of regret. He'd been in a bad mood for the last few weeks, but he didn't have time for apologies. The business he'd acquired a fortnight ago was about to go belly up. If it did it would put a small dent in his personal fortune and a much bigger one in the pockets of the thirty people who'd be on the dole by Christmas. As the woman staring daggers at him was one of them, he considered her hurt pride acceptable collateral damage. 'The ball starts at eight. I'll pick you up at seven-thirty.'

'I can't go,' she said with frigid control. 'I have other commitments.'

So she had a boyfriend. His sympathy dried up as he walked round the desk. 'If you've got a date, break it.'

Serena stood her ground with effort. She would not be bullied into this. The very idea of being forced to spend an evening with this man made her pulse pound like a timpani drum.

'I didn't say I had a date,' she said. 'I said I had other commitments.'

'What other commitments?'

'My five-year-old son.'

The words shot out and echoed into silence. He folded his arms across his chest and frowned as his gaze swept over her. Serena forced herself not to notice how his shirtsleeves stretched across his biceps.

'How old are you?' he asked at last.

She clutched the notepad tighter. 'I'm twenty-one.' She didn't like the way he was looking at her, as if he'd seen her for the first time.

'That must have been tough,' he said softly. 'Having a child at sixteen.'

'Not at all.' She thrust her chin out. She didn't want his pity. 'Sammy's the best thing that ever happened to me. I adore him.'

He smiled. And she realised she'd never seen him smile before. She would definitely have remembered the slow, sensuous curve of his lips, the way the blue of his eyes deepened and intensified. It was doing something very peculiar to her heart-rate—and her thigh muscles.

'I can see that,' he said. 'Sammy's a lucky fellow.'

Serena swallowed, her anger fading to leave something much more disturbing in its wake. Damn. Tracy was right. He *was* a hunk.

'The thing is, I'm a single mum. So I can't go to—'

'Do you have a regular sitter for Sammy?' he interrupted.

She nodded. 'Tina next door.' Why did the way he said her son's name make her heart pound even harder?

'Give her a call. I'll pay.'

'But she might not be available.' What was she agreeing to? 'And even if she is, I don't have anything to wear.' The Winter Ball, held in a top London hotel, was the swankiest, most exclusive event of the Christmas season. Serena didn't do swanky *or* exclusive.

He glanced at his watch. 'I'll get a personal shopper to bring a selection of suitable gowns and accessories to your place.'

He smiled at her again—and every coherent thought flew right out of her head.

'I can't…' Her breath caught as he stroked a finger down her cheek.

'You know, you're very pretty when you're perplexed.'

She was sure she should take offence at that one. But strong fingers cupped her elbow as he steered her to the door and she lost the power of speech completely.

'You'd better head home,' he said, leading her out of the office. 'You've got a lot to do before seven-thirty.'

She hadn't managed to utter a single objection before the door shut behind her.

* * *

As the long black limousine glided down Holland Park Avenue, Serena stared out at the night-time expanse of Kensington Gardens, far too aware of the man sitting beside her.

Get a grip, woman. You are not Cinderella and Jack Strider is no Prince Charming.

It was the same mantra she'd been repeating to herself all afternoon and evening.

While listening to Tracy's excited chatter about 'Serena's big date with the boss'.

While selecting a breathtaking designer gown from the selection laid out on her sagging sofa cushions by the personal shopper.

While watching her teenage babysitter Tina mime a thumping heart from behind Jack's back as he stepped into her tiny living room, his white dress shirt dazzling against the tailored black tux.

But her daydream had got so much worse when Sammy had popped out from behind her skirts with a childish scowl on his face and shouted, 'I don't want you to take my mummy out. What if you lose her?'

She'd expected Jack to reprimand Sammy for his rudeness—had been ready to defend her son. But to her astonishment Jack had crouched down, until his eyes were level with Sammy's.

'I promise I'll take very good care of your mummy,' he'd said gently. 'And bring her home safe and sound.' He held out his hand. 'You want to shake on it?'

Her son, who had always yearned for male approval, had stared at Jack's hand with something akin to awe before it folded around his.

'If you want,' Sammy had said, his voice eager with hope, 'you could come to Christmas dinner?'

A slow grin had formed on Jack's lips. 'I'd love to.'

The scene had continued to prey on Serena's mind after Jack had ushered her into the limo. She never would have expected him to be so considerate with her son. Even so, she knew not to read too much into it.

She sighed. 'Thank you for being so nice to Sammy. Don't worry—I'll explain to him you can't come on Christmas Day.'

'Serena, look at me.' He blew out a breath as she turned. 'I wasn't being nice—I like Sammy. And I intend to take him up on his invitation.'

'You're coming to Christmas dinner?' She swallowed, feeling her cheeks heat, not sure what to make of the anticipation she felt.

He nodded, smiling. 'But if I bring the turkey, you'll have to cook it.'

The hotel looked like a dignified fairytale castle in its festive finery. Two massive spruce trees accented with silver bows flanked the pillared entrance, and fairy lights sparkled like tinsel teardrops round the ornate brass lettering. Serena peered out of the limousine, her eyes widening as they eased to a stop on the hotel's forecourt. A liveried doorman, resplendent in red wool and gold brocade, offered a hand as she stepped onto the midnight-blue runner.

Frosty air made goosebumps prickle on the flesh exposed where her gown plunged. She pulled the matching wrap tight. Rich turquoise velvet caressed her skin as Jack's palm settled on her naked back.

'Here goes,' he whispered, his breath brushing her earlobe.

She sent him a nervous smile, twisting the diamond solitaire he had slipped on her finger as they'd cruised up Park Lane. He smiled back—and all her nerve-endings tingled.

She took a shaky breath as he guided her into the hotel's marble lobby.

She mustn't get carried away. She knew that.

But as the night wore on Serena found it harder and harder to cling on to reality.

Every time Jack introduced her as his fiancée with fierce pride roughening his voice. Every time he held her so close she could smell the musky scent of his aftershave. Every time he waltzed her across the ballroom floor and swung her into a giddy turn. She felt special, important, cherished—for the first time in her life.

And, as the minutes ticked into hours, she couldn't help falling deeper under the romantic spell.

'No more champagne for you, madam.' Jack lifted the flute from Serena's fingers and grinned as her throaty giggle bubbled out. Those mermaid eyes sparkled with an innocent, artless desire that had been tying his stomach in knots all evening. God, she was beautiful. Bright, witty and warm. Forget fascinated. Now he'd begun to uncover her secrets he was well and truly captivated.

He wanted her so much it was a miracle he hadn't dragged her into some quiet corner and ravished her already. But right alongside the lust was an urge to protect—a need to be careful with her that stunned him. He'd never felt this way about any woman before. The thought made him cautious, even a little wary, but he couldn't wait much longer.

Placing their glasses on a nearby table, he framed her face, pushed wayward curls back as he bent his head. 'Kiss me, Serena.'

Her eyes went round as he skimmed his thumbs down the line of her throat and felt the pulse hammering in her neck.

Her lips parted on a breathy sob.

'I need you,' he murmured.

Serena's hands fisted in Jack's shirt as his lips slanted across hers, his words swirling at the edge of her consciousness. She swayed and clung on as he dragged her close and his tongue plundered. Every pulse-point throbbed with intoxicating pain, desperate pleasure, as she tumbled headfirst into erotic fantasy.

He wanted her. He needed her. *He loved her*, her mind sang.

But as she flattened her hands the diamond in her fake ring

winked against the dark cloth of his lapel. *Remember none of this is real*, her mind taunted.

She pushed him away, scrambled back.

'Don't…' she cried, as the dream that had seduced her all evening shattered.

His head lifted. 'What's wrong?'

'Don't pretend to care about me,' she said, as bitter tears seeped over her lids. 'To need me when you don't.'

'What are you talking about?'

He looked so gorgeous, so sexy, so confused—and so far out of her league. How could she have lost sight of that?

'It isn't fair, Jack.' She gulped down a jerking sob. 'I'm a single mum from Shepherd's Bush. I've never worn a designer gown before. I've never danced all night at a ball until my feet hurt. And I haven't made love since I lost my virginity to Sammy's father,' she blurted out, her humiliation complete. 'I'm a complete push-over. If you wanted to seduce me all you had to do was ask. There's no need to pretend you want more than that.'

She ran out of the ballroom, her heart breaking into jagged shards.

'Stop! Serena!' She heard the pained shout above the chatter of departing revellers and the muted strains of orchestral music. And kept on running.

Strong fingers clamped on her wrist and hauled her back. She struggled, only to be anchored against an unyielding male chest.

'Hold still.' He swore softly and held her chin, forcing her to look at him. 'You're right about one thing. I do want to seduce you,' he said. 'So consider yourself asked.'

She gave an astonished gasp as he planted a smacking kiss on her lips.

'But you're wrong about everything else,' he said, searching her face.

Serena stilled. What was it she could see shining in his eyes?

'I *do* want more than your body,' he said, his voice husky, his chest rising and falling in time with her own staggered breathing. 'Much, much more. I don't know if I'm falling in love, because I have no idea how that feels.'

For the first time since she'd met him, he looked unsure of himself.

'But I want the chance to find out. Don't you?'

'It's only been one night,' she whispered, hope blossoming inside her.

'I guess that's all it takes,' he said, before sealing the deal with a demanding kiss.

The following Christmas, and all the Christmases to come, Serena and Jack left their children with a babysitter to attend the Winter Ball. They danced until Serena's feet hurt, made love in the Honeymoon Suite until the wintry dawn broke over Hyde Park, and rejoiced in a fantasy that had started out as a lie one enchanted Christmas evening—and turned into heart-stopping truth.

* * * * *

THE CINDERELLA VALENTINE

Liz Fielding ★

Liz Fielding was born with itchy feet. She made it to Zambia before her twenty-first birthday and, gathering her own special hero and a couple of children on the way, lived in Botswana, Kenya and Bahrain – with pauses for sightseeing pretty much everywhere in between. She finally came to a full stop in a tiny Welsh village cradled by misty hills and, these days, mostly leaves her pen to do the travelling. When she's not sorting out the lives and loves of her characters, she potters in the garden, reads her favourite authors and spends a lot of time wondering "What if...?". For news of upcoming books – and to sign up for her occasional newsletter – visit Liz's website at www. lizfielding.com.

Liz says...

"The most romantic gift I have ever received was a pair of pearl earrings, made from pearls fished from the Bahrain pearl beds and given to me by my husband, on the occasion of the birth of our daughter."

If you're looking for some Christmas magic, don't miss Liz's new book, *Christmas Angel for the Billionaire* – **available next month in Mills & Boon® Romance!**

THE CINDERELLA VALENTINE

POLLY had allowed herself plenty of time. She was leaving nothing to chance. She'd even used two alarm clocks, set at five-minute intervals, both of which had performed on cue. Emma Valentine had come through for her with a life and a sanity-saving job at Bella Lucia, her famous family's chic, elegant, A-list group of restaurants. Hard work, but big tips. This was not the day to turn over and go back sleep.

The bus—incredibly—arrived on time and dropped her off at a spot a mere two-minutes walk away from the classic, ornate Georgian building in the heart of Chelsea, where the first of the fabulous Bella Lucia restaurants had opened fifty years earlier.

For once in her life, Polly hadn't messed up.

Even the sun was shining.

"Excuse me?" Polly turned to see a harassed mother encumbered by a three-year-old, a baby and a buggy struggling to get off the bus. "Would you mind…?"

In an all's-right-with-my-world glow, Polly took the buggy and did what she'd done a hundred times when babysitting her nieces and nephews—flicked it open.

The buggy didn't open. It sprang wide like a hungry tiger, taking a chunk out of her tights. As she bent to check the damage, the three-year-old generously thrust the rusk he'd been chewing into her. A thick beige smear appeared on the front of her waistcoat. She was already off balance when a speeding motorbike, skimming the curb to dodge the traffic, finished the job and dumped her in the road.

It could have been worse.

She could have fallen under a bus.

All was not lost, Polly thought, as she picked herself up. She was early. With luck she'd be able to slip into the staff washroom, clean up and change into the spare pair of tights that she'd fortuitously slipped into her bag before Mr. Valentine saw her. She scooped up a strand of hair that had sprung loose, tucked it behind her ear, rang the bell on the wrought-iron gate that guarded the rear entrance and was buzzed through.

It was only then that she discovered what she should have known the minute the buggy attacked her: she had carelessly left her luck, like a forgotten umbrella, on the bus. Not missed until the heavens opened up and she actually needed it. Right now the sun was shining, but, as the man blocking her dash to the staff washroom slowly turned, she could have sworn she heard a clap of thunder.

Maybe that was because he bore more than a passing resemblance to the devil himself.

His hair, a pelt of thick, crisp curls, was a glossy black. His nose proclaimed that his ancestors had once ruled the known world. His brows were bold, straight, dark and not even the sensual curve of his lower lip could override the impression that he was more used to giving than taking orders.

All he lacked was a pair of little horns, although curls that thick could hide a lot. His eyes, the colour of warm treacle, might have softened the image, but they were regarding her with a long, critical look that took in her hair—she could feel her own curls springing free of pins loosened by her fall—the sticky smear of rusk decorating her left breast, her torn tights.

"Polly Bright," she said quickly, getting that in before he could voice what he was so plainly thinking. She met his eyes head on, and offered her hand in the manner of a woman whom, despite appearances to the contrary, knew what she was doing.

He did not take it.

Wise move, she decided, realizing too late that, in her attempt to save herself, she'd placed her hand in a patch of oil.

"It's my first day," she added, but with rather less conviction.

"No, Miss Bright," he replied as, with the slightest movement of one hand, he addressed her appearance, "it is not."

Polly, entranced by the soft, seductive, fall-into-bed accent that matched the Roman nose and Mediterranean colouring, was, for a moment, oblivious. Then what he'd actually said sank in.

Not?

Not! Oh, no, she wasn't going to take that, allow this long-legged demon to dismiss her without even giving her a chance to explain. This job was too important. It was an opportunity to get back on her feet, to prove to her family that she wasn't a complete screw-up. It was a chance to start again…

The familiar sounds of a kitchen gearing up to serve a hundred plus diners reached her and, name-dropping like mad, she said, "Emma Valentine will vouch for me."

Polly had met Emma Valentine, the Chelsea BL's chef, when she'd been booked to give a cookery master-class at Polly's catering college. Not that Polly was taking part; her exclusion was punishment for a piece of nonsense involving an ice sculpture. Polly had found Emma in the student washroom, throwing up from nerves; she'd fetched her some ginger ale, distracted her with the woeful tale of "Little Willy," made Emma laugh so much that she'd taken Polly into the class as her assistant leaving the principal with no option but to accept this fait accompli.

"Or Mr. Robert Valentine," Polly continued. Emma would be up to her eyes at this time of day. "He interviewed me."

"Mr. Valentine is at the Mayfair office this morning and his daughter is in Meridia organizing the coronation banquet."

In other words, what kind of nerve did she have thinking either of them would have spare time to pull her irons out of the fire?

"Max Valentine is in the office," he offered, with a touch of amusement. "Maybe you'd prefer to have this conversation with him?"

"No!" She'd met Max when she'd come for her interview. He was scary, unlike his father who was a sucker for a smile. "No," she repeated, "I'm sure he's busy." "Then I'm sorry, Miss Bright, but all you have is me."

Well, if life gave you lemons, you made lemonade. She tried the "sucker" smile.

"And you are?"

"Luc Bellisario. I may not be a Valentine, but Bella Lucia was my great-aunt, if that makes me an acceptable alternative?"

Seductive sarcasm, she noted, but then he was not just some uppity Italian waiter with a power complex. Not even an Italian restaurant manager with a power complex. He was family…

"This lunchtime I am acting manager of this restaurant," he continued, without waiting for her to confirm that he was. "And you, Miss Bright, are not in any state to polish its floor, let alone serve food to the people who dine here."

"Mr. Bellisario…" She pulled out all the stops, reprising the smile that had worked so well on Robert Valentine. "Luc." Then, with a sweeping gesture that took in her bedraggled appearance, she appealed to his sense of fair play. "You don't imagine that I set out from home looking like this, do you?"

"That," he replied, unmoved, "is beside the point."

"No!" Then, because actually he was right, "Well, yes, obviously it is, but I had an accident."

As he frowned, his brows drew down at the centre, emphasizing the devilish look, drawing attention to his eyes. They were, she realized, threaded with streaks of gold lightning.

"What kind of accident? Are you hurt?"

"Hurt? Oh, er, no." Surprised into a genuine smile by this evidence that he was, after all, human, she said, "I had an argument with a buggy." She raised her leg, apparently to display the damage, but well aware that they were one of her better features. The buggy, she realised belatedly, had taken more than nylon.

"You are bleeding." His expression softened a little and the devil took on a different role. Pure temptation.

"Oh, no," she said, not entirely in response to this statement. Men, even sexy Italians, had been banished from her life. Then, using his concern to her advantage, she said, "Well, not much." She rubbed at her elbow. "A bit of a bump when I fell off the pavement, that's all. The motorcycle barely touched me…" She ground to a halt as she realized she was coating her shirtsleeve with oil.

About to assure him that all she needed to do was clean up and she'd be ready to go, she decided to save her breath. Luc Bellisario, rot-his-socks, was right. Who, in his right mind, would let a disaster like her practice the dangerous art of silver service in a restaurant full of the rich and famous?

"Okay," she said.

"Okay?" he repeated, totally Italian. Totally gorgeous.

"I give up. There's always an opening at Burgers-R-Us."

Luc watched the woman rescue a pale blonde corkscrew curl that had escaped its pin, smearing more oil on her cheek as she tucked it behind her ear. She was a disaster, no question, and after learning that Robert Valentine had employed her, his first response had been nothing short of astonishment.

His second had been to send her home. Losing a day's pay—more importantly, a day's tips—would give her time to dwell on the standards required from staff working in a restaurant like Bella Lucia.

His third....His third had been purely physical as she'd smiled—the real smile, not the one calculated to turn him into her slave—eclipsing the late September sun, heating him down to the bone. It was a raw, totally male reaction that went a long way to explaining why Robert Valentine—Luc's cousin had made meeting beautiful women his life's work—had employed her.

"Wait," he said.

She stopped, looked back over her shoulder, blew another escaping curl from her face. Had she any idea how sexy that was?

Well, obviously. Like her first smile, it was a move calculated to snag his attention, keep him hooked. It was working.

"What?" she demanded. Then, when he didn't answer, "Don't tell me, you want me to leave the uniform?"

He swallowed, fighting the image of her peeling it off, piece by piece and dropping it at his feet.

"Would there be any point?" he asked, striving manfully for cutting sarcasm. "It's only fit for the dustbin."

She was trouble.

He should do everyone a favour and let her go, but in a month he'd be back in Italy, stepping into his father's shoes. Assuming the role to which he'd been born. Trapped....

The word dropped into his mind like a stone weight.

He blocked it out. Concentrated on the problem facing him.

Miss Polly Bright.

Luc saw, behind her sparky, couldn't-care-less in-your-face attitude, a loss of hope that tugged at something deep inside him. Something that he couldn't bring himself to crush.

"Come," he said, turning abruptly, and walking towards the housekeeper's room, resisted the urge to look back, check that she had obeyed him.

She'd followed.

"Housekeeping will find a dressing for your leg and a clean uniform. When you're fit to be seen, come to the restaurant and report to Michael, the head waiter." He came close to smiling.

"I warn you, he won't be impressed by a smile and unlike me, he won't give you a second chance."

"You won't regret it, Luc," she said, earnestly. Then, "Mr. Bellisario."

"Be sure," he warned her. "You'll be sorry if I do."

All through the busy lunchtime, the rush of media stars, artists, the unexpected arrival of a minor royal whose party had to be found room in an already packed restaurant, Luc kept an eye on her.

Polly wasn't slick. He didn't know what she'd told Robert about her previous experience, but it certainly hadn't been as a waitress at the luxury end of the business, he decided, after witnessing a couple of close calls with the silver service. Far from irritating high profile diners who were used to the best, however, they responded to her startled "oops" with good humour, encouraging her efforts, tipping her extravagantly.

Watching her might be wrecking his nerves, but she had a way about her, a warmth that people responded to. A smile that could melt permafrost.

Max Valentine joined him, followed his gaze. "Isn't that Emma's friend? How's she doing?"

"Living dangerously. If she gets through lunch without tipping a bowl of soup into someone's lap, it'll be a miracle."

"Oh, great, that's all we need. A lawsuit." Then, "Look, Dad wants me at head office and he warned me it's likely to be a long one. I realise it's your evening off, but I wondered if you could stand in for me?"

"No problem."

"Thanks, Luc." Then, "Keep an eye on that girl."

That wasn't a problem, either. It was looking away he was finding difficult.

Polly made it through her first day on pure adrenaline. It would have been easier if Luc Bellisario hadn't been watching every move, making it plain that he thought she was a disaster waiting to happen. It hadn't and by the end of the week, even the perfectionist head waiter had given her a nod of approval.

But the devil just didn't quit. Every time she looked up, it seemed, his dark eyes were fixed on her. Every time he spoke to her, he had found something to criticize. Her hair, mostly.

Today, though, she really was in trouble. At one of her tables, a woman whose face was a permanent fixture on the front pages of the gossip magazines, had drunk her way steadily through a bottle of wine, waiting for a lunch date who never appeared, not touching the bread, the herb-flavoured olive oil, the tiny antipasto appetizers that Polly had brought, hoping to tempt the woman to eat something….

Luc, a sixth sense alerting him to trouble, looked for Polly. But for once she wasn't causing the drama—she had diffused it. She calmly, lent an arm to the infamous diner as if she was a dowager rather than just unsteady on her feet. Luc moved to help, but Polly stopped him with a keep-back I-can-handle-this look, and helped the woman move towards the rear exit to escape the paparazzi who were outside hoping for a gift like this.

It was nearly an hour before she returned.

"Where the devil have you been?" Luc demanded, when she finally appeared. By then he was almost out of his mind with worry.

"Sorry. I didn't have any money with me so I had to walk back."

"What!"

Misunderstanding him, she was instantly on the defensive, "I had to make sure that poor woman got home safely."

"It's a pity she didn't have the same thought for you."

"She was distraught." Then, "So? Am I in trouble, Mr. Bellisario? Do I get shot for desertion in the face of the dessert trolley?"

"Nothing that painless, Polly. Your punishment is to sit next to me at lunch."

For a moment she looked beaten, but she rallied. "Brave man."

He thought that foolhardy probably better described his action as sat beside him at the staff lunch table. He was much too close to the fine spirals of hair that had worked free of the pins that never could quite restrain them. Much too close, altogether.

"Tell me," he said, in an effort to distract himself, "what were you doing before you worked here?"

So, that was what he was after. Digging into her background to find some reason to get rid of her.

"Not this," Polly said, and since there was no point in pretending, listed all the jobs she'd had in the last year—always two at a time—cooking fast food, slow food, pub food just to pay back the bank, keep a roof over her head.

This had the effect of rendering Luc momentarily speechless. A relief. She could resist his good looks—if she closed her eyes—but his voice never failed to reduce her bones to putty.

"You're a cook?" he asked, while she helped herself to a spoonful of risotto. She wasn't planning a long lunch.

"According to any number of gold-edged certificates with my name on them," she assured him. "In fact until a year ago I was a partner in a catering business I started straight from college."

"So?"

She looked at him. The lightning in his eyes had softened to flecks of gold and she discovered that it wasn't just his voice....

"What happened?"

She swallowed, concentrated very hard, remembered how to speak. "One of my partners had a baby."

"And the other?"

She swallowed, took a slow breath. "Was the father," she said. It had been a year. She was over it, she told herself. Looking into Luc Bellisario's eyes, she could even believe it. "They wanted their capital back. It was tied up in the equipment."

"You had to sell it?"

"Yes." At a thumping loss, which she'd carried. She'd have done anything to escape… "This is my way back. Emma told me about the tips your people earn. A year and I'll be able to start over." This time on her own. Then, "Is that it, Mr. Bellisario? Inquisition over? Because I'm done here."

"Luc," he said. Then stood as she pushed back her chair, "We got off to a bad start, Polly, but I want you know that I appreciate what you did today."

"Oh," she said, doing her best to ignore her stupid heart doing that stupid little fluttery thing.

"Just…"

Too soon….

"What!" she demanded.

"Next time take a taxi," he said, with unexpected warmth. "We'll pay."

He'd misjudged her, Luc realized, as she walked away. He now watched her, not for mistakes, but for the pleasure of it. Nearby, Robert Valentine, his attention caught by a burst of laughter, smiled. "Pretty little thing, isn't she?"

"More than that, sir. A lot more than that." She'd had a setback, but was determined to start again. That took courage. Heart.

"Polly…."

"Luc, if it's about what happened with the princess…"

Three weeks and she hadn't dropped anything. Not that she still didn't get the wobbles when she caught Luc looking at her—not from nerves, but because now he looked away. But today, he hadn't been fast enough and she'd been surprised to see something in his expression, something almost tender and she'd come close to spilling some chocolate confection into the lap of a minor royal. Not that Her Highness had complained. On the contrary, she'd smiled away Polly's apology, and said, "My dear, if that man smiled at me like that, I wouldn't drop just my pudding…"

"No. That was not your fault."

He knew what he'd done, then…

"Are you going out? Lunch is about to be served."

"Thanks, but I could do with a break from food." And sitting next to him. Since that first occasion, the place had been left for her, as if everyone could see that she wanted to be there— even if she refused to admit it to herself. "You can enjoy your lunch for once without holding your breath, wondering if I'm going to tip something down myself."

"Instead I'll be worrying that you're being attacked by a buggy, or run down by a motorbike," he said, his voice grave, even while those little gold flecks were dancing in his eyes.

She caught her breath and stifled the laugh that responded to the way the corner of his mouth tilted up in an invitation to join him in a little self-mockery.

No. She really wasn't going to be that stupid. He would be leaving soon. Going back to Italy. She stuffed another brick in the wall guarding her heart and said,

"I'm sorry, Luc, but right now all I want is some air."

"You've been working non-stop for three hours and you've got a tough evening ahead of you. You can't do that on fresh air."

"I'll pick up a sandwich."

"That's not enough. You need proper food."

Confronted with his Michelangelo good looks, liquid Italian accent and spare broad-shouldered, narrow-hipped figure, bricks were useless and a girl had to save herself any way she could. "You do realize," she said, "that you sound exactly like your mother?"

This affront to his masculinity was supposed to drive him away. Instead, with a wry lift of his left brow said, "You've met her." Then, before she could recover, he took her elbow, opened the door for her and said, "Very well, fresh air first, then we eat," and refusing to take no for an answer, he steered her out into the street. Smooth and silky as chef's ice cream, she thought. First the freeze, then the sweetness as it thawed on the tongue. "Besides, someone has to ride shotgun on your uniform."

It was the delicious combination of the American expression and Italian accent that got her.

"What?" he demanded. "What did I say?"

She shook her head as she pulled her lips hard back against her teeth in an attempt to smother the burst of nerve-fuelled laughter. Then, losing it, "You're a fan of spaghetti westerns?"

It took him a moment, but then she discovered that despite all evidence to the contrary, Luc Bellisario knew how to laugh. And when he laughed he looked younger, less threatening. But a whole lot more dangerous. Yet she still found herself walking along the King's Road with him.

While she'd planned to do nothing more than window shop, enjoying exotic and beautiful things she couldn't begin to afford, Luc apparently had other ideas, a destination in mind. But when he turned a corner into a narrow street, away from the shops, opened a gate that led down to a basement flat, produced a key and opened the door, she dug her heels in.

"You won't get much fresh air pounding the pavement, Polly. I have a small garden. You can sit in the sun and I will make you lunch." His smile was reassuring, his hand extended like a lifeline. And for the first time in a year, she was hungry.

"Small?" she exclaimed, a moment later when he'd ushered her through to a courtyard where a two-seater bench—there wasn't room for anything bigger—occupied the only space that wasn't filled with pots of sweet-scented culinary herbs standing, hanging everywhere. "This is pocket handkerchief-sized, but fabulous." And while Polly the woman suspected she was making a mistake, Polly the cook didn't care as she plucked a warm leaf of basil, and rubbed it between her fingers to release the scent. "A touch of home in London?" she said, taking the cold drink he passed to her.

"If you forget the sea, the boats, the long wide beach," he said, wryly.

"It sounds lovely."

"There's an ancient square where people gather in the

evening. Mountains." He made broad, encompassing gesture. "Everything."

"You must miss it," she said, settling herself on the bench. "But you're going back soon."

He joined her, leaning back into the seat, not quite touching her. "Next month. The Bellisario family is in the restaurant business, although not on the grand scale of the Valentines. Not yet. I came here to learn from them so that when I go home and step into my father's shoes…."

He didn't look that excited at the prospect. And in a heartbeat, she found herself wanting to reach out, touch his hand. Invite his confidence.

"And you, Polly?" he asked, before she did anything so reckless. Turning the attention from himself to her. "What are your plans?"

"Not to step into my father's shoes, that's for sure. I'm the family failure."

"Your catering business? That is not failure, that's experience."

"You could say that." Then, because she wanted him to understand, wanted him to know everything… "One of my partners was my fiancé, Luc. The baby…."

He was the one who took her hand. Stopped her. "I was so busy building an empire that I didn't notice what was going on under my nose. I'm too stupid to live, let alone be entrusted with a business."

"No…." Then, softly, "He was the stupid one, Polly."

And he should know. He could teach her a thing or two about stupid, Luc thought, as Polly closed her eyes, effectively closing the subject as she lifted her face to a sun that continued to shine on into October, suspending autumn in a perfect Indian summer. At least she'd had the courage to follow her dream, while he would be living the one his father had invented for him: to emulate his famous cousins, the Valentines, taking their own restaurants into a new level of luxury, elegance.

When Max had asked him to delay his departure to give them all a little breathing room, he'd grabbed at it. Anything to delay the inevitable.

His father had understood. The Valentine family was in turmoil with skeletons falling out of every closet. Grey faces, long meetings, Stephanie with a face like thunder after a confrontation with her stepfather, Robert Valentine. Debts had to be paid. Honor demanded it….

And how much honor was there in living a lie when with Polly's example—with the hope of Polly at his side—his own dream beckoned so much more brightly.

Reluctantly, he let go of her hand and, leaving her to drink in the sun, went into the kitchen and began to assemble a simple lunch. The sooner it was done, the sooner they could return to the restaurant. To sanity.

"What are you doing?"

He glanced round. She was flushed from the sun, her mouth sweet as the fat cherries that grew in his grandmother's orchard. "Making lunch. Nothing as exciting as a sandwich," he said, unable to resist teasing her a little. "Just pasta, wild mushrooms, a little cream."

"Ambrosia," she said, laughing. "Food from the gods."

"I… No…" Flustered, quite possibly blushing—the devil had lost his cool—he said, "My grandmother taught me to cook." Then, "I need parsley…."

"I'll get it." And when she returned, she took a teacloth, tucked it around her waist. He moved over. There was just enough room for the two of them at the stove.

"Polly…." As she glanced up from chopping the herbs, as he'd known she would, a stray curl bobbing over one eye. She blew it away. No, he realized, she had no idea just how sexy that was or she wouldn't risk it here, alone with him…

"Yes?" she prompted, when he didn't say any more.

"Nothing," he said. "Just Polly." Then, "What kind of name is that?"

"It's short for Mary."

"How can it be short for Mary? It's longer."

"I guess it's one of those things you have to be British to understand."

"Mary." This time she just carried on chopping, using the razor sharp knife like the professional she undoubtedly was and without warning the dream in his head, the one he'd buried so deep that he'd almost forgotten it, dissolved into the one that had been haunting him ever since Polly Bright had stuck out an oily hand and introduced herself, smiling at him.

"Maria…" She scooped up the herbs, dropped them into the pan of mushrooms.

"Bella Maria."

And this time when she looked up, he bent to kiss that smile.

He just might have retained his hold on sanity if she had not kissed him back. If her kiss had not been the one his soul had been waiting for, if she had not been the woman who would complete his dreams, making anything seem possible.

A kiss, one kiss, was all it had taken to break down the wall she had spent the past year building around her heart.

No. Three weeks of looks that had moved from cold to a sizzling heat. From tight smiles to tender ones. Three weeks of looks and one kiss.

And a little pasta with mushrooms and cream served by a man who looked not like the devil, but Adonis.

After he'd kissed her, he hadn't said a word. He had simply served her lunch and then walked her back to the restaurant. And that evening, all through the long hours while they cleared and laid the tables for the next day, he didn't look at her once. She understood that. If he had, if their gazes had met, she'd have crumpled up into a little pile of mush right there on the floor.

But then, at the end of the evening, she waited for him.

Michael said, "If you're looking for Luc, he's holed up with

Max. It looked as if it was going to be a long one. Can it keep until tomorrow?"

"Yes. Yes, of course."

Except that tomorrow, Luc Bellisario was not there.

It was Robert Valentine who broke the news that he'd returned to Italy. "Luc put his plans on hold to help us out over a difficult few weeks. He'll be a tough act to follow, but…."

She stopped listening.

He'd left without a word. Gone home to his small Italian town by the sea where his father's shoes were waiting for him. She would have walked out then, but she owed Emma for the chance she'd been given. It wasn't as if she had to see him. But she kept on looking up, expecting to see him…

Polly gave a week's notice and for six days she performed like a well-oiled automaton, on the outside at least. She was the perfect waitress. Efficient, calm, invisible. Not an "oops" or a dropped pea. Not much laughter, either. All emotional responses had been shut down. What was there to get emotional about? One kiss. What was that?

Nothing, she told herself and was congratulating herself over how well she was holding everything to together—just this last day to get through—when the restaurant door opened bringing in a rumble of the thunder that had been threatening to bring the Indian summer to an end, a draft of cool air. And something else….

Luc.

When she looked up he was standing there, watching her and six days of perfection came to an end as the tray she was carrying slid from her hands.

Luc was beside her even as Michael moved in smoothly to restore order. Beside her, murmuring softly, reassuringly. "Cara…forgive me…. I could not speak…." With his arm about her, he swept her into the office, closing the door, held her as she cried out, tried to escape…. "Before I could speak to you I had to talk to my father. Say what I should have told him long ago. That his dreams are not my dreams. That I cannot walk in his shoes. Only then could I come back for you, my Bella Maria."

"You're giving it all up?"

"I'm surrendering my father's dream for one of my own, Polly. A small restaurant overlooking a sheltered bay." He was so close that she could hardly breathe.

"How did he take it?"

"Philosophically. And my sister is very, very happy."

"Oh. So, this restaurant…."

"Somewhere full of warmth, life, where the food touches the soul. Is that a dream you could share?"

"What you're saying," she said, carefully, "is that you're looking for a cook?"

"What I'm saying is that I would like you to be my partner." He took an envelope from his pocket, took out a document. "Here are the deeds."

She glanced at them, saw the name—Bella Maria.

She was shaking, close to tears. "And if I say no?" she whispered.

"Then I will keep asking you," he said, "like this…" He brushed his mouth against hers, melting the bones in her legs so that she was forced to lean into him for support.

"I'm not sure…." she said. Then, he'd kissed her again. "This may take some time."

"Come to Italy, my Bella Maria," Luc said, taking her hand, leading her into a new life, a shared dream, "and I'll take as long as you need."

* * * * *

KISS ME, KATE

Alison Kent

Alison Kent was a born reader, but it wasn't until the age of thirty that she decided she wanted to be a writer when she grew up. Five years and a mental library of industry knowledge later, she had the most basic grasp of "how-to" and her first book in print.

Three years after that, she found a permanent home at Mills & Boon. With her first three novels in print, she took a break from writing romance novels and spent a few months living one, finding her own hero and practising every technique she'd learned from a lifetime of reading the best "how-to" manuals around! She now writes for both the Mills & Boon® Blaze® and Kensington Brava lines, and is a partner in Access Romance and DreamForge Media.

And the rest, as they say, is history. With the encouragement of her new master, er, husband, Alison is now back at work writing the stories she loves to read – the fantasies that show readers the way love was meant to be. Alison lives in a Houston, Texas, suburb with her hero, four vagabond kids and a dog named Smith.

And she actually manages to write in the midst of all that madness. Readers can contact Alison through her website at http://www.alisonkent.com.

Did you know...?

Alison sold her first book to Mills & Boon in America, live on national television!

KISS ME, KATE

"WHAT do you mean you only booked one room?"

"What I said. This trip is just to get a look at the place, so we can decide whether or not it'll work. I'd rather save the big bucks for the gift. Once we decide on one. If that ever happens."

"Just great. Now you don't want to work with me on something as important as this honeymoon gift for our parents? Not that you backing out on the planning particularly surprises me..."

"Did I say I didn't want to work with you, as impossible as that is? And what's with the crack about not being surprised I'd back out? You're acting like I dump on you on a regular basis."

He didn't. He never had. But Josh Sawyer was so close to walking out on Kate Holloway that he didn't need a ruler to measure the distance, or a clock to count the seconds it would take to kiss her goodbye.

Doing so, unfortunately, would defeat the purpose of having

knowingly reserved the single room, but since this entire venture was about to go south in a bucket of lard, he wasn't sure it mattered.

At least he'd walk away with a kiss. That was all he really wanted. Scratch that. He wanted more. He'd wanted more for a very long time.

And he was pretty damn sure he hadn't been imagining the reciprocal signals Miss Kate had been broadcasting all this time...for the last twelve months...since his mother had started dating her father.

No. This was more a case of her being backed into a corner. Not of her trying to squirm her way out. And that wasn't the sort of squirming he'd invited Kate to join him in at Manhattan's Hush hotel.

"Fine," she finally said, stepping away from the French doors that opened onto the room's balcony. "I'll call the reservations desk myself."

Good luck, he thought, dropping into one of the room's plush armchairs, squaring one leg over the other, lacing his hands behind his head. He'd asked about the crowd milling in the Hush lobby when picking up his key card this afternoon.

The place was booked to the rafters. A celebrity wedding. Kate was stuck.

He watched her reach for the bedside phone and dial, her back to him as if pretending he wasn't in the room. She'd been held up in court today until four, and hadn't been able to get away to meet him any earlier.

The situation had played nicely into his plans.

While he'd been scoping out the room's amenities, she'd been on a train from Hartford into the city. And judging by her tone of voice since arriving, she'd used that time to build up a nice head of steam.

"Are you sure? I'll take anything, the basement, the kitchen, the back of the bar."

Josh chuckled under his breath, earning himself a nice

steamy glare. Eyes narrowed, Kate turned to the side just enough to deliver the look. She stood with one arm crossed over her middle, the other elbow propped on top, the phone still held to her ear.

She was all business in her navy pumps and navy suit, her tiny pearl earrings and the tight braid holding her dark wavy hair to her head. And that was the thing that had intrigued him since the day they'd met.

He saw beneath her armor to the free spirit she was hiding. Was it some kind of crime to want to get to the bottom of who she really was? To see if they fit as well in real time as they did in his very active mind?

"No, I understand. Thank you for trying," she said, carefully placing the receiver in the cradle when he could see she wanted to slam it down.

"Look, Kate." He sat forward, knees spread, hands laced between. "This isn't the disaster you're making it out to be."

"There's one bed, Josh." She faced him from across the room as she perched carefully on the edge. "The potential for disaster is huge."

At her admission, his gut began to tighten. He'd been right. There was life beneath the corporate shell. She wasn't the cold fish with a hard heart the rest of his family believed. She was alive and feeling, and he was going to find the chink in her protective gear before the weekend was done.

"Now, now. It probably won't seem that way after you eat. We have reservations for dinner at Amuse Bouche at nine."

She pursed her lips, glanced at her watch then got to her feet. "I'll take a quick shower and change."

He pushed to his feet, rubbing his palms over his thighs and smoothing down the denim of his jeans. "Why don't you meet me in the bar when you're ready?"

She lifted a brow, took him in from head to toe. "You're not going to change?"

Ah, now *there* was the uppity Miss Kate he'd gotten to know the past twelve months. He reached into the armoire where he'd hung the few things he'd figured would do better not being shoved in a drawer, and pulled an unstructured black jacket from a hanger, shrugging it on over his black T-shirt. "Better?"

Kate rolled her eyes, picked up her toiletries case, walked into the bathroom and shut the door. Once he heard her turn the lock, he laughed. Then he headed for the elevator. He continued to laugh all the way down the hall.

He couldn't wait to get the weekend started.

Kate listened to the door latch as Josh left the room, then sat on the edge of the huge whirlpool tub and buried her face in her hands. What in the world was she doing here? They could have worked out this parental wedding-gift business through email and text messaging. As a last resort, she could have picked up the phone and given him a call.

But, no. She'd agreed to spend the weekend with him at Hush to see if the hotel would meet their gift-giving needs. Now they were stuck sharing a room, and all she'd done to object was argue like a shrew before picking up the phone and pretending to call the front desk.

She was such a phony. And such a chicken. Josh Sawyer was everything she'd spent her life trying to outrun—even though he was everything she wanted.

He was big and bad, and obviously didn't care what anyone thought—about the way he dressed straight off thrift-store racks, or wore his dark blond hair too long and too shaggy, or never seemed to remember to shave. He was a complete heathen, and she was crazy about him.

So crazy she feared she'd fallen in love.

She got to her feet, peeled off her pantyhose, shimmied out of her skirt and tossed her blouse and blazer with the rest of her clothes to the floor.

Standing in front of the bathroom's huge mirrors, wearing nothing but sensible white cotton underwear, she wondered if she would actually be able to follow through with her plan to seduce him.

So far, things hadn't gone so well. Obviously. She didn't know why she found it so easy to stand in front of a jury and argue a case, but coming face-to-face with Josh brought on such a flurry of nerves that her claws came out in force.

It was all about self-preservation. She knew that. She'd chosen poorly in the past and feared that wanting Josh the way she did was a twisted effort at throwing caution to the wind—a thought that had her glancing at her toiletries case.

Tucked in the bottom and wrapped protectively in tissue paper was a pair of black satin panties with a cutaway crotch and a matching pushup bra without cups. Even picturing herself wearing the set in the privacy of her bedroom where she'd only once had the courage to try it on, was enough to make her knees—and other body parts—tremble.

Thinking about wearing them for Josh…she shuddered, stripped out of the rest of her things, and stepped into the shower—a very icy, very cold shower.

When Kate walked into Erotique where Josh sat in a plush leather chair at one of the bar's low tables, he caught himself staring at the gorgeous woman with lust in his heart. When it registered that the gorgeous woman was Kate, lust took a sharp turn south.

He was used to the pumps and the pearls, to practical suits and seeing her in dress pants and sweater sets. But this… this…oh, he could get used to this.

Her hair, held back from her face with a simple jeweled band, hung to her shoulders in waves. She wore strappy black heels of at least three inches, and a little black dress that added even more length to her fabulous and oh-so-long legs.

She was beyond gorgeous, and he felt like a putz. He should have gone to more of an effort to gussy up for her the way she'd obviously done for him. If she had done it for him…

He signaled for the server dressed in black tuxedo pants, a

cummerbund and a hot pink, sleeveless, tuxedo-styled shirt. Even the help looked better than he did. "The lady will have…"

"A vodka Collins, please," Kate said, settling into the second chair at the table and crossing her legs, the back and forth swinging motion of her dangling foot holding his attention way too long.

"A refill for me," he found his voice to add, and the server smiled and headed for the bar. In another lifetime, Josh would have watched her go, would have enjoyed the sway of her hips in those perfectly tight pants.

But this was the here and now, and he only had eyes for Kate.

"You look…great," he finally said when they'd both been staring at each other and silent too long. "You ought to wear that more often."

"How do you know that I don't?"

He didn't know any such thing. But he couldn't picture the Kate he'd spent time with this last year at family dinners and outings and holiday functions dressing like this for any reason…except to mow down a man.

And even from where he flailed flat on his back, he couldn't help but wonder when she'd changed her mind, because thirty minutes ago she'd been all about putting distance between them.

The server returned with their drinks, and Josh sat forward. His elbows on his knees, he cradled the highball glass in both hands. His voice was low when he spoke. "Well, now that you mention it, I don't know. The only Kate I've met is the one you've let me see."

"There's only one Kate, Josh." She ran a fingertip around the rim of her glass. "There's only me."

"I'm not so sure," he said. "Seems I was talking to another one up in the room a while ago."

She dropped her gaze from his, smiling softly as she stared into her drink. "I owe you an apology. It's been a tough week, and then to get here and find out we'd be sharing a room…"

She lifted her lashes, her dark eyes sparkling. "I wasn't ready for that. At least not earlier."

Implying she was ready for it now? "I don't get it. What weren't you ready for?" And why snap his head off back there in the room, if she was going to have this very welcome change of heart? A test. That was it. Some *Cosmo* tip thing about how to try a man's mettle.

But then she took a deep breath, uncrossed her legs and with a trembling hand, set her drink on the table. And he swore her eyes were watering when she said, "For us, Josh. I wasn't ready for us. For facing this thing we have between us."

He swallowed hard, set his drink next to hers and raked both hands back through his hair. He'd been all prepared to seduce her, yet here she was, placing herself in his hands, making all of this way too easy.

And what was he doing instead of grabbing the bull by the horns? He was shaking in his boots, that's what.

He didn't want her to know that particular truth, and so he quietly asked, "What thing might that be, Kate?"

Her smile was worldly and wise, and spoke of heat and female secrets. It was also his undoing. "There's a reason you and I are the center of attention any time our families get together."

"You mean the sniping and bickering?" What had gone on upstairs was nothing in the grand scheme of the Kate and Josh show. "The low-down sarcasm and underhanded insults?"

She cocked her head to one side. "And all of it done with pulses racing and temperatures rising. Most people call it foreplay."

She got to him with the talk of foreplay. Not surprising. Josh had always been easy to fluster. He would never admit it. He might not even know it. But she was an expert witness. She'd seen it happen time and again—more often than not when she was the one doing the flustering.

What better time than the present to play her upper hand.

They'd moved from Erotique to Amuse Bouche at dinner's appointed time. Josh had ordered man food—steak and potatoes. She'd ordered play food—succulent broiled shrimp.

She wouldn't eat half of what was on her plate. Eating wasn't the point. The point was to watch Josh squirm—and to see how good an actress she really was by keeping him from finding out that she was doing the same.

"What's your impression so far?" she asked, picking up an asparagus spear with her fingers and closing her lips around the tip.

"My impression of what? The food? The service?" He paused, his eyes darkening. "The way you eat with your fingers?"

She licked clean the pads of her index finger and thumb, laughing softly and hoping he didn't pick up on the quiver that was all about nerves. Her stomach knotted and rolled. "No. Your impression of the hotel. Do you think our parents would enjoy a stay here? Or do you think they'd prefer a quieter place to celebrate their marriage?"

He cleared his throat, tossed his napkin to the table. "Depends if anyone's going to be fingering their food."

She reached for a shrimp, picked it up by the tail, swirled it through the side of clarified butter. "Does it bother you that much?"

He waited until she'd wrapped her tongue around the curl of the shrimp before he nodded. "Yeah," he said, his voice gruff and throaty. "It bothers me a lot. Please. Don't stop."

Her heart fluttered. She nearly choked when she tried to swallow. And when she reached for her wineglass, Josh snagged her wrist and stopped her.

He held her for several long seconds, neither one of them speaking, neither moving except to breathe. She felt his pulse in his thumb where his fingers ringed her wrist, and was certain he felt hers there where it raced beneath her skin.

And then he was on his feet, circling the table, pulling her up, taking possession of her chair, and tugging her into his lap. He didn't give her time to object—not that she would have—or time to do anything but brace her hands against his chest. He used his palm on the back of her head to bring her mouth to his.

His tongue was insistent against her lips and she opened to take him in. He tasted like red wine and steak sauce, and he kissed her like he would never be able to get enough. He stole her breath, and she dug her fingers into the balls of his shoulders, thankful for the privacy of the alcove where they sat, even while not caring at all that anyone walking by could see them.

She'd wanted this far too long. The feel of Josh beneath her, the hard strength in his thighs, the pressure of his hand on the back of her head…she wanted it all, had dreamed of it all. And so she kissed him back.

She wrapped her arms around his neck, threaded her fingers into his shaggy hair, enjoyed the scrape of his day's growth of beard against her face. He was hungry, his body growing tight, his desire evident.

He brought a hand up between them to cover her breast, groaning deeply, filling her mouth with the sound as he discovered how much of her body her choice of lingerie left exposed.

"Kate, what the hell are you wearing?" He found her nipple and teased it. "Or what are you not wearing?"

"Something I thought you might like," she whispered against his mouth.

"Like to see? Or like to get you out of?" he asked, tendering kisses along the line of her jaw, moving to the hollow of her throat where he pressed his lips to her pulse, his hand wriggling between their bodies.

"Well, there's not a lot there to get me out of." Oh, what was he doing there with his finger and thumb? "Or to see, really."

"I have a feeling there's a whole lot I'm going to want to see." He moved his mouth to her earlobe and nibbled. "And I'm not talking about what you're wearing."

Was she ready for this? To have her dreams come true? Would what she had to offer be enough for this man?

"I'm just not sure…"

She stiffened before he could finish.

"…if we should maybe…"

She pulled back, unable to look him in the eye.

"…skip the rest of dinner and finish up with dessert in the room."

Oh, no. She was not letting him get off—so to speak—quite that easy.

She got to her feet, and when he did the same, she stepped around him, returning to her chair, leaving him standing alone.

He shook his head and tugged his jacket together over the fly of his jeans. Then, while she signaled for their server, he circled the table and sat.

"Is there anything else I can get you this evening?" the young man asked when he arrived.

"Just the check," Josh answered, nearly growling.

"Yes, you can," Kate quickly countered. "I'd like a serving of your most decadent dessert. Something with chocolate or caramel sauce. Or with strawberries and whipped cream."

"I've got just the thing," the server said with a smile, but she cut him off before he could rattle off his spiel.

"Great. Could you add it to our check, please?" she asked, turning to Josh as she added, "And have it delivered to our room?"

The woman was going to be the death of him if first she didn't drive him over the edge. She hadn't let him close since they'd left the restaurant. She'd kept her distance on the walk to the elevator, in the elevator, on the walk from the elevator to the room.

And now that they were *in* the room, what was she doing? Hiding in the bathroom, damn female.

Room service had delivered her order, and he kept waiting for her to come out and dive in, seeing as how she'd dumped him for dessert the minute he'd said the word.

When he heard the bathroom door open, he picked up the covered bowl in one hand, picked up the spoon in the other and turned to give her what she wanted. Only he suddenly wasn't so sure he knew what that was.

If he'd thought the Kate who had walked into the bar was gorgeous, this Kate brought him to his knees. She'd pulled the band from her hair and wore a sheer black robe over a bra and panties that left nothing to the imagination.

She walked toward him. He retreated, backing into one of the room's plush armchairs. Still holding the bowl and spoon, he sat. Kate came closer, a brow lifted, the corner of her mouth quirked upward, and climbed up to straddle his lap.

She took the bowl from his hand, dropped the cover to the floor, breathed deeply of the chocolate and caramel and marshmallow confection. Then grinning as she reached for the spoon, she said, "There. That's better."

"What's better?" he choked out.

"Your hands. They're empty now."

Oh. That. He didn't know where to start. Kate made it easy by dipping a spoon into the bowl and drizzling chocolate sauce over the slope of one breast. His hands holding her hips, he leaned forward and licked it from her skin, burying his face in her cleavage and breathing in.

Then just as quickly he set her away. Not because he wanted to. Because he had to. "Tell me something, Kate. What are we doing here?"

She cocked her head to one side. And though she did seem sure of herself, he sensed a hesitation, a tremor of uncertainty where he held her. "We're having dessert, Josh. That's all."

"*Is* it all?" he had to ask. He wanted her. Hell, she made for the perfect dessert. But before he gobbled her up, he had to know if this was about satisfying more than lust. "I need to know if this is a game or a weekend fling or a payback for some insult I've forgotten making or—"

"Shh." She pressed her fingertips to his lips. "You're making me nervous. Men aren't supposed to analyze. They're supposed to—"

"What?" he asked, cutting her off. "We're supposed to jump a woman's bones without thinking?"

"Most men do."

"Uh-uh-uh. Generalizations can get you into trouble, sweet Katie."

She looked down, swirled the spoon through the brownie and marshmallow and caramel confection. "Okay. Most men I've known do."

He reached for her hand, wrapped his fingers around hers that held the spoon. "You know me, sweetheart. And I don't."

Her eyes suddenly grew damp. "Oh, Josh. I'm so scared."

Uh-oh. Panic. "Of me?"

She shook her head. "Of the way I can't stop thinking about you. Of the way I pick fights because I know you'll stick around to argue."

"Katie, I swear. I'll stick around even if you never say another word. I'm crazy about you." Emotion clogged his throat, and he swallowed. "I've been crazy about you forever."

"Then could I have my hand back?" she asked, laughing softly. "So we can get started with dessert?"

He started without her, sliding his free hand between her legs where her cutaway panties left her exposed. He cupped her there, feeling her warmth and her wetness.

She shuddered, shivered, pulled her hand from his and dipped into the pooling sauce, spooning the bite into his mouth.

Then she leaned forward to kiss him, sharing the sweetness, sliding her tongue into his mouth, moaning as he found her wet and ready and slipped a finger inside.

He stroked her, played her; the kiss grew frantic as her pleasure peaked. She squirmed on his lap, spilling melted marshmallow and caramel and chocolate all over the both of them. That was it. Enough.

He set the bowl and spoon on the side table, hoisted her up in his arms, carried her across the room and laid her back on the bed. She was sticky and sweet, and he licked her clean, loving the taste of her skin and her body's moisture more than he'd ever love any dessert.

Moments later, she came apart, crying out his name. It was the most beautiful thing he'd heard in his life.

"This isn't going to be a one-sided relationship, you know," Kate said, leaning back into Josh's damp chest.

He tightened his hold across her middle, pulling her close. "I'm a patient man. Hell, I've waited a year for you already."

She slapped his knee beneath the water. "You have not."

"Oh, yes I have."

He couldn't be serious. "I thought you couldn't stand me."

"Didn't mean I didn't want to get you into bed."

"What?" Water splashed everywhere as she turned around in the huge tub to face him. "You couldn't stand me but you wanted to sleep with me?"

"There's a thin line between love and hate, sweetheart," he said, his dimples breaking in the shadow of his beard.

That caught her off guard. His use of the "L" word. The way his eyes had softened as he looked at her. "Josh?"

"Kate?"

"I think I love you."

"Considering I know I love you, that's damn good news."

"Oh, Josh." She launched herself forward, threw her arms around his neck in the biggest hug she could manage. How could she be this lucky? "Why did we waste so much time fighting?"

"A lot of people would call that foreplay," he said, winking at her when she stuck out her tongue. "Of course, now that we're here, feel free to cut to the chase."

Shaking her head, she pressed her lips together and fought a smile. "You are incorrigible."

"Actually, I'm horny."

She reached beneath the water between his legs and found him thick and full. "So I see."

"I'd rather you feel."

"Isn't that what I'm doing?"

"Yeah, but not fast enough."

"You said you were a patient man."

"I lied," he said, all hint of teasing gone. "I love you. I want you. I need you. Now, kiss me, Kate, before I go blind."

She did, filled with such emotion that when she opened her mouth over his, she sobbed. He calmed her with long strokes of his hand down her back, urging her closer, asking her with his hands and his mouth to love him.

Braced on her knees, she took him inside, sliding down his length until they were joined completely, fully, until they were one. When he began to move beneath her, she followed, the yin to the yang of his motion.

"Do you know how good you feel?" she asked him, whispering the words against his cheek and swearing nothing had ever felt this amazing.

"Not half as good as you do, I'm pretty damn sure."

Breathless, she laughed. "Wanna bet?"

"And have you beat the pants off me? I don't think so."

"Your pants are off already."

"Hmm. I wondered why I felt so naked," he teased, hissing in a breath when she moved just right. "There. Do that again and keep doing it again."

"Greedy pig," she managed to get out before sensation took her away.

"You better believe it." He pushed up. "And you better get used to it. I've waited for you this long, it'll be a hell of a while before I get my fill."

Oh, did she ever know the feeling. She shivered as he tensed beneath her. "Josh?"

He closed his eyes and groaned. His hands gripped her hips and held tight. "This isn't a good time, Kate."

"I just wanted you to know—"

"Really, not a good time."

"—that I don't mind—"

"Not good. Trust me."

"—having to share one room."

"I knew you wouldn't." He gasped. He wheezed. "That's why I only booked one."

He surged upward, taking her with him; together they climbed to the stars. Minutes later, when they'd made their way down and she lay collapsed against his chest, their bodies still joined, she told him the truth.

"I know. I called reservations last week to check."

"And you came anyway."

"Of course I did. I love you."

And when he reached between her legs, she came again.

* * * * *

THE MISTRESS'S SECRET

Julia James

Julia lives in England with her family. Mills & Boon® novels were Julia's first "grown up" books she read as a teenager ("Alongside Georgette Heyer and Daphne du Maurier") and she's been reading them ever since.

Julia adores the English countryside ("And the Celtic countryside!"), in all its seasons, and is fascinated by all things historical, from castles to cottages. She also has a special love for the Mediterranean ("The most perfect landscape after England!") – she considers both are ideal settings for romance stories! Since becoming a romance writer, she has, she says, had the great good fortune to start discovering the Caribbean as well, and is happy to report that those magical, beautiful islands are also ideal settings for romance stories! "One of the best things about writing romance is that it gives you a great excuse to take holidays in fabulous places!" says Julia. "All in the name of research, of course!"

Her first stab at novel writing was Regency romances – "But alas, no one wanted to publish them!" she says. She put her writing aside until her family commitments were clear, and then renewed her love-affair with contemporary romances. "My writing partner and I made a pact not to give in until we were published – and we both succeeded! Natasha Oakley writes for Mills & Boon® Romance, and we faithfully read each other's works-in-progress and give each other a lot of free advice and encouragement!"

In between writing Julia enjoys walking, gardening, needlework and baking "extremely gooey chocolate cakes" – and trying to stay fit!

Julia says...

"My greatest goals as a romance writer are to write the kind of novels I love to read - the kind I just can't put down! And to affirm, over and over again, the power and triumph of love, the grace by which we live. I truly believe love stories are a force for good in this world."

THE MISTRESS'S SECRET

ALANNA RICHARDS leafed idly along the racks of cocktail dresses. Each carried a top designer label and was swathed in protective plastic. A wry, almost self-mocking smile hovered around her mouth. Once she had a wardrobe of such dresses. Each more beautiful than the last. Her smile took on a touch of strain. But then, it had been essential that she look as good as she possibly could. Every day.

Every night.

Her smile stilled. Memories, long banished, suddenly haunted her. A face—dark-eyed, desiring.

Abruptly she dropped her hand and started to walk forward again across soft deep carpet. It was time to find Maggie and the boys. It had been stupid of her to indulge in such weakness, however brief. Her memories were locked tightly away. Maybe, one day, when she was an old woman, she would take them out. But until that time, so far ahead of her, it was not safe. Not safe at all.

Eyes straight ahead, she started for the archway that led through to the escalator lobby of the huge, world famous London department store. It catered to the rich—the very rich—and once Alanna had been a regular customer.

Now it was as much as she could bear to enter its portals again. Not that it had been her idea. Maggie had enthused over the idea of making a special visit up to town with the boys to see the store's magically decorated Christmas toy department— "Not to buy, of course," Alanna's friend and fellow single mother had laughed. "Just to look. Ben and Nicky would adore it!"

They had, too—delighting in the lavish display of toys and the wonderful Christmas decorations, and content merely to look. Both children were used to "only looking" when it came to toys. Neither Alanna nor Maggie had money to spare for expensive playthings.

For a moment regret hovered in her mind. Had she been rash to give away Nikos's money as she had?

No—she lifted her chin resolutely—it had been the right thing to do. The only thing! It had been money she'd had no right to—none at all. The little she had kept had been enough to keep her and Nicky out of state support. Next year, when Nicky started school, she would be able to work during the school day, and then her finances would ease a little.

But never again—her eyes wandered sideways one last time to a mannequin wearing a glittering evening dress that didn't even have a price displayed—would she ever wear anything like that...

Not like that female there, she thought, her gaze lighting on a chicly clad blonde wearing what was obviously a designer suit, pursing her lips thoughtfully over the evening dress. The woman was about her age, she thought, a few years under thirty, and she had that polished perfection about her that told Alanna immediately that she spent her days doing nothing but having her hair and nails done and making herself look fabulous.

The way I used to spend my days...

She paused momentarily to study the woman. Yes, she

thought, her lips tightening, I used to be just like that. Checking out the very best in clothes. So that I could look my very best.

For Leon.

Memory leaped back, seizing her throat, making her breath catch chokingly. It was this place that had done it, reminded her of that beautiful, expensive world she'd once, so briefly, inhabited. The sight of these glamorous, expensive clothes had ripped away that fragile—terrifyingly fragile—barrier that she had erected day by day…year by year…against a single man, a single name.

Leon Andreakos.

Greek.

Rich.

Gorgeous.

Fantastically, wonderfully, irresistibly gorgeous. All six foot two of him. From the top of his silky, sable hair to his long, lithe legs. And everything in between. The most fantastic male she'd ever set eyes on. Ever would set eyes on. Ever could set eyes on.

Whom she would never see again.

His face was in front of her again, tormenting her memory—that arrogant tilt of the head; the high, sculpted cheekbones; and those eyes, so dark, swept by eyelashes so thick and long that they were wasted on a man. But nothing, nothing at all, was wasted on Leon Andreakos. Not an inch of that toned, muscled flesh that she had once known so intimately…

Her mouth twisted.

No, she had never *known* Leon Andreakos. She had known his body—and he had known hers…oh, how he had known hers!—but she had never known the man. He had never permitted that. Always, always, even in the tempest of their physical union, even at the more intense moments of their shared sensuality, he had kept that distance between them, never letting her close that gap, always, always holding her just far enough away.

There was a hardness now in her eyes, and behind the hardness, a pain that would never leave her. After all, what man like Leon Andreakos would ever let his mistress become emotionally close to him?

Let alone fall in love with him.

She shut her eyes, feeling the pain sweep over her. Pain she had pushed aside nearly five long bitter years ago because what was the use of feeling it? She could weep and agonize over loving Leon Andreakos all she liked, but he would never love her, and so what was the point of all her pain, all her wasted love?

And it wasn't just that Leon Andreakos didn't love her.

He hated her.

She'd seen that hatred, seen it loud and clear and spearing from his eyes as if it were a knife to plunge deep into her heart. Hatred for what she had done to him, to his family...to his brother.

Another emotion flushed through her like acid eating her from the inside. She had tried to stop that emotion, too, but it was no use; it came flooding back, rocking her with the force of it.

Guilt.

Guilt over Nikos, who was dead because of her.

She forced her eyes open. Making the real world come back. Not the world that haunted her, the sickening memories of that terrible, deadly night when Leon Andreakos's brother had died.

Her eyes rested on the first thing they saw—that chicly dressed blonde who was reaching out her hand, fingering the fabric of the evening gown while she considered whether or not it would sufficiently adorn her beauty. Then, as Alanna's gaze rested on her, half-blind still, torn still between memory and reality, the woman's head turned. A smile lit her face. Of greeting, of pleasure...of satisfaction.

A man was walking into the department, walking with lean, long strides up to the beautiful blonde, who was smiling at him...and he was smiling at her. Smiling at the beautiful woman who was gracing his arm in the clothes he had bought her, gracing his bed in return for those clothes...

Faintness washed over Alanna. The room swam, and she felt her legs weaken, her whole body weaken.

It couldn't be…. But it was.

Blood drummed in her ears like a crashing tide.

For the first time in over four long, endless years she was looking at Leon Andreakos again.

CHAPTER TWO

ALANNA could not move. Not a muscle. She could only stand, paralyzed, while in front of her, Leon Andreakos walked up to the woman who was his current mistress.

Leon Andreakos, whom she had not set eyes on for nearly five long years, whose mistress she had once been in another lifetime, another existence…

The lush surroundings of the store's eveningwear department vanished. The years vanished. She was standing, once again, behind the counter of the gift shop in the lobby of the expensive west end hotel while the most fabulous man she had ever laid eyes on walked up to her.

He came up to the counter and smiled at her. And in that moment, that single moment, she felt her heart swoop like a bird plunging from the topmost branch of the tree. To abase herself at his feet in worship of his male perfection, his sensual, sexual potency.

"Would you gift wrap a scarf for me?" His eyes flickered briefly to her and then moved to the flowing cascade of silk scarves that hung from a display at the end of the counter. Long fingers moved swiftly and then selected one patterned in muted grays and soft pinks. "This one, I think."

He removed it and draped it on the counter in front of her. His eyes came back to her. An eyebrow rose.

"If you please?"

The prompt jolted her. Jolted her out of the total daze that had overcome her as she had stared, mesmerized at this most devastating-looking man. Tall, with dark, Mediterranean looks, dressed in a charcoal business suit that hugged every line of his lean body, and eyes…oh, eyes that made her heart swoop again—this time right up to the clouds, to the sky beyond…

"Yes—yes, of course, sir," she managed in a voice suddenly far too tight, too faint. "Um…do you want to have it delivered to your room, or do you wish to wait?"

How she had got out that second sentence she did not know. She didn't know anything suddenly, not a thing—only that she just wanted to stare and stare at the face of the man in front of her.

It was his eyes…no, his mouth…no, everything, just everything! Everything just made her want to gaze and gaze at him. His eyes were so dark, but they had fleck of light in them, and she wanted to drown in them. His mouth was sculpted, perfect, but there was a mobility to it that made her insides weak…

"I'll wait—if you don't take too long."

It was his voice! That's what it was, Alanna thought, desperate to try to make her brain work again, make it reason… when all it wanted to do was to dissolve into formless goo. His voice—deep, accented. *What accent?* She forced herself to think as she heard her own voice murmuring, "Of course, sir," as she reached under the counter for the silver tissue paper. She felt her hand fumbling and dragged her eyes away. She couldn't just stand here staring at this man…she had to gift wrap the scarf. It was what he was waiting for her to do.

How she managed it she did not know. The man did not move, simply stood there, immobile, his eyes resting on her bowed head as her fingers fumbled hopelessly with the task. Usually she was deft and nimble with gift wrapping; today she was hopeless. And it was because of him.

And all the while he said nothing, just waited, and she could hear his impatience mounting.

He glanced at his watch once, she could tell, saw from the corner of her eye the swift lift of his wrist, the faint flash of gold.

Finally it was done, and she gave the last ribbon one final curl with the edge of her scissors. With relief she reached for the snipped off tag and flashed it through the bar-code reader and got on with printing out the invoice. The cost of the scarves still astounded her—she could have bought an entire outfit for the price of one of these hand-painted silken works of art. But then everything about working in this luxury gift shop in this five-star hotel still astounded her—that people really existed who could afford what the shop stocked, who could afford to stay at the hotel in the first place.

This man certainly could. She had come to recognize money when it walked around the lobby, and this man was a walking gold mine. Everything about him shrieked it, from his superb tailored business suit to the tips of his Italian handmade shoes.

Just as everything about him shrieked that he was the most gorgeous male she'd ever seen.

And she was going to have to look at him again. She couldn't complete the transaction keeping her head bowed. With huge effort, as if she were lifting a great weight, she looked up at him.

"Would you prefer to pay here, sir, or shall I charge it to your room?"

As her gaze met his she felt her heart do that terrifying, enthralling swoop again, and a tiny gasp escaped her constricted throat.

For a second his eyes narrowed, as if focusing on her properly for the first time, and then, in the next instant, he smiled again.

That palpable aura of impatience vanished. Completely vanished. In its place his eyes washed over her.

Caressing her…

The swoop came again from a greater height, and she gave that little gasp again. Something changed in his eye—amusement, that was it.

And it devastated her even more.

"Charge it to my room," he instructed in that deep, accented voice. "1209."

"And the name, sir?" she asked, her voice still faint. She needed a name to countercheck against the reservations computer in case of fraud. He took the payment slip she offered him and scrawled across the signature line.

"Andreakos. Leon Andreakos." He picked up the gift-wrapped scarf. *"Kalispera, thespinis,"* he murmured in his deep, accented voice and walked out.

Greek, she thought weakly. He's Greek.

Greek.

Rich.

Gorgeous.

And now, almost five years since she had first had her life turned upside down by Leon Andreakos, she was seeing him again.

Alanna went on standing, paralyzed, every muscle frozen.

And slowly, like in some hideous slow motion, she saw him reach the woman, saw his gaze flicker past her to head beyond the blonde toward her like some dire, deadly missile…where it came to rest.

For a moment, just a brief instant, he did not recognize her. Then, as the night-dark eyes focused, they hardened. Like steel. Like the blade of a knife ripping into her exposed, defenceless flesh.

She reeled. It was like a blow to the heart—without mercy.

Ignoring his current mistress, he stalked across to his former mistress, his heavy tread silent over the thick, soft carpet. The blonde glared, irritated by his distraction by another woman—and such a woman. Wearing nothing but a jersey and trousers, not in the least fashionable, bought off the rack from a budget chain store. Utterly unworthy of the perfection that was Leon Andreakos.

Alanna stood there, waiting. Waiting for Leon Andreakos,

who had once been all the world to her, and to whom she was now nothing, worse than nothing.

He stopped dead. His eyes were glittering obsidian. Full of loathing.

"What the hell are you doing here?" he snarled.

CHAPTER THREE

HIS VOICE was the same—deep and accented, but filled now with a cold anger as Leon Andreakos demanded to know the reason why his cast-off mistress from five long years ago dared to be in his presence again. He had banished Alanna from his life—from his family—from further contaminating any Andreakos at all.

Alanna felt hysteria beading in her stricken throat. Dear God, did he think she had waylaid him here on purpose? A man she had never thought to set eyes on again for the rest of her life? As she stared at him, totally frozen, she saw him glance at an inconspicuous man standing some little ways away by the exit to the escalator lobby.

His bodyguard. Leon Andreakos always had a bodyguard in tow. He was a wealthy man. Very wealthy. Such men were a target. A target for thieves, kidnappers—and greedy, gold-digging women.

That's what Leon had thought her, Alanna knew. One more in the long line of beautiful women who used their beauty to get their greedy little fingers inside his wallet. Get him to shower his money on them.

Self-condemnation shadowed her eyes. Leon had been right about her in that—she'd been overwhelmed by his wealth, incredulous that he should lavish so much of it down upon her, to whom luxury had been totally unknown. After a lifetime of perpetual scrimping and saving, with barely enough for essentials, let alone anything else, she had gone wild as his mistress, she knew, lapping up the luxurious lifestyle with Leon like a kitten standing four-paw in a bowl of cream.

She had revelled in the clothes he'd bought her, the gifts he'd given her, the places he'd taken her to. Revelled in the whole wonderful, magical bliss of being the woman in Leon Andreakos's life, envied by all other women—yet he had chosen her, just ordinary her, had plucked her out of the hotel gift shop and selected her for his bed. And she had gone willingly, eagerly, helplessly, the thought of turning down his wonderful, magical invitation never even a possibility. Because what woman could possibly turn down Leon Andreakos?

"Well?" Leon's harsh voice cut through her self-recrimination. Like some hideous mocking replay of the very first time he'd ever spoken to her in the hotel gift shop, Alanna was unable to reply, unable to force her voice to work. But she had to speak, say something, anything. Even though her limbs felt like water and her bones like soft wax.

"Nothing—" The word mumbled from her. She swallowed and said it again, clearer this time. "Nothing."

The memory of the last time he had spoken to her assailed her. The very last words he had said to her as he had barred her from his brother Nikos's funeral.

"Whore! Murdering whore!"

She stumbled past him, but a hand shot out, closing over her arm like a steel band, fingers digging into her flesh.

"Let me go!"

For one long, devastating, soul-consuming moment she stared into his night-dark eyes.

And in that one moment the present was ripped away, back, back into the past they had once had together.

Torment and bliss. Agony and ecstasy. All at the same time.

Oh Leon, Leon—how I loved you once! How I would have thrown myself at your feet! But you didn't want me—you didn't want me for anything except your bed. And you thought that all I wanted from you was your money...

His eyes seared into hers, and in that flash of fire she knew, with a hollowing of her insides, that it was not just his wealth that had overwhelmed her. It had been him—every inch of him, every pulse of his raw, potent sexuality that could melt her bones, pool her like honey in his arms with a single touch, a single kiss....

The memory of his very first kiss flared in her. He had come back to the gift shop the following evening...

He placed the scarf, loosely folded within the opened wrapping tissue, in front of her.

"Is it faulty?" she asked anxiously.

He gave a caustic smile—but not at her.

"The wrong color, so I was informed." There was a bite beneath the accent. He was annoyed; she could tell.

"Would you like to exchange it?" she offered. She tried to slow the sudden rapid beating of her heart that had happened the moment he'd walked back into the gift shop. Tried to stop her eyes from just gazing helplessly at him. She'd thought of him all night. Tossing and turning in the narrow bed in the poky flat in the dreary part of London that was all she could afford on her meagre wages. His face kept appearing in front of her closed eyes, and she could not banish it. Did not want to. Wanted to keep thinking about it, thinking about him—dreaming about him.

Now he was here in the gift shop again, in the flesh, and her pulse was racing.

Suddenly, quite abruptly, it slowed to a halt. He picked up the scarf and reached forward. With a casual gesture he draped it around her neck, his fingers lifting her hair free.

She thought she would faint. Her eyes widened helplessly, her breath catching in a little gasp in her throat as she gazed at him.

He smiled down at her. The annoyance was gone. In its place amusement...and speculation.

"On you," he said, the husk in his voice melting her bones, "the color is perfect."

Then, still holding the ends of the scarf, he drew her forward and lowered his head....

His kiss was bliss, his mouth moving with slow appropriation over her lips. There wasn't breath left in her body.

As he let her go he went on smiling down at her.

"Come and have dinner with me," he said.

And she went. Just like that. Without thought, without question. Closing up the shop and following him out into the hotel lobby as meekly as a lamb. The only thing she managed to say, half terrified that it would make him change his mind, was, "I'm not properly dressed!"

He paused and glanced at her neat gray pencil skirt, her crisp white high-necked blouse.

His eyes washed over her, draining even more breath from her.

"You look very...demure." The expression in his eyes changed minutely, and she felt heat flushing through her. "It has its own allure." He nodded imperiously. "Come."

And so it had begun. He had seduced her that very night, wining and dining her in the finest restaurant, where every bite had tasted like ambrosia, then taking her back to the hotel, back up to his suite, removing her crisp white blouse, button by button, slipping her narrow skirt down over her slim hips and slender thighs. And when she had been naked, completely naked, he had taken her to bed—and paradise. A paradise that had lasted for six exquisite months before the bitter, bitter end had come.

And now, nearly five long years later, a single glance from Leon Andreakos's night-dark eyes could relight the ashes of passion she had thought quenched for ever.

Then the flash of fire was gone, and he thrust her from him.

On legs like jelly Alanna stumbled away from him, desperate to escape. Shock was shooting through her, making her heart seize up, her every movement jerky and uncontrolled. How she got out of there she didn't know, but as she gained the escalator lobby, felt the soft carpet give way to the clack of stone beneath her winter boots, she felt as if a tank had just rolled over her. Crushing the life from her.

As she stepped onto the up escalator, clutching the hand rail for support, her whole body still trembling, heart racing, chest heaving, she quite failed to notice a suited, inconspicuous figure following her out of the dress department.

Under clear orders from Leon Andreakos.

CHAPTER FOUR

LEON ANDREAKOS glanced at the out-of-town address printed on the memo his security agency had forwarded to him, then let the paper drop again.

No, he would not follow it up. Would never again have anything to do with the woman who had destroyed his brother Nikos.

Just Nikos?

The question mocked at him, and he crushed it aside. No, he had not let Alanna Richards destroy him! He had felt nothing for her but desire—that was all.

She had been his mistress—that was all.

True, she had been different—engagingly different—from his usual female fare. It wasn't just that her natural, unforced beauty had caught his connoisseur's eye the first time he had seen her in that hotel gift shop, or that her wide-eyed gaze had reflected her immediate response to him. It was that usually his mistresses were seductive, sophisticated and very sexually experienced. Alanna had been none of these things.

Oh, there had been some fumbling boy, so he had learned from her faltering lips, who had taken her virginity in a tipsy teenage congress, but all she had learned from the experience was how not to have sex. At his skilled hands she had learned the art of pleasure from a master—and had proved an apt and ardent pupil. He had enjoyed teaching her—had enjoyed taking her on that journey to the paradise of the senses, had found, indeed, that she had extended that paradise for him in ways he had never previously experienced.

He had not expected that. He had seduced her simply because her predecessor had foolishly chosen to try to manipulate him, something he never tolerated in a woman, and because Alanna had been such a refreshing contrast.

Memory flickered at him—how she had gazed in wonder at him, her dark hair a cloud around her lovely face, blue eyes huge, pupils dilated, body trembling whenever he touched her...

Roughly he pushed the memo away from him, and stood up. It hadn't just been *him* she'd gazed in wonder at, but at the things he'd bought her, too! His mouth tightened. He'd been amused at first—amused by her stunned reaction to his showering down his wealth on her. Buying her beautiful clothes, taking her to beautiful places, bestowing a luxury lifestyle on her. She had revelled in it, adored it!

A hard light glinted in his dark eyes.

She had become greedy. Wanted more. And hadn't been fussy how she'd got it. First she'd tried to trap him, and then, when he'd made it clear he wasn't about to hand her a lifetime's golden meal ticket, she'd made Nikos her target.

Screwed up, malleable, vulnerable Nikos—and she'd got her greedy little claws into him and hadn't let go. Not until he had married her. And then she had destroyed him.

Betrayed him within weeks of their wedding—and it had killed Nikos. Killed his brother...

He thrust the memo into his desk drawer and strode out of his office. Seeing Alanna again had been nothing more than chance—ill chance.

So what if he'd felt, like the blade of a knife, desire stab through him at the sight of her, standing there, as lovely as she ever had been, her hair a cloud around her face, her eyes as wide and as brilliant for him as they had ever been? Making every other woman he'd been with since seem cloying, boring—pointless.

He would not remember it. Would not remember her. He'd worked her out of his system, and she was gone now. History. She'd taken Nikos's money and had cleared out nearly five long years ago—and good riddance to her! He would never think about her again.

Alanna emptied out the washing-up bowl and rinsed round the sink. Then she turned her attention to drying the dishes. Nicky was asleep in bed, tired out from an afternoon spent with his pal Ben at the municipal swimming pool. She gave a fond smile. Money might be punishingly tight, but her son was having a good childhood, for all that. She was making sure of it.

Her smile wavered. Her son would grow up without a father, and although that was increasingly common these days—look at her friend Maggie, promptly abandoned by her waste-of-space boyfriend the moment she'd told him she was pregnant—it was a source of perpetual guilt for her. But what kind of father would Nikos have made, even if he'd lived?

She sighed heavily. What was the point of thinking about that? Nikos was dead. And though she would feel responsible for his death to the end of her days, she must not think about the past. It was gone, over. Nikos was dead. And Leon—Leon might as well be.

Certainly she was dead to him.

Seeing him again like that before Christmas had been traumatic, but she'd gotten over it. She'd gotten over him the first time around. She'd had to—she'd had no choice. And this time—three months ago now, since that brief, awful encounter at the department store that had lasted just a couple of minutes, no more—she'd gotten over that, too. She'd had to. Nothing had changed. Leon Andreakos still hated her.

She felt her heart squeeze the way it used to in those first nightmare months after she'd fled his bed, and went on drying up. She had Nicky. A new life with him. A blessing beyond all grace.

The buzz of the doorbell made her head lift sharply. Who on earth? Not Maggie at this time of night. Ben would be asleep as well. So who?

Cautiously, because although the small block of flats was in a quiet part of town, you could never be too careful these days, she walked down the narrow hallway to the front door. The buzz came again, impatient. Peremptory. She peered through the fish eye, but all she could make out was a man in a suit, face distorted. He seemed respectable, but for all that she opened the door slowly on the chain.

"Alanna?"

Blackness folded over her eyes.

The voice—deep, accented.

"Alanna, open up."

Not a request. An order. A hand, large, square, long-fingered, pressed insistently against his side of the door.

Like a zombie she opened the door to him. To Leon Andreakos.

She stared at him blankly.

"What are you doing here?"

Her voice was a thread.

His eyes, so dark—condemning—looked down at her. No expression.

But in their depths, something she had not seen for an eternity of lonely nights.

Desire.

He stepped inside. She couldn't stop him. Felt her knees buckling. He saw her reaction and a smile slashed across his face. Cynical. Mocking.

But it was not her he was mocking. It was himself.

He looked down at her, his eyes filled with a dark fire.

She stood there, completely incapable of movement. Silently, saying not a word, he slid his hand around her neck, stroking the nape softly with the tips of his fingers, his other hand drawing her against his long, lean body, his hand hard on her spine.

Sensation, like a hot flood, drenched through her.

"I still want you—" said Leon Andreakos as he lowered his mouth to hers.

For an instant, so brief it scarcely existed, she tried to resist. Then she gave a moan, low in her throat, and was lost.

Arousal surged through Leon. *Thee mou* but he wanted her! Wanted the feel of her lissom body pressed against him, wanted the warmth of her mouth opened to him, wanted to knead and stroke those soft, rounded breasts...

He'd tried not to want her. Tried for three months to not think about her—not to remember her. But seeing her again like that, out of the blue, had relit a flame he'd thought he'd doused five long years ago as he lowered his brother into his untimely grave.

And the flame was burning now, searing through him, firing his blood. Alanna Richards had destroyed his brother, but right now he didn't care. He would have her one more time.

Right now.

CHAPTER FIVE

ALANNA was drowning, drowning in bliss, in sensation, as Leon possessed her mouth with his. Conscious thought had gone, submerged totally in this flood of hot, hungry desire that was consuming her very soul. Oh, after so long, so long, she had Leon again in her arms, wrapping him against her, pressing against his hard, muscled body, yielding her mouth to his as he plundered its sweetness, fingers spearing into her hair. Her hips strained forward, feeling with shocked excitement his instant response to her stimulus.

There were no words, none. How could there be words? she thought as her body took her over, yielding to what it so desperately longed to do—recover what had been lost so long ago....

His hand was moving to her waist, sliding between their tight-pressed bodies, seeking the zipper on her jeans. He was moving her, moving her backward—

"Where?" It was all he said, hardly lifting his mouth from hers.

"In here." The words gasped from her, and she let him steer her into her darkened bedroom.

It was insanity, madness. She had to stop him—she had to! She had to stop herself...

But she could not. A power greater than she could resist possessed her.

Silently, without words, only with touch, he stripped the clothes from her, tumbled her down upon the bed.

"I have to have you."

The words grated from him. And in the dark, without words, only with touch—hot, hungry touch—he took her.

Fire scorched through them, urging them to wild, wanton consummation. His possession was total, absolute. Her passion total, absolute. The whiteout of desire blinding them both, convulsing their bodies in one final, extreme urgency of ultimate sensation.

She cried out, smothering her cry in his shoulder, nails digging into his back without volition, only with need, absolute need. He surged within her one last time, head lifting, eyes blinded, for one long, endless moment that held eternity in it.

Then he lay, still and heavy, on her panting, exhausted body.

Her heart pounded, and slowly, very slowly, she realized what she had done. But before she even put mental thought to the emotion that now sluiced through her like a cold draft, he had thrown himself back off her, lying staring up into the dark. She could feel his bare arm against her arm, he was still that close—but as distant as the stars.

He said something in Greek that she did not understand. Then, in English this time, he said, "I'll set you up in a flat in London. I'll have to be discreet about you this time around. Even my father must not know that I've taken you back—let alone my mother."

His voice was harsh.

Bile rose in her throat. Horror at what she had just let happen. Disbelief that it had happened. And beneath the horror and the disbelief her body still throbbed, uncaring of anything but itself, its own needs and demands.

Hating herself, her body, she rolled jerkily to her side, swinging her legs to the ground and pushing herself upright. A hand shot out, imprisoning the hand she was using to lever herself up.

"Let me go!" Her voice was low, hissing.

He gave a grating laugh.

"I cannot! There is no question of it. Understand that. You should never have let me see you again. I have fought this for three months—and I have lost. I will take you back, make you my mistress again!"

There was a choking sound in her throat.

"You're insane!"

He laughed again. She turned round to look at him. In the dim light the planes of his face were etched starkly. His eyes blazed with a black light.

"Yes," he acknowledged, "I am. Insane to want you like this—insane to take you back. After everything you did to me. And yet I do, God help me. I want you—greedy, treacherous, faithless—but I don't care! You destroyed my brother, and I don't care! He wasn't even cold in his grave when you ran, taking all his money with you. And I don't care!"

His other hand snaked around her waist, hauling her down against him. Every muscle in his body was tensed, she could tell, and so were hers. His eyes burned into hers. "You looked so demure that first time I saw you—I had to teach you everything. So how is it, *how,* that you do this to me?" His hand moved, splaying down over the smooth curve of her hip, starting to caress her.

This time she found the strength to pull away. For a moment, so brief, he resisted the attempt. Then, abruptly, he let her go. She got to her feet unsteadily, horribly conscious of her nakedness—his.

"I want you to go," she said in a shaky husk. "Just get out. Go!"

He stood up. Totally unconcerned by his nudity, his superb body glistening in the half light. She felt her insides turn over and jolted backward with a step. His eyes glanced dismissively around the small bedroom and into the narrow hallway beyond.

"You've sunk low," said Leon, his dismissive glance coming back. "You must have blown Nikos's money in a big way to be reduced to this dump. Well, I'll bank roll you again, but—"

"Get out!" Her voice was a shriek. She groped for her clothes, finding her baggy sweatshirt and pulling it over her head. It came down to mid-thigh, concealing the essentials.

As for Leon, he simply started to dress again as calmly as if nothing had happened.

"You always were greedy for Andreakos money," he said, his tone almost conversational, as Alanna stood there, heart pounding, limbs trembling and emotion bucketing through her like a hurricane.

How could he be doing this to her? *How?* She was over him, over. But he'd walked in and without a word taken her to bed...

She started to shiver, but not with cold. Disbelief was washing through her just as his words—so cruel, so hateful—were washing over her.

"You'll have an allowance but nothing more," he was saying as he shrugged on the shirt she had all but torn off him. "I'll be generous—but don't even think of getting more out of me this time around! Tell me—" he jerked his head up and looked at her across the bed, as he calmly did up his cuffs "—just how long did it take you to spend Nikos's money? One year? Two? Or has it only just run out? Was that why you'd gone clothes shopping that day when I saw you? To tart yourself up again so you could catch another sucker at a Christmas party? Looks like you didn't get lucky…"

The sneer was open, and suddenly, quite suddenly, Alanna's shaking stopped. In its place anger, raw and vehement, burned through her. She whirled around, flicked on the bedside lamp, then yanked open a wardrobe door and tugged out a large cardboard box from the base. Thrusting her hand inside, she pulled free an envelope with a letter still inside.

She hurled it at Leon.

"Read it!" she snarled. "Go on, read it!"

With a faint frown he picked up the envelope, pulling out the letter and opening it up.

She watched his face change. His eyes snapped to hers. The letter dropped from nerveless fingers to the bed, the printed heading from the famous London's children's hospital quite visible.

"You gave it away. You gave Nikos's money away."

His voice was blank.

She stood, chest heaving still.

Then, into the absolute silence between them, another sound was heard from beyond the bedroom.

"Mum-my!"

Shock etched Leon's face.

CHAPTER SIX

As NICKY'S plaintive cry came again, Alanna galvanized into action. She hurried from the room, intent only on reaching Nicky. Her yelling must have woken him. Panic started to engulf her. She had to get Leon out of the flat. Had to get rid of him totally.

She'd been an idiot to throw that letter at him from the hospital thanking her for so magnificent a donation—but something had snapped inside her as he'd rained down such vile insults on her head. But Nicky calling out was an even worse disaster.

Nicky was sitting up in bed, half distressed at being woken, still half sleepy. She sat down on the bed and cuddled him up to her, sheltering him from view.

"It's all right, darling, just lie down and go to sleep again. It was just something noisy on the telly, that's all."

But Nicky was craning his neck to try to stare over her shoulder.

She heard something in Greek behind her and froze. Then heavy tread across the shabby carpet.

"You have a *child?*"

She didn't let go of Nicky and kept her back to Leon.

"Yes." Her teeth were gritted, stomach hollowing with fear. "I met…someone else. My—my son is three. Just turned three."

Her voice was strained. Would Leon believe her?

Nicky was squirming in her arms, defying her attempt to lay him back down again.

"Who's that man?" he demanded.

"Just someone visiting Mummy. Lie down, poppet." Desperately she urged him back down on the pillow, but he struggled upright.

"I'm not a poppet," he said distinctly, "I'm Nicky. And I'm not three, Mummy. I'm *four!*"

There was a rasp, a sharp intake of breath behind her, and then the room flooded with light. She blinked, blinded by the brightness. Footsteps, rapid, urgent, a hand on her shoulder, pulling her away from her son so that his face was visible.

His face—with his dark, Andreakos eyes, his black hair, his Mediterranean skin tone. Only the shape of his face was hers.

"Thee mou—"

Leon's voice shook. His brother's eyes looked up at him out of his nephew's face.

* * *

Alanna stirred the coffee in her mug round and round with the teaspoon. She wanted to drink it, was desperate for the caffeine—desperate for anything that might act upon her savaged nerves—but it was too hot. On the far side of the kitchen table, palms square on the surface, leaning menacingly toward her, Leon loomed like an unholy presence.

Alanna hunched into her chair.

"Give me one good reason why you hid him! One!"

His voice cut at her, and the teaspoon jerked in her grip.

One good reason? She could give him a dozen!

"I'd have thought it was obvious," she said tightly. She lifted her eyes, like dead weights, to Leon's.

He was glaring down at her. There was anger in his face—but more, much more. She could not tell what it was. She had never seen such emotions in him before. She was used to only three emotions: amusement, enjoying her naïveté as he had at the beginning of their relationship when she'd been so impressed by him and the world he lived in; alternating with desire, when his eyes had taken on an expression she learned to know well, sending tremors through her, liquefying her.

And then, at the end, anger. Nothing but anger.

Anger that had slain her.

It was slaying her again…but this time she had an answer. The only one she could give.

"Do you think," she said leadenly, "that it would have been good news? Knowing that I left Greece pregnant? *Do you?*"

Something flashed in his eyes. Then it was gone.

"It would have been consolation to my parents—"

She gave a harsh, ugly laugh.

"Fine consolation! With me as their grandson's mother?"

"They'll accept you. For their grandson's sake."

Her mouth fell open as the import of what he had just said hit her.

"What do you mean—they *will* accept me?"

His lips pressed together.

"We shall be flying to Greece without delay."

Alanna stared.

"Are you mad?" Her voice was hollow.

"Are *you* mad," he echoed harshly, "to imagine I will leave my nephew here, to be raised in this dump?"

"There's nothing wrong with this flat! It's clean and in a quiet part of town! It's all I could afford once I'd—"

Her voice broke off.

Another emotion worked in Leon's face. He stood up.

"Why did you do it, Alanna?" There was something strange about his voice.

She shut her eyes, then opened them again. She looked at Leon but did not see him. Saw only the tormented face of his brother— her husband. Who had married her to save her—and himself.

And doomed them both.

"How could I keep it?" she answered brokenly, staring down into her coffee, unable to keep looking at Leon.

A sound like a rasp came from his throat.

"How? Very easily I imagine! It's what you married him for—his money!"

Her fingers tightened on the teaspoon. She lifted her head.

"For financial security—and I kept enough to ensure that!"

His mouth tightened, and he glanced involuntarily around the little kitchen at the old fashioned appliances, which she was not able to afford to replace, and the worn vinyl flooring.

She met his eyes. "I'd been poor before, Leon," she said quietly. "It wasn't so hard to go back to being poor. And Nicky is having a good childhood—I don't have to work; I can be with him all the time. This is a decent suburb; he's having a normal life. I know it's not normal by your standards, but for most of the population this is perfectly adequate. When he goes to school I'll start working, and that will bring in more money as Nicky grows older."

"And when he asks for his father?"

The question was harsh—her answer strained.

"Many children now have no fathers. There's no stigma."

His brows drew together. He looked formidable suddenly, and she felt a tremor go through her.

"Stigma? Why should there be a stigma in being the son of my brother—and his wife?"

Her fingers clenched. "I—I meant…" Her voice trailed off.

Leon's eyes rested on her like weights.

"The point is irrelevant. All that is relevant is that the child needs a father—and he will have one."

Her gaze stretched, uncomprehendingly.

"He will have me," said Leon. "As his stepfather I will adopt him, and he will grow up as my son. And you—" a sardonic note entered his voice "—you will attain the very goal you once longed for. You will be my wife after all!"

As he spoke, every last shred of color drained from her face.

The dream she had once had so long ago had just turned into a nightmare.

CHAPTER SEVEN

"You don't mean that—you can't." Alanna's voice was faint.

Shock was starting to take over—shock upon shock. She couldn't cope, not with what had happened in the space of less than an hour…

An hour ago her life had been normal. Now Leon Andreakos had stormed back into her life, demanding her body. And her child. She had given him the former…but could she do the latter?

Leon rested dark, implacable eyes on her as she sat at the kitchen table, her coffee cooling in front of her.

"But I do. I will raise my brother's son as my own." His expression changed. "Why this show of reluctance? I am granting you what you dreamed of—I'm making you my wife."

"That dream ended a long time ago when I realized what a fool I'd been."

His mouth tightened. "A fool to think you could trap me into marriage. So that you could spend even more of my money." His hand slashed through the air. "But enough! As my wife, as my nephew's mother, you will be treated accordingly. And at least—" his eyes filled with an expression she knew well, one that made the breath catch in her throat, her limbs quicken "—I know that in bed we shall be as good as we always were…"

She got to her feet, sharply pushing her chair back.

"No, I'm not marrying you. Never!"

He leaned back in his chair—he seemed unconcerned.

"Then you will face a custody battle that will make you wish you had never been born."

She swayed.

"No court will take him from his mother!" Her voice came out high pitched with fear.

His face hardened. "Do you think your past makes for edifying reading? You were my pampered mistress for six months! You lapped up everything I gave you—greedy for more. You were prepared to conceive a child purely to force me to marry you. And when I called your bluff, you eloped with my twenty-two-year-old brother to try the same trick on him. You knew full well he'd already had years of psychiatric treatment, but all you cared about was persuading him to marry you and get you pregnant. And within a month—a month—of marrying him he found you with another man! A man so depraved he drew a knife on Nikos and used it."

"He died, too," she whispered, her voice a thread. "They died together, falling down the stairs as they struggled…"

Sickness was washing over her, wave after wave, as the nightmare vision returned and she witnessed again in her head that hideous, terrifying struggle at the top of the long flight of stone stairs in Nikos's house in Athens. Heard her voice, screaming, screaming…

"I should never have married him…" Guilt crushed her. "That's why I gave his money away… Nikos died because of me. I had no right to his money."

She turned away.

Hands came over her shoulders, heavy, yet not hard.

"Did bearing his child make you realize what you had done? Did it finally put some shred of morality into you? Some fragment of remorse?"

There was that same strange note in Leon's voice as when she had shown him the letter from the children's hospital.

He turned her around, lifting her chin to look at him. His face was sombre.

"You cannot deprive Nikos's son of his birthright because of your guilt. He has a right to the life he would have had, had Nikos lived. And Nicky—Nicky has a right to a father, Alanna. I will be a father to him. Your guilt has made you run, hide. But it has to stop now. You must see that."

His words had drained the color from her face, the breath from her body. His dark eyes bored into hers as if he would see into the heart of her.

She felt immobile, as if too much had happened too soon. Too many emotions, too much feeling—emotions that Leon couldn't, mustn't discover—draining from her all present capacity for feeling more right now.

He spoke, measuring each word.

"I do not offer you forgiveness; I cannot be that generous, but you should know that I understand why you sought sex with another man."

She stilled, tensing all through her body.

"You do?" She dared not ask, but breathed the question at him.

He nodded. The self-mocking look was back in his eye, as if he almost hated himself.

"I taught you passion in my arms—you did not find it in my

brother's. He was, I know…inept…with women. After what
we shared you would not have found him…satisfying."

A shadow passed in her eye, and she looked away.

"Do you deny it?" he demanded. He turned her face back
toward him. "Then you lie—to me, to yourself." Long fingers
stroked her cheek, and she felt her heart give a crazy lurch. "Five
years since I last possessed you," he said in a low voice, "and
the flame burns as strongly as ever it did. And now—" his mouth
lowered, grazing over her lips, and she felt her spine dissolve
"—it can keep burning. Marriage," he breathed, as his mouth
moved on hers again, "is the perfect answer. Nicky gets a father,
you get the wealth you always craved and I—" he opened her
mouth, deepening his kiss, folding her against his body "—I get
you."

"In you go!"

Nicky squealed with glee as Leon settled him in beside him
in the miniature train. His uncle pulled down the safety bar and
put his arm around his shoulder.

"We're off!" he exclaimed as the ride began.

Alanna stood behind the railing, watching the little train
moving slowly at first, then gathering speed as it raced up the
incline through the "mountain" to twist and turn and loop
back round and round.

Spring sunshine bathed the theme park in fresh light, the newly
budded leaves on the trees and bushes telling of winter's end and
the summer to come. Warm days. An end to chill and loneliness.

She felt strange, unreal. Welling with an emotion that threatened to overspill, flood right through her life. Three days had
passed since Leon had arrived at her door—but it might have
been three months or three years.

He had stayed the night, taking her back to bed, caressing
away every last shred of resistance until she was melting honey
in his arms. And he had slept with her afterward, holding her
tight against him as if he feared she might run away in the
night, taking Nicky with her…

But she had not run. Had watched, heart full, as Nicky had come into the bedroom in the morning, demanding to know why "that man" was still there. And Leon had sat up and had made Alanna sit up, too, with his arm around her shoulder and had invited Nicky—and the teddy bear he was clutching—to sit on the bed beside them because he had something to tell him.

And she had watched, wide-eyed, emotions keyed up so tight that she could hardly breathe, as Leon had told him he was his father's brother, and he would like to marry his mother and take them both to Greece to meet his grandparents and stay in a house with a swimming pool...

Nicky had listened, dark eyes huge.

"A swimming pool?" he had breathed, unable to believe such good fortune.

Leon had nodded.

"Are we going today?" Nicky had asked, eager to be off on such an amazing adventure.

"Today we are going to London. I am going to buy a ring for your mother, so we can be married soon, and get a passport for you, so you can come to Greece." He had turned to Alanna. "I take it he needs a passport? Alanna?"

His voice had changed. She had been sitting there against the pillows, staring at them, emotion working in her eyes.

He had touched her cheek. "It will be all right," he had murmured.

The softness in his voice had nearly undone her.

Then Nicky had recalled his attention. "Are you going to eat breakfast with us?" he had asked. "I eat toast for breakfast. Made with brown bread," he'd added virtuously.

Leon had grinned at him.

"You will grow up strong and healthy!"

Nicky had grinned back, well pleased with such a notion.

Now Alanna watched the pair of them twist and turn on the ride, Nicky shouting with laughter and Leon, too.

Something clutched at her heart.

I have to do this, she thought. I did not ask for it. It came to me, unasked. I will suffer—but it does not matter. Only Nicky matters.

The bond between Nicky and Leon had been instant. Instinctive. There had been no shyness, no reticence. Nicky had simply enfolded Leon into his life—and let Leon enfold him into his.

As she watched them bonding so instantly, her heart had crushed and had known a rightness, a relief that told her there could be no other way. Nicky needed Leon—*deserved* him.

And she knew, with a kind of overwhelming inevitability, that there was one more secret she would have to tell him.

Whatever it cost her.

She prayed for strength. Strength to endure the love she still felt for Leon Andreakos, would feel till the end of her days— a man who did not love her. Who never had. Who never could.

But who *must* love Nicky…

CHAPTER EIGHT

ALANNA stared at the pearls in their velvet case as she sat in the wide leather seat of the executive jet winging toward Athens.

"Let me put them on you." There was a husk in Leon's voice.

"No—no, there's no need. They're exquisite, I can see." Her voice was strained.

"What's wrong, Alanna? You used to love my giving you jewelry."

The husk had gone. There was only sharpness now. And questioning.

She lifted her head to look at him.

"Perhaps I've outgrown my greed at last," she answered.

He stilled. "And perhaps," he answered back slowly, "you were never as greedy as I thought you. Perhaps I never realized how deprived a life you'd led. Never realized—" his expression changed "—how unreal my wealth was to you."

"I was like a kid in a candy store," she said, and her eyes slipped away from him, looking out over the cloudscape, remembering, "being handed the most fabulous sweets in the shop by Prince Charming himself. I didn't—I didn't mean to be greedy...but I was. I took everything you gave me and revelled in it."

She swallowed, a hard knot in her throat, and looked back at him, straight in the eye. "But I won't be greedy any more. So please...please don't give me jewels. I'm only your wife for Nicky's sake; I know that. I...won't—won't...presume, Leon. I learned that lesson a long time ago."

She felt her emotions swell and stood up.

"I—I just want to check on Nicky. Make sure he's all right."

She hurried off to the sleeping cabin at the rear of the plane where an exhausted Nicky slept after the excitement of his mother's wedding to his wonderful new Uncle Leon. Alanna's throat tightened.

I've got to tell Leon, she thought. I've got to tell him about Nicky. The truth...

As soon as the ordeal of meeting Leon's parents is over...

Leon stared after her. He felt his heart scrape. He had married for Nicky's sake, but not just for him, he knew.

Alanna—so soft in his arms, glowing with passion. Hungry for him. Starving...

It was like it had been at the beginning, but it was more. She felt remorse, he knew—had given away Nikos's money, raising Nicky on a pittance.

She'd had the guts, the courage to do that...

And even now, as his bride, she only wanted him to spend his money on Nicky.

His heart squeezed. Nicky—the child of his heart, even if not of his loins. He was drawn to him by a love that had been instant, all consuming.

And Alanna came with him, the little boy he loved already....

Alanna...

His heart squeezed again.

I will make this marriage work! Thee mou *but I will do so!*

As tense as a board, holding Nicky's hand, Alanna stood as Leon's parents hurried toward them across the huge, ornate drawing room of the Andreakos mansion in Athens.

What if they rejected Nicky for being her son? The woman they blamed for Nikos's death.

There was a volley of excited Greek, and then Leon's father scooped up Nicky, hugging him close.

In wonder, Alanna saw tears on his cheeks. And then his wife was there, kissing Nicky, calling herself his Ya-ya who loved him already and forever.

Champagne was uncorked, fizzing lemonade for Nicky, more Greek, more exclamations, and then, suddenly, switching to English, Leon's mother turned to her.

"Oh, my dear, how you have suffered for our sakes! But now we beg your forgiveness for the wrong we did you when Nikos died."

The room went completely and utterly silent.

Then, into the silence, Leon's father spoke.

"Nicky, come and see the swimming pool."

Happily, Nicky put his hand into his grandfather's and was led away. Leon's mother paused. Her eyes were huge.

She touched Alanna's wrist. Her voice full of emotion.

"We never knew the truth about my poor Nikos...till recently. The son of a friend let it slip. And when we knew the truth, we understood. Understood why he died. That it was not your fault! But Leon, Leon does not know. You must tell him, my child, so that he may have the happiness that he, too, deserves—as you deserve yours."

She kissed Alanna and followed her husband and her grandson from the room.

As the door clicked behind her, Leon spoke.

"Tell me what? What do I not know about Nikos?"

She moved away from him. Shock was still buckling through her.

"Tell me!" The urgency in Leon's voice demanded an answer.

She swallowed. His parents wanted her to tell him. Tell him the secret she had promised Nikos she would keep for ever—as she had.

Until now.

She took a deep, shuddering breath.

"Nikos was gay," she said. "And terrified of it, of discovery. That's why he had so much psychiatric treatment. He married me to hide it. On—on the night that he died, the man who came to the house was not my lover. He was Nikos's. He came in a jealous rage, demented that Nikos had married. After—after they had both died in each other's arms, I could not add to your parents' grief, to yours, by telling what I had promised Nikos never to tell…"

"So you let us think the man was your lover and took the blame for Nikos's death." Leon's voice fell like a tolling bell.

"It was all that I could do. I felt so guilty…"

"Guilty! What cause was there for you to feel guilty?"

She shut her eyes, then opened them.

"Because I knew I should never have married him, despite his pleas. He begged me—that morning, when he came to your apartment, and discovered…"

She broke off.

"Discovered *what?"* Leon's eyes burned into hers.

"Discovered I was leaving you."

He stared.

"*Leaving* me? You left me to marry Nikos!"

Slowly she shook her head.

"No. I was leaving you anyway." She looked him in the eye and told him her heart's secret, hidden for so long. "I—I'd fallen in love with you, Leon. I dreamed, like an idiot, of being your wife one day. But you only wanted me to be your mistress. I…couldn't bear it. I'm sorry."

There was silence all around them. In a grating voice, Leon spoke.

"Why not tell me you loved me?"

Alanna gave a bitter, hollow laugh.

"You'd just told me not to think of getting pregnant to extract a wedding ring from you. I didn't think you'd be interested in hearing that I was in love with you."

"I thought you married Nikos for his money, but when you inherited it you gave it away. So that was not the reason, was it?"

Now. Tell him now! The final secret!

She took a breath. Then, his expression as tormented as if the devils of hell were taunting him, he spoke.

"If Nikos was gay, how did you conceive Nicky?" His eyes were bleak, but understanding began to dawn in them. "You were already pregnant—by me. And you dared not tell me because I'd warned you not to get pregnant! So you married my brother to be the father to Nicky you thought I would not be."

His face was broken, ravaged. Pain clutched at Alanna. She ran to him, catching his hands.

"I should have told you—trusted you to be a father to Nicky, even if you never married me, never loved me! And you had every reason to think me greedy, mercenary, wanting your money."

"You've proved to me you are not in love with money. Giving Nikos's wealth away and living in poverty," he ground out. "My distrust of you drove you away. I lost both you and my son."

His bitter self-accusation lacerated her.

She swallowed. "Seeing you with Nicky shows me how wrong I was to keep him from you. You love him dearly already! As for me—" she took a breath "—I will be as good a wife to you as I can, and not...bother you with my feelings."

He stared at her. "Are you telling me," he said in a slow, disbelieving voice, "that you are still in love with me...after all I did to you?"

She gave a painful smile. "Love isn't something you turn on or off. It's just...there. But I won't annoy you with it, I promise you."

Something changed in his eyes. For the first time since his mother had dropped her bombshell, Alanna saw them lighten.

More than lighten.

Gleam.

His hold on her hands loosened, and he brought each hand up to his lips and kissed them. The tension in his shoulders eased.

"You may...*annoy* me with your love any time you want, Alanna *mou*. For it is a gift to me I do not deserve and can only wonder at."

Something moved in his face, an expression that suddenly made Alanna's heart skip a beat. Then, drawing her hands against his heart, he lowered his mouth to hers.

The kiss was light and sweet and healing.

As he drew back, he spoke.

"When I thought it was my money you loved, not me, I was hurt, angry. It made me lash out when you married Nikos, and when he died I turned my feelings for you into hatred—but they were never that. Never that. And now..." He took a deep, shuddering breath. "Now you have given me a second chance and two most precious, precious gifts. My son and your heart. And I will treasure them both all my days for as long as I live, my sweet, beloved wife, my own one. My dearest love."

Tears welled in her eyes, and her heart swelled with wonder

and joy. He kissed away her tears, cradling her against him for long moments. Then, setting her back, he took her hand.

"Let us find our son—and our new life together."

She went with him, her hand, trustingly, in his, radiant with joy.

* * * * *

THE DUKE'S DILEMMA
Margaret Moore

Margaret Moore realised once that she actually began her writing career at the age of eight, when she and a friend would make up stories featuring a lovely, spirited damsel (played by a scantily attired fashion doll) and a handsome, misunderstood thief nicknamed "The Red Sheikh" (portrayed by a red-haired male fashion doll in a red cape).

She also loved to read, especially Trixie Belden books, the Golden Book Encyclopedia and the Narnia stories of CS Lewis.

Then Margaret discovered Errol Flynn. He was, she admits, her first "crush" and she was shattered to discover he was long dead. Her next "crush" was on that reticent, emotionally controlled Vulcan, Mr Spock. Obviously, "fantasy men" have been a part of her life for a very long time!

Later, she graduated with distinction from the University of Toronto with a bachelor of arts degree in English literature. Margaret had no intention of being a writer; it just seemed wonderful to be able to get a degree for reading. During that time, she also became a Leading Wren with the Royal Canadian Naval Reserve, where she learned to use a variety of weapons and had the weepy experience of being tear-gassed. She has also been an award-winning public speaker, a synchronised swimmer, an archer, and studied fencing and ballroom dancing, as well as being a wife and mum.

Margaret currently lives in Toronto, Ontario, Canada, with her husband of over twenty years, two children and three cats.

Margaret's new historical romance,
***My Lord's Desire*, is available now from**
Mills & Boon® Super Historical

THE DUKE'S DILEMMA

CHARLOTTE winced as an inebriated party-goer stepped on her foot, but she kept moving determinedly toward the doors that led to the balcony. The Duncans would be delighted with their party; it was clearly *the* event of the season, and their daughter had been successfully launched into society.

Unfortunately, the noise, the heat, and the crowd combined with Charlotte's pounding headache to make her want to escape for a breath of fresh air. Reaching the balcony doors, she opened them to find two people engaged in a passionate kiss.

"I'm sorry." The words escaped her mouth before she realized it would have been better to make an exit without being noticed. The couple jumped apart.

Charlotte felt the blood drain from her face as she stared at her fiancé. "John! I thought you were dead!"

Two azure blue eyes flashed in a face so handsome it could take a woman's breath away. "John *is* dead. I'm James."

Charlotte breathed again. Of course this wasn't John. John was dead, and by his own hand. This was his twin brother, who had gone off to fight with Wellington while John had stayed home. This was the brother who had stayed in Europe after her fiancé's death, who had written that terrible, accusing letter that had arrived when she was still full of sorrow and remorse.

This was the brother who knew so little of her relationship with John, yet who derided her, and blamed her for something she had not foreseen. She would have prevented John's death if she could have; she did not need to feel more guilt from someone who had not seen his brother in over five years.

And who was now the Duke of Broverhampton, heir to a vast estate and fortune, as well as the title.

As Charlotte fought to regain her composure, James's gaze meandered over her simple silk gown, lingering for the briefest of moments on the embroidery around the neckline—or her breasts—before returning to her blushing cheeks.

Angered by his impertinent scrutiny, she quickly closed the doors behind her, shutting out the music heralding the start of a quadrille. She wanted no one to hear them, or come out to see what was going on. And she wanted to know what the long-absent James was doing on the Duncans' balcony with her cousin, Dulcabella—besides the obvious.

Dulcie Duncan giggled and swayed, clearly the worse for the powerful punch full of rum, which was how their family had made their fortune, one large enough to overcome the stigma of having earned it in trade. The Duncan Distillery had even been granted a Royal Warrant to supply rum to the British Navy.

"I just came out for a breath of air and he grabbed me and kissed me," Dulcie explained with a sodden grin. "I quite liked it."

"Indeed?" Charlotte inquired as she regarded James, not

troubling to hide her annoyance. "I daresay you did, for I have heard that the duke is quite accomplished in that, if nothing else." She took hold of her cousin's arm, intending to lead her inside. "Come along, Dulcie. I think you should bid good-night to your guests."

"Running away, are we?" James calmly inquired in his deep, husky voice—the thing that distinguished him most from John. Otherwise, both men had the same dark hair, chiseled cheekbones, and brilliant blue eyes.

Charlotte slowly wheeled around to face him. "I think if there is a person here who could be accused of running away, it would not be me, Your Grace."

She watched as her words brought, for the briefest of moments, a look of what might have been remorse to those bright blue eyes. Yet if the Duke of Broverhampton felt anything deep in his cold heart in response to her accusation—one she had been waiting years to make—it was quickly gone, replaced by the cool tranquillity he had always possessed, even in his youth. John had been all fire and light and music; James had been dark and silent and cold as snow in January.

Her cousin feebly yanked her arm out of Charlotte's grasp, the action making her totter like a pile of teacups. "I want to schtay right here!" Dulcie protested as she grabbed on to James's black waistcoat.

"I think you should retire, cousin," Charlotte said with a tone of firm command.

Dulcie pouted and stamped her slippered foot. "I don't want to."

"Dulcie, I really think you ought—"

"Well I don't!" *Stamp!*

Out of the corner of her eye, Charlotte saw James's lips jerk up into a smug grin, as if he was enjoying this show of defiance from the usually docile Dulcie.

"Dulcabella, you should go before the ladies begin to gossip about the time you have been out here and with whom. Unless you want your season ruined before it is well under way, I suggest you go back into the ballroom, and preferably to bed. You have had too much punch."

Charlotte's words finally seemed to penetrate Dulcie's drink-befuddled brain. She swallowed hard, then lurched back into the ballroom.

Charlotte was about to follow her when James barred her way. He reached back and closed the balcony doors. "Let me pass," she ordered.

He shook his head and stepped closer. "I have waited a long time to have a moment's word with you."

She inched away from him, until her back was against the wall and the ivy covering it. The foliage wasn't the only reason the flesh there tickled, as James came closer until his body was mere inches from hers.

Summoning her courage, Charlotte squared her shoulders. She would not let James's predatory attitude frighten her. "If the wait was troublesome, perhaps you should have returned to England sooner. There was nothing to prevent you, especially when you inherited your title and the family fortune."

"A fortune you did not get your greedy hands on, after all."

Charlotte gasped. "I was not marrying your brother for his wealth!"

James's face betrayed his skepticism. "No?"

"Certainly not!"

He sidled closer, trapping her between the wall and his broad-shouldered body like a doe run to ground between a cliff and a pack of dogs. "Then why did you agree to marry him?" he asked in a husky whisper.

"Because...because I loved him!" She put her palms on James's chest and shoved, but it was like trying to budge a boulder.

He caught her hands in his powerful grasp. "Love?" he scoffed. "What do you know of love but this?" he demanded as he hauled her close and captured her mouth with his.

CHAPTER TWO

SHE HAD thought James cold? She had thought him lacking in passion? As James's lips moved over Charlotte's with firm and fiery purpose, she realized how wrong she had been.

How very, *very* wrong…

Which did not give him leave to kiss her, or her to enjoy it.

Before she could shove him away, the balcony doors burst open. "Charlotte!" Uncle Malcolm cried as he stepped outside. "What are you doing?"

While she stared, equally horrified, at her uncle and the well-dressed people crowding behind him, James moved away. He faced her uncle and quite calmly adjusted the cuffs of his waistcoat. "We were kissing."

Uncle Malcolm's jowls quivered with an indignation that matched Charlotte's, now that the initial shock of discovery had passed. "Then, sir, you have not behaved like a gentleman!"

"Indeed, he has not," Charlotte seconded, preparing to march past James, her uncle, and through the avidly curious onlookers. She could hear the scandalized whispers that would follow in her wake. Her reputation was already sullied by her fiancé's death, for surely the love of a good woman should have saved him from such despair. Therefore, the reasoning went, there must be some flaw in her. And now, to be found kissing her late fiancé's brother—!

James's hand held her back and he looked into her eyes, his gaze searching. "I have never claimed to be a gentleman."

"How could you, since you are not? Now let me go!"

He did not loosen his grasp as he once again faced her uncle, whose cheeks were getting progressively more flushed. "Gentleman or not, I am quite prepared to do the honorable thing, Mr. Duncan, and marry your niece."

Charlotte stared at James. She couldn't marry him! She

hated him! And she had done nothing wrong here to cause her to be imprisoned in a marriage. "I would rather die!"

"Like John?"

His words pierced her heart like the thrust of a rapier. "How…how dare you!" she whispered as tears of anger and dismay leaped into her eyes.

"I dare because you as good as held the gun that killed him when you broke his heart."

"*I?*" she gasped, incredulous. "I broke *his* heart?"

"Your Grace, Charlotte," Uncle Malcolm said, obviously attempting to control his temper, "this is hardly the time or place for such accusations. I suggest you retire, Charlotte. As for you, Your Grace, you will please leave my house. You may call upon me at my offices tomorrow morning, where we shall discuss what is to be done. Now, Your Grace, I give you good night."

James, the Duke of Broverhampton, smiled and inclined his head, then strode through the crowd which parted for him as they might a pauper who had intruded into their midst.

Sitting in his barouche outside the offices of the Duncan Distillery, makers of Fine Rum and purveyors to the Royal Navy by the appointment of His Majesty, King George III, James wondered—and not for the first time—what the devil he was doing here. He should order his driver to take him home. Or to his club. Or even the closest tavern. Anything but beard old Malcolm Duncan in his den and explain that he did *not* wish to marry Charlotte. The offer had been made in the heat of the moment.

And what heat. What unexpected, overwhelming heat. Charlotte clearly possessed the ability to drive a man to passionate ecstasy, if that was how she kissed when she supposedly did not want to be kissed.

Or maybe she had. Could it be that despite her apparent animosity, she was setting her sights on the man who now had the wealth she craved? He mustn't forget that she was a greedy, grasping creature who had broken his brother's heart and destroyed his spirit when John had realized she was only marrying him for his title and money. That knowledge, and his shame at being duped, had driven John to take his life.

If he married her as he had impulsively suggested because of some last, lingering vestige of chivalry called forth by the vulgar fascination on the faces of the guests last night, he might be playing right into her soft, yet avaricious, hands.

Therefore, he must go to Mr. Duncan and rescind his offer. Such a thing would not enhance his reputation, but he could not concern himself with that.

What he should concern himself with was making sure Charlotte knew *he* knew the kind of woman she was, despite his momentary lapse into forgetfulness, and that he intended to make sure the rest of the world knew it, too. That was why he had followed her out onto the balcony, or thought he had.

He had mistaken Dulcie for Charlotte. The cousins looked enough alike that, attired in similar gowns and with their blond hair done in similarly Grecian styles, it was easy to mistake one for the other, especially across a crowded ballroom.

So he had followed "Charlotte" and could not resist the urge to announce his presence with a kiss, only to realize the moment his mouth touched Dulcie's that either he was kissing the wrong woman—for it was no secret that Charlotte didn't drink because her father had died after falling from his horse while inebriated—or else he had his lips on a rum bottle.

Whatever had happened last night, he finally decided, he could not and would not marry Charlotte.

He alighted from the barouche and strode into the distillery, heading directly for Duncan's office. He marched past the startled bevy of clerks perched on stools as they toiled at their high desks and entered the office without so much as a rap on the door.

To find that Charlotte was already there. Or maybe it was Dulcie facing her father with her whole body rigid, her hands on her hips, and her bonnet's white feather dancing.

The young woman whirled around to face him, and he discovered it was indeed Charlotte. "What do you want?" she demanded, glaring at him.

As always when faced with a nerve-racking situation—which was always the situation when he was near the vivacious Charlotte—he summoned up a mask of calm indifference, and answered truthfully. "I've come to tell your esteemed uncle that I have changed my mind and cannot marry you."

Her green eyes flickered and a sardonic smile curved her full lips. "Good, because I am here to tell him the same thing."

How her emerald green eyes sparkled like jewels when she was angry! How lovely she looked in that charming ensemble, including the ridiculous plume bobbing about like a writer's quill penning a screed of its own volition. "Excellent. Then we are agreed."

"Yes!"

"So I see no need to remain here any longer."

"Nor do I," Charlotte declared, pushing her way past him and slamming the office door with a bang like a cannon shot that probably sent the clerks scrambling for cover.

Taking a deep breath, James bowed at the openmouthed Mr. Duncan. "Good day to you, sir, and I regret any inconvenience."

Before he could turn away, Duncan heaved himself to his feet with surprising speed. "Not so fast, Your Grace. I would speak with you."

James suppressed a sigh as he waited for the man to proceed. No doubt Duncan intended to berate him, and soundly, too.

"You will either marry my niece, or I shall take you to court for breach of promise."

CHAPTER THREE

JAMES stared, slack-jawed, at Charlotte's uncle. "Breach of promise?" he repeated in an incredulous whisper.

Malcolm Duncan smiled with malicious pleasure. "Exactly. Several people heard you offer to marry her last night."

"She didn't accept!"

Duncan waved his plump hand dismissively as he returned to his seat. "Women are fickle creatures, apt to change their minds."

"But you can't be serious! She hates me."

"Does she?"

James's eyes widened even more, and even though his mind told him it must not, the small, hidden place in his heart where his hope had been buried cracked open. Charlotte had been living with her uncle since her father's demise years ago; it could be he knew her well enough...

It didn't matter. "Of course," he replied, burying the long-denied hope back where it belonged. "You heard her say she'd rather die than marry me."

"Well, be that as it may," Duncan said, leaning back in his chair and steepling his fingers, "the fact is, you've compromised my niece's honor. Your family has already done her harm, and it's about time one of you made it right."

"My family did *her* harm?"

"Aye," Duncan said, grave and firm as the bricks of his distillery. "She loved your brother and she was heartbroken when he died. And she's blamed herself for far too long for what your brother did. Her reputation has suffered for it, too."

"She did *not* love my brother, and she *is* to blame for what John did," James protested, every line of John's last letter bemoaning his anguish and shame burned into his brain. If Charlotte mourned anything, it was the loss of his brother's money.

Duncan eyed him shrewdly, as if James were a merchant trying to sell him something of dubious quality. "Whatever you think of the past, it is last night I am most concerned with today. You compromised Charlotte's honor, and you will do the honorable thing, one way or another, or you'll be hearing from my solicitor."

"I can afford the best solicitor in London to fight the suit."

"Aye, I have no doubt, but fighting me will cost you a pretty penny, especially as these things can drag on for so long. In the meantime, no woman of character will trust you, should you wish to marry and create an heir. Of course, if you plan to remain a bachelor all your days, that may not trouble you."

James did not plan to remain a bachelor. He wanted children, and not simply to provide an heir. He liked children. Many nights as he lay awake listening to his comrades in arms snoring and snorting and tossing and turning, he had envisioned leading the life of a country gentleman, surrounded by a loving family, married to…his brother's fiancée. He flushed and pushed away that shameful memory. "Do you intend to threaten Charlotte into agreeing, too? Will you sue her, as well?"

"Charlotte will do what is best for her."

James scowled. "Of that I have no doubt," he said as he strode to the door. When he went out, he slammed it even harder than Charlotte had.

"But, Papa, I don't understand," Dulcie pouted a fortnight later as she sat on the arm of her father's chair in his mahogany-paneled study, which smelled faintly of cheroots and pomade. "Why did you invite him to dinner again? Charlotte refuses to see him, and he sits here scowling like a bear whenever he comes. Why, they *loathe* each other!"

"Of course they do," her father replied with a chortle as he chucked his beloved, but not overly intelligent, daughter on her round little chin. "I don't intend that they should marry. I have other plans for the duke."

He eyed Dulcie so significantly, even she caught on. "*Me?*" she squeaked. "You want him to marry *me?*"

"Yes." He patted her arm. "The more annoyed he gets with Charlotte, the lovelier and more pleasant you will seem."

Dulcie pouted again. "I thought I *was* pretty and pleasant."

"Oh, you are, my dear, you are, and the duke can hardly fail to notice that fact every time he comes here."

Dulcie's pale forehead wrinkled with a frown. "Yet you said you'd sue him if he doesn't marry Charlotte."

"Only to ensure that he would stay in London and visit us. The moment he tells me he would rather marry you instead, all talk of breach of promise will be quite forgotten."

Dulcie toyed with her rings and didn't meet her father's gaze. "That seems a bit hard on Charlotte, Papa, using her to lure the duke here to fall in love with me."

"All's fair in love and war, my dear. Indeed, we are really doing her a favor." He warmed to his subject. "The gossip will go against her if the duke doesn't at least seem to be doing the honorable thing, but if he jilts her in your favor, she'll appear to be the one hard done by. All the ladies will sympathize with her, even those who were so quick to blame her in that other unfortunate business."

Dulcie continued to frown. "What if they blame me for stealing the duke away?"

"They won't," he assured her. "If there's any blame in this, it will attach to him." He gave his daughter an indulgent smile. "Besides, what does it matter what they say if you marry a duke in the end?"

CHAPTER FOUR

CHARLOTTE looked unseeing out the tall, narrow windows of the town house in Mayfair. She felt like a prisoner in her home—or at least, her uncle's home. She had never been completely comfortable living with her uncle and cousin, but after her father's death, she had no other alternative. Now, with the unwelcome presence of the Duke of Broverhampton haunting her like a ghost, she felt more imprisoned than ever.

She heard a small sound and turned away from the window, to find Dulcie standing near her dressing table.

"Yes?" she asked, noting that her usually placid cousin looked worried and uncertain. Perhaps the strain of this forced marriage nonsense was wearing on her, too.

"The duke is coming to dinner again."

"So I heard from the downstairs maid."

Dulcie chewed her lip and gazed at her beseechingly. "Charlotte, do you really not want to marry him?"

"No." *Not now. Not under these circumstances, although there had been a time....* "I do not understand why he doesn't just let Uncle Malcolm sue him for breach of promise. I am more than ready to give evidence that I would be pleased to release him from his promise, such as it was. He can afford a good solicitor and surely that has to be more appealing to him than continuing this sham."

Obviously relieved, Dulcie's words came out in a torrential rush. "Papa thinks if the duke keeps coming here and you don't see him, but he sees me, he might...that is, he might change his mind about marrying you and ask to marry me instead. He's threatened to sue the duke not to ensure you marry him, but to keep him coming here."

Charlotte stared at her, confused—and yet, knowing Uncle Malcolm and his crafty mind, this could very well be true. "If this is so, why are you telling me, Dulcie?"

Her cousin straightened her slender shoulders and her doelike brown eyes shone with more resolve than Charlotte had ever suspected she possessed. "Because I like you, Charlotte. You've been like a sister to me, and I don't agree with Papa's plan."

Charlotte's heart swelled. She had no idea Dulcie cared for her so much and she hurried to embrace her. "I appreciate your affection, and your honesty, Dulcie," she murmured, while also cursing herself for ever thinking ill of her cousin.

"If you can win the duke's heart, you are welcome to it." She silenced the nagging little voice in her heart that told her she was lying. "And you are kind to tell me that I am but bait." She drew back and regarded Dulcie gravely. "Shall I end this charade, then?"

Just as grave, Dulcie nodded. "Yes, please. If I cannot attract his notice by better means, I do not deserve it."

Listening at the top of the stairs, Charlotte hurried toward the drawing room the moment she heard the butler usher James toward it. Dulcie would be at least another hour dressing, her uncle several minutes. This was her best chance to have a private word with the duke.

Despite her determination, she hesitated on the threshold when she saw him. He had one arm draped across the ornately carved marble mantel and was staring at the flames in the hearth, a look of such despondency on his face, she could scarcely believe this was the arrogant James Ellery.

All this time, she thought he must be enraged over the situation, or disgusted, or frustrated. She had never imagined he would ever feel despair, about anything. She had always believed him different from John in that, as well.

He must have heard her, for he looked up, and was immediately once more the coolly indifferent nobleman. "So, you have finally decided to venture down from your tower, Rapunzel."

She perched on the scarlet velvet seat of a gilded chair. "You must ignore my uncle's threat of a lawsuit and stop coming here."

"Perhaps it amuses me to allow people to think I have a vestige of honor, after all, by agreeing to marry you," he said as he sat on the brocade sofa opposite her.

"He doesn't really want to sue you."

That caused the duke to raise an inquisitive brow. "Then he is a finer actor than I gave him credit for, for he certainly conducts himself as if he does."

"He wants you to fall in love with Dulcie, and he thinks the threat of legal action, which compels you to appear to be engaged to me, and which therefore requires you to call here, is an excellent way to throw the two of you together."

For a moment, James looked incredulous, then his lip curled in a sneer. "He does, does he?"

"Now that you know that, you can drop this pretense of an engagement between us. I'm sure once he understands you cannot be bullied, he will reconsider suing you."

"My reason for continuing to call here has little to do with any man's ability to bully me, and more to do with my enjoyment of your discomfort that this engagement causes you— some small recompense for the pain you caused my brother."

Annoyed that he persisted in blaming her for his brother's death, she jumped to her feet, her hands balling into fists at her sides. "How many times must I tell you I did nothing to cause him pain? I was as shocked as anyone when he killed himself, and I have spent hours and hours thinking over all that I said and did in the days before, wondering if there was something I could have done to prevent it, but I saw no signs that he was so despondent. I thought he was happy we were to be married."

"Then you, madam, are either the most coldhearted, calculating woman...or the most accomplished liar...I have ever met." James rose and reached into his jacket pocket, pulling out an old, creased piece of paper. "Read John's own words, and find yourself condemned as a scheming fortune hunter who never loved him. Hear from John himself how that discovery humiliated and destroyed him until he could not bear to live."

He thrust the paper at her. "You may keep this. I will never forget what he says in this letter if I live a hundred years. And to think that once I—"

He fell silent, then turned on his heel and marched from the room.

CHAPTER FIVE

A FEW minutes later, Charlotte dashed into the street. She could see the carriage with the ducal crest rounding the corner and took off after it like a Bow Street Runner pursuing a thief, John's plaintive letter clutched in her hand.

Mercifully, the carriage had to wait to let another, even finer, vehicle pass before turning into the next street. Regardless of the startled coachman, or anyone else who could observe her, Charlotte ran up to the carriage and pounded on the door. "James, you must let me explain!"

The window of the carriage came down with a crash, and James's angry face appeared. "If you have read the letter, there is nothing to explain."

"Yes, there is," she insisted, "and I shall scream if you don't let me in!"

For a moment it looked as if James was going to refuse, but then he said, "Stand out of the way." He opened the door and kicked out the folding steps for her to climb inside.

"You'll catch your death running about London without a wrap," he noted as she scrambled onto the seat opposite him in a decidedly unladylike fashion.

"I don't care."

After closing the door, James knocked on the roof of the carriage. "Drive on, Charles," he ordered, and the carriage lurched into motion. "Well, Charlotte, this will certainly set the tongues to wagging, even more than our embrace. Is that your intention?"

"I had no idea John had found my diary. He should not have read it."

James frowned. "Oh, so my brother's curiosity excuses your behavior?"

"He read my private thoughts, which he had no right to do. Even so, I would have explained if he had asked me."

"What possible explanation could there be but the obvious. John was very clear about what he found in your diary—your obvious passion for another man, your desire to be with him, your dismay that you could not. Surely you cannot fault him for believing you did not love him, the man you had pledged to marry? What else was he, or any wealthy, titled man of reason to think but that you were marrying him for those things, and not himself?"

"That's not it." Now that the time had come to tell the whole truth, Charlotte hardly knew where to begin. Or if she should even try. And yet she could not forget what he had implied only moments ago, something that had made her heart race even as she read John's letter. If she did not tell James everything now, she might regret it for the rest of her lonely life.

"The diary John found was not a recent one. I haven't kept one for three years, well before I became engaged to your brother. I did love another man then, passionately. But nothing came of it. I thought he didn't care for me, for he never paid me much attention. When he went away, I thought that was the end of it. I *believed* it was the end of it, and still believing it, conceived an affection for John. I did care for him, truly, and it breaks my heart anew to realize that he died because he didn't believe that."

"Maybe your passion for this unknown lover was not as dead as you claimed," James replied. "The diary alone would not have been enough to cause John such despair. There must have been something else."

"You have been away a long time, James. John was not the lad you left when he took his life. He was jealous of any man who glanced at me, and nothing I said seemed to alleviate his fears. He would rage at me, and for no reason. Any little thing would set him off. Even if he had never found the diary, he might have despaired of my love enough to end his life anyway."

"Then you no longer love this man you wrote about?"

"I thought I did not," she said, her gaze searching his face. "I thought he did not love me."

Willing himself to feel nothing—not envy as he had felt for John when he had announced his engagement, or remorse for keeping his feelings buried for so long—James turned to stare out the window. "I'll order Charles to return you to your uncle's house. Our engagement is officially over, and I'll leave you alone. You are free, Charlotte."

"Oh, James," she cried, moving to sit beside him and taking his face between her chilly palms as the letter fluttered to the floor. "It was *you* I wrote about in the diary. After you went away, I thought I could forget you and what I felt for you, that I could love John, that we could be happy. I was devastated when he died. You must believe me, James." Her hands dropped limply to her lap. "But now I see that you are right, too. I *did* deceive him." She raised her stricken eyes to look at him. "Yet I didn't know it, because I was deceiving myself, too. I didn't realize that I agreed to marry John because he was so much like you."

Finally, she had confessed—but it was not at all what he had expected. Nor was she the only one guilty of keeping secrets that had led to such disastrous consequences.

Full of remorse for all that he had done and not done, James grabbed her hands and clasped them between his. "I do believe you, Charlotte, and I'm so sorry for how I've misjudged and mistreated you. I've loved you for years, but I was too shy to say so. You always seemed so bold, so confident, I thought you would laugh at me. And then when I realized how John felt about you, I was sure I didn't stand a chance, so I went away. If I had stayed home and made my feelings known, how different things might have been! John would still be alive and we could have been married."

"While we cannot bring John back, we are engaged now," she reminded him.

By God, she was right. They were engaged. They could be married. There would be scandal and gossip and rumors, but he didn't care. All he cared about was Charlotte as he pulled her close and kissed her. All the passion and desire and yearning he had been trying to hide and destroy for years burst free. She returned his kiss with the same heated passion, the same fierce desire, the same anxious yearning.

"Poor uncle!" she murmured a few moments later, arching her neck as James's lips slid slowly lower. "He will be so disappointed."

"Right now, I don't give a damn about the man."

"And if it hadn't been for dear Dulcie…"

James drew back, a slight frown darkening his face. "I must say, Miss Duncan, I am not pleased that you can ignore my kisses."

"I'm not ignoring them," she said, putting her finger between his cravat and his shirt as she gave him a devilish smile. "I'm enjoying them very much. I'm just feeling rather sorry for Dulcie."

He watched her proceed to pull off his cravat. "If it will make you feel better, there's a fine young gentleman I know I can invite to the wedding and make sure your cousin meets. I think they would make a lovely couple."

"That does make me feel better," Charlotte whispered as she gathered a fistful of his shirt and pulled him to her. "Now let me see if you can ignore *my* kisses."

He didn't even try. Indeed, they would have made love then and there if the coach had not tottered to a halt.

"If you come into my house now and with your gown in such a state, it will cause a great scandal, Charlotte," he panted, his words grave, but his eyes dancing with joy as they moved apart.

Charlotte laughed merrily, and not a little breathlessly. "You are in a state of *dishabille* yourself, Your Grace," she said as she threw open the carriage door and caution to the wind. "And I don't care if all the world knows we are in love."

* * * * *

THE CHRISTMAS CRUSH

Pamela Toth

When she was growing up in Seattle, USA bestselling author **Pamela Toth** planned to be an artist, not a writer. She majored in graphic design at the University of Washington. It was only after her mother, a librarian, had given her a stack of romances that Pam began to dream about a writing career.

Her plans were postponed while she raised two daughters and worked full time. After being laid off from her job, fate stepped in. A close friend was acquainted with mystery writer Meg Chittenden, who wrote for the Superromance line at the time. Meg steered Pam to a fledgling local chapter of Romance Writers of America, but it still took three years and several false starts before her first book sale. For the next twenty years, she belonged to a close-knit group of published writers while penning romances for several series.

A year after her divorce, a chance remark by an acquaintance led her to a coffee date with her boyfriend from high school. After spending three decades apart, they are now happily married in a condo near Seattle with a view of Mt Rainier and a new Birman kitten named Coco.

When Pam isn't travelling with her husband, who recently retired, she loves spending time with her two grown daughters, serving on the board of her condo association, antiquing, gardening, cross-stitching and reading. The stack of books beside her chair includes thrillers, mysteries, women's fiction and biographies as well as romances by her favourite authors. Her future plans include a cruise to Alaska and learning to quilt – and writing more romances, of course.

THE CHRISTMAS CRUSH

"WILL SANTA CLAUS bring me everything I ask for?" Six-year-old Molly poked her arm into the sleeve of the red coat Lana MacDonald had found at the consignment store. Molly's cheeks were flushed and her blue eyes, so like her father's, sparkled with excitement.

Lana felt a familiar surge of love for her daughter. "If he did, what would you ask for next year?" she teased as they left their apartment. Lana was in a hurry to get to the storefront in downtown Crescent Cove that had been turned into Santa's workshop. She hoped the line of eager children didn't stretch all the way down Harbor Avenue.

"It doesn't really matter what Santa brings me," Molly said after Lana had secured her in the back seat and slid behind the wheel. "Daddy will buy what Santa forgets."

Lana tensed as she turned the key in the ignition, but the engine sputtered to life. The car needed a tune-up as well as a couple of new tires, but all would just have to wait. Molly was spending Christmas with her father, so she and Lana were celebrating early. Most of Molly's presents were wrapped and hidden away in the back of Lana's closet.

She tried to not resent Mike for spoiling their daughter, just as she struggled against turning the holiday into a gift-giving competition. Not that she could win. Mike's job in Silicone Valley paid a lot better than hers at the senior care center. Even with monthly child support checks, Lana had to budget carefully—hence the choice between gifts and tires. But Molly would only be a child for a short time and as far as Lana was concerned, her happiest memories were *not* going to be of lavish holidays spent with her father and his new family.

"You're lucky to have a daddy who loves you so much," Lana said diplomatically. "That's more important than the presents he buys."

"I know," Molly agreed. "If you get another husband, you'll still love me, won't you?" she asked as Lana found a parking space right downtown.

It wasn't hard to figure out what had provoked Molly's question. Mike and his young wife Charlene had a two-year-old boy and another baby on the way. No wonder Molly felt displaced! He might be a dynamic sales manager, but when it came to his daughter, the man was clueless.

Lana helped Molly from the car and gave her a quick, fierce hug. "No matter what happens, I will always love you with every cell in my being, and so will your father." It was Lana whom he had stopped loving only four years after he had vowed to do so forever.

Molly squirmed impatiently. "That's what you always say. If you had more babies, I could take care of them just like my dolls."

Lana clasped Molly's hand tightly as they walked quickly down the street. The downtown shops were open late during the Winter Festival, their windows filled with colored lights and holiday goods. Red and white twinkle lights were strung between the old-fashioned brass street lamps.

The historical district with its quaint shops stretched along the waterfront. The sidewalks were crowded with tourists as well as locals, and a group of Victorian carolers sang on the corner. A ferry leaving the terminal sounded its mournful horn as it began its journey back across Puget Sound. The evening air was cool and smelled of salt, but the rain had stopped and stars twinkled overhead.

"I like it being just you and me," Lana told Molly after exchanging friendly nods with a teller from the bank. The other woman's arm was linked through her husband's, giving Lana a brief pang. This was the season for families, but hers was broken. "I'm in no hurry to remarry," she muttered to herself as much as Molly, who skipped along at her side.

Between work and raising her daughter, Lana had no time for a social life. Her feelings for Mike had died after he left her for Charlene four years ago, but the idea of dating again filled Lana with dread. Online profiles, blind dates, awkward dinners, painful small talk and rejection. Who needed any of that?

"Patty Finnigan's mom has a boyfriend," Molly said, holding tight to Lana's hand as they sidestepped a trio of teenagers. "Patty said they're getting twin babies after Christmas."

From what Lana had heard, Heather Finnigan's live-in lover spent more time with his motorcycle than he did with her. Once Heather had confided to Lana that she couldn't stand being alone. Lana had felt sad for her.

"Oh, Mommy, look!" Molly exclaimed, stopping at the entrance to Santa's workshop. "It's beautiful."

The doorway and windows had been decorated with blinking lights, pine bows and artificial snow. An oversized elf in a green tunic and pointy hat held open the door. "Welcome to the North Pole!" he cried boisterously over the holiday music from inside, then handed Lana a form to sign for a photo with Santa. "No obligation to buy," he added.

The Merchants' Association had outdone itself this year. Sitting on a golden throne on a raised dais in the center of the room was Santa, surrounded by two more elves and a photographer. A woman at a side table collected orders and money. The best part for Lana was that the line of parents waiting with their children wasn't long.

Molly hung back, suddenly shy. "I don't think I want to talk to Santa right now."

"It's okay," Lana reassured her, glancing around. "Isn't that one of your friends with her dad?"

"It's Sarah," Molly replied, brightening instantly. "Hi, Sarah!"

Sarah waved and her father smiled when he recognized Lana. One of Santa's helpers escorted Sarah up the red-carpeted steps to Santa.

Molly tugged on Lana's arm. "Mommy, why is Santa staring at you?" she whispered loudly. "Did you come here when you were a little girl like me?"

Todd Elsoe's jaw itched beneath the scratchy beard, the heavy red suit was too warm and his big toe throbbed like a bad tooth. Earlier this evening a little boy in a Seahawks sweater had jumped off Todd's lap and landed on his foot, just because he wouldn't promise the kid a new Xbox. Todd didn't believe in making promises that parents might not keep.

When he glanced up to see how many more children were waiting in line, a glimpse of long, red-gold hair as bright as a flame grabbed his attention. Since high school he'd always been partial to that color. As he stared, the woman turned, and he could see her face.

Lana.

"Santa?" A little girl wearing glasses tugged on Todd's sleeve. Reluctantly he shifted his attention to the job at hand. At the last minute his uncle who played Santa each year had recruited Todd to fill in when he came down with the flu. Todd wanted to carry on the family tradition and help the kids keep their fantasies for as long as they could before they realized what a cold place this world could be.

"Ho, ho, ho!" he exclaimed after he had recovered from the shock of seeing Lana again. His assistant gave him the little girl's name. "And what do you want for Christmas, Sarah?" he asked.

CHAPTER TWO

WHEN MOLLY'S turn came, she marched confidently up the carpeted steps while Lana watched with a burst of pride. Coming to see Santa was a tradition she and her daughter shared.

This year Santa looked younger than usual in his white wig and fake beard. When he'd stared briefly at Lana, she had felt a jolt of awareness that Mrs. Claus, stuck back at the North Pole, might not have appreciated. Lana gave Molly a reassuring smile as Santa repeated his ho-ho-ho's in a booming voice.

"Big smile now," said the photographer, snapping their picture.

Lana wished she could tell who Santa really was, but all she could see was gray eyes and dark lashes behind his wire spectacles. If his hair was dark, too, she hoped it wasn't black like Mike's. Not that it mattered, not to her.

"Tell me what you'd like me to leave under your tree," Santa said to Molly while Lana's hand tightened convulsively around her purse strap. She hoped the expensive doll in her closet still topped her daughter's list.

The carol that was playing came abruptly to an end. It was then that Molly, in a clear, high voice, announced, "What I want more than anything is a new boyfriend for my mommy. Then she won't be lonely anymore."

Awkward laughter rippled through the room and people looked curiously at Lana as she cringed. For a moment, Santa appeared speechless. "I might not have room for him in my sleigh," he said, recovering quickly. "Why don't you tell me what you'd like me to bring you instead."

Lana had no idea what Molly replied with. Head high, she was too busy trying to ignore the whispering behind her in line without bursting into tears. When Molly was done, Lana grabbed her hand and hurried past the other parents and the woman taking money; their expressions seemed full of pity.

"Mommy, Mommy, what's wrong?" Molly exclaimed when they reached the sidewalk. "Are you mad at me?"

Guilt halted Lana's flight and she crouched in front of Molly, who looked ready to cry. What kind of mother would spoil her daughter's joy because of a little embarrassment? Molly hadn't done it deliberately.

"Oh, sweetie, I'm not mad." Lana stroked her long, dark hair. "It was so warm in there that I needed some air, that's all."

"Do you feel better now?" Molly asked anxiously.

"Much." This wasn't the place to discuss Molly's comment. "Let's go home," Lana suggested. "We'll have cocoa with marshmallows to warm us up."

A few moments later, as Lana drove uphill through the sudden rain shower, the steering wheel pulled hard to the right and the tire began to thump.

"Mommy, why are you stopping?" Molly exclaimed as Lana eased the car to the shoulder of the dark road and turned on her four-ways. "Is something wrong?"

"I think we've got a flat tire," Lana replied. "Stay here while I check." There were no street lights along this stretch, so she grabbed a flashlight from the glove box and peered around cautiously before unlocking the door.

The scattered houses sat far back from the road, their lights hidden behind tall hedges. There was no other traffic.

Lana checked the front tire, confirmed her suspicion, then got back inside. "I was right." She dug her cell phone from her purse. "It's flat." Roadside assistance wouldn't be cheap, but it beat fighting the tire alone in the rain.

"Who are you calling?" Molly asked, sounding worried.

"No one, unfortunately." Lana glared at her phone with disgust. There weren't many cell towers in the area, making service both intermittent and unreliable. Tonight they were out of luck.

Now what? The apartment was too far away to walk and she dared not leave Molly alone in the car, so the only choices were to make their way down one of the long driveways or to wait for another car. Neither possibility thrilled Lana, even in a small town like Crescent Cove. She wasn't paranoid, but the idea of putting Molly at risk was petrifying.

"Will somebody come and help us?" Molly asked in a tiny, worried voice.

"Yes, of course." Lana tried to sound reassuring. "We'll just have to sit here for a little while."

She hadn't seen another car since they turned off the main road. In this part of town at this time of the evening, people were home watching TV, not driving around in the dark and the rain. She planned to wait a half hour and then start knocking on doors.

Before she could suggest a guessing game, Molly's voice broke the silence. "Mommy, I think I have to go potty."

Todd couldn't wait to get home so he could take off his uncle's itchy red suit and flop in front of his new plasma TV. In the three months since Todd had moved back from Seattle, he'd sold his old house, bought a condo and gone into business with a childhood friend. So far the signs indicated that he had made the right choice in leaving the urban architectural firm where he had been considered a rising star.

All the signs, at least, until he'd looked up tonight and seen the object of his unwavering adolescent obsession, Lana Larson. Head cheerleader, homecoming queen and, without a doubt, the prettiest girl who had ever strolled the hallowed halls of Crescent Cove High. And the most unattainable dream that a gangly, awkward, dorky nerd like Todd could have had back then. Driving through the dark in his SUV, he could remember how totally besotted he'd been.

Had she known about his crush? He could only hope she hadn't. Even though she'd been one of the nicest girls in school, the thought of her pity was enough, even a decade later, to make him squirm in his heated leather seat. Despite adding a couple more inches to his string bean height, bulking up considerably and having laser eye surgery, inside he was still a nerd. Some things never changed.

He turned onto the curving shortcut to the bluff while he reviewed the evening. When his uncle had asked him to step in, Todd had figured playing Santa might be fun. He liked kids, even looked forward to having his own. Seeing Lana had been a bonus, and then even more surprising, her little girl asked him to bring her mom a boyfriend. Last Todd had heard, Lana married her high school steady, Mike MacDonald. Iron Mike had been part of a group of thick-necked jocks who'd made Todd's life—if not miserable—then a lot less fun than it might have been without their bullying.

As Todd drove around a bend, his memories of Lana in her cheer uniform were interrupted by the sight of a car on the shoulder, flashers blinking. He could see someone inside, so he put his plans for a cold beer and mindless TV on hold and pulled over behind the other car.

CHAPTER THREE

"SOMEONE'S stopping to help us!" Molly clapped her hands as another pair of headlights shone through the back window. "We're saved."

Lana hoped her daughter was right and some harmless older couple had stopped to give aid. She and Molly had only been sitting here for a few minutes, but at least Molly's need for a bathroom hadn't yet reached the critical zone.

In her mirror Lana saw a big red shape emerge from the other car. With her door locked, she lowered her window cautiously.

"Good evening. Car trouble?"

Lana recognized his voice instantly. She had been right about the dark hair, but without his disguise Santa was far more attractive than she had imagined.

"I've got a flat tire," she explained. "It was raining so hard that I didn't want to get out of the car." She hadn't even noticed that the shower had ended.

"I'll take a look," he offered. "You stay put."

"Thank you for stopping." She had no intention of getting out of the car. "I'll be happy to pay you." Not *that* happy, since payday wasn't until next week, but she wasn't exposing herself or her child to danger, even if it was dressed up like Old Saint Nick.

Todd was disappointed that she didn't recognize him, even without his glasses. It was hard for him to believe that he was near enough to the former Lana Larson to touch her.

"You're still as pretty as ever," he blurted. As her eyes widened, he felt like a total geek. *Way to go, Todd.* "I mean, you haven't changed."

Her eyes narrowed, suspicious. "Do I know you?"

"Of course you do, Mommy," exclaimed the precocious little girl from the back seat. "He's Santa Claus." She peered through the window. "Where's your beard?" she demanded. "You're supposed to have a beard."

He glanced helplessly at Lana. "I, um..." His mind had turned to mush. Help, he mouthed silently.

Who are you? she mouthed back.

He glanced distractedly between her and her daughter. Now

what? Before he could reply, another car came around the bend. When it pulled up beside them, he saw that it was a patrol car.

"Everything okay here?" the deputy asked through his open window. "Ma'am?" He smirked as he looked Todd up and down. "Santa?"

Todd considered letting Officer Friendly change her flat, but just then the deputy's radio crackled to life.

"Miz MacDonald, do you want me to call roadside assistance before I leave for this other scene?" he asked.

She glanced up at Todd, obviously seeking assurance. Did she think Santa was going to mug her in front of her kid?

Part of Todd knew he wasn't being fair. What had he expected, that she jump out of the car and throw her arms around him? And say what? *You're the nerdy boy who used to stare at me!*

"Save your money, Lana," he said gruffly. "My name's Todd Elsoe. We went to school together. If your spare's good, I'll have it changed in ten minutes."

"Since you two know each other, I'm outta here." The deputy's words barely registered with Lana. She was too busy staring up at her would-be rescuer.

"You're Todd?" she blurted as the cruiser drove off. "I never would have known it was you." Immediately she realized her total lack of tact. She barely remembered him, except that he'd been quiet and brainy. She hoped he'd never heard the comments some of her friends made about him or the other "nerds."

"I guess I've put on some weight." He held out the loose-fitting red jacket. "Even without the padding."

"Mommy, I really have to go potty. I don't think I can wait."

"I'm sorry, sweetie," Lana replied, feeling a jab of guilt for getting her priorities scrambled just because a hunky guy had shown up. "Just a few more minutes, okay?" She hit the trunk release button and unfastened her seat belt. "I'll help you," she told Todd.

He held open her door politely. "Do you live very far?" he

asked. "I could run you home and then we can come back to fix the tire."

It was nice of him to offer, but Lana didn't know him anymore, hadn't ever known him very well and hadn't spared him a single thought since graduation. Didn't people always say the serial killer next door seemed like *such* a nice, regular guy? Still, the deputy had seen them together, in case she disappeared.

"Mommy, can we?" Molly asked, making up Lana's mind. "Please?"

"We live right at the top of the hill in that red brick apartment building," Lana told Todd as she grabbed her keys and her purse, then freed Molly.

In moments they were settled into Todd's SUV. The leather seats and fancy dash indicated that he must be doing well. As soon as he parked, Lana hurried Molly out of the SUV.

"We'll be right back," Lana told him, keys in hand as Molly fidgeted beside her.

"I'll be here," he replied with a grin that threatened to curl Lana's toes. "Don't keep your daughter waiting."

"Why is he wearing a Santa suit if his name is Todd?" Molly asked when they came back out and Lana locked the front door. "He even sounds like Santa."

Lana was relieved to see Todd leaning against the silver SUV. She hadn't really believed he might leave without them, but one never knew for sure what other people would do. She was tempted to tell Molly to ask him why he was dressed the way he was, but that wouldn't be fair, especially after he'd been so helpful. She still couldn't get over how much he'd changed. Even in the baggy clothes, she could tell he was broader through the shoulders and chest. His face was different, too, and not just because he wasn't wearing glasses. It was leaner, with angles replacing the unformed curves of youth.

"Santa needs spare suits in case his gets torn or something," she improvised as she and Molly approached him. "Since he wears it for hours and hours on Christmas Eve, each one has to be broken in, just like your new shoes."

As he opened their doors, Todd shot Lana an appreciative glance. "So he has guys like me to wear them for him," he added.

"So you know Santa!" Molly exclaimed when he got behind the wheel.

He glanced in the mirror at her as he headed back down the hill. "I certainly do," he said. "When I saw him tonight, he told me about you."

Molly looked entranced. "Did he tell you what I asked for?"

CHAPTER FOUR

"DID SANTA tell you what I asked him to bring me?" Molly repeated to Todd.

"Oh, no," he said quickly, lips twitching. "That's confidential, but he did say it was memorable."

Todd probably saw Lana as pathetic! Everyone in town knew her husband had left her for a younger, prettier woman. Todd had seen Lana's car and the building where she lived. It certainly wasn't a slum, but it was old and their unit was small; it was the best she could do.

"Will you tell Santa hi for me when you take back his suit?" Molly asked him as he made a U-turn in order to pull back in behind Lana's car.

"I sure will," he replied. "Why don't you stay right there while your mom and I change that tire?"

"Then you can tell Santa that I did what I was told," Molly replied.

He winked at Lana. "It's a deal."

When Lana unlocked her trunk and reached for the jack, Todd touched her arm. "Why don't you let me do that," he suggested quietly. "I'd hate to see you get dirt on your jacket."

She glanced down at her light blue parka. "What about your pretty red suit?" Todd's grin sent a shiver through her, but it wasn't because of the cold night air.

"It's my Uncle Hank's spare," he said quietly, lifting out the jack. "Go sit with Molly."

A few moments later, he returned the tools and her tire to the trunk, so Lana helped Molly from his SUV.

"Why did the tire get flat?" Molly asked him

Todd wiped his hands on a rag. "A tire's like a balloon," he said after shutting the trunk. "A big nail made a hole for the air to escape."

"I can't thank you enough," Lana told him.

"It was really good to see you again and to meet Molly."

"You, too." Lana stared up at him for an awkward moment, torn between the wish that he would say something more and the need to put the unexpected meeting behind her. As attractive as Todd had turned out, he wasn't for her.

She quickly settled Molly in the backseat, thanking him again when he held open the driver's door. They exchanged holiday wishes and he walked back to his SUV. Lana wasn't surprised when he followed her up the hill. It meant nothing, since he'd been going that way in the first place.

When she reached her building, he drove on by. She glanced back in time to see him wave. Maybe she would run into him again, but probably not. Even in a small community like Crescent Cove, a struggling single mom and a successful bachelor wouldn't normally run in the same circles.

"I guess you'll have something to tell the other kids at school tomorrow," she told Molly after they'd entered their apartment. Their little adventure was over.

It was only later as Lana drifted off to sleep that Todd's image reappeared. This time he wasn't wearing a Santa suit.

He wasn't wearing anything at all except a smile and a pair of tight red briefs.

"Ho, ho, ho," he said, brandishing a sprig of mistletoe. "Come to Santa, sweetheart."

The next morning Todd stuck his head into his partner's office to say hello. "What have you heard lately about Lana Larson?" he asked Gary Perkins after they had discussed an early conference call with an out-of-state client.

All the way home last night, Todd had chewed himself out for letting Lana get away without asking for her number. So what if she shot him down? It wouldn't have been the first time he'd felt the sting of rejection. In high school he'd been the poster boy for failure with girls. Even though he'd had a couple of mildly serious relationships since then, he had yet to experience anything as intense as his adolescent feelings for Lana.

Standing by the window overlooking the distant bay, Gary considered Todd's question. Like Todd, Gary had grown up in Crescent Cove and gotten a degree at the University of Washington in nearby Seattle. Unlike Todd, he'd married a coed and brought her back with him right after graduation.

"Why are you asking about Lana?" he asked. "Don't tell me you're planning on looking her up again?"

Todd wished he'd kept his mouth shut. Back in school, Gary had known all about his obsession with his dream girl. Reluctantly he filled Gary in on the events of the night before, omitting Molly's request that he bring her mom a boyfriend. Gary might be amused, but Todd had seen Lana's expression. To her it hadn't been funny.

"Some guys have all the luck," Gary grumbled. "The last time I stopped to help someone, it was a ninety-year-old man who was deaf as a post and smelled of mothballs." He shrugged. "You knew Lana and Mike split up, didn't you?"

"That's what I figured. Any idea what happened?" Gossip wasn't Todd's usual style, but he couldn't suppress his curiosity.

Gary shook his head. "Why does a bright woman like Lana never see through a jerk like MacDonald? It was that old story of the wife being the last to know he was seeing a coworker. I think he married her."

Todd felt a surge of anger on Lana's behalf. Mike deserved a broken nose, for Molly as well as her mother. Divorce was tough on kids; Todd knew that firsthand. "How long ago did it happen?"

Gary shrugged. "A few years ago, I guess."

"Does Mike still live around here?" Todd realized his hands had bunched into fists. Deliberately he relaxed them. Just because he wasn't the wimp he used to be didn't mean he needed an assault charge in his resume. Besides, it wasn't his business.

"I don't think so." Gary frowned. "Can't say I've heard anything since the split. Lana must keep a low profile."

A phone rang in the outer office and their assistant, Gail, answered the call.

"You're single, she's single. You going to call her?" Gary challenged with a grin.

Todd shrugged. The idea stirred up feelings of insecurity he hadn't felt for years. Gail appeared in the doorway. "Gary, your nine o'clock is here."

"Keep me posted," Gary told Todd before they filed out of his office. As Gary greeted his visitor, Todd took the opportunity to slip back to his own office. He had a full day's work and he had to get back downtown by five for his volunteer gig. With luck, he'd be too busy to moon over Lana.

CHAPTER FIVE

"WHAT DID YOU do in school today?" Lana asked Molly as they walked hand-in-hand across the courtyard from Mrs.

Pickering's apartment. Lana was lucky to have found the older woman to watch Molly after school while Lana was at work.

"I can't tell you," Molly replied. "It's a surprise."

The kids were probably working on something for their parents. "Shall we order a pizza for dinner?" Lana asked, sure of Molly's reply. Right now pizza was her favorite food.

"Yea!" Molly cheered. "I want ham and black olives."

As they were about to go up the stairs, Lana noticed a silver SUV pull into one of the guest parking spots. She'd never paid any attention to that make and color until the other night, but now they seemed to be all over the place.

"Come on, Mommy," Molly urged, tugging on her arm. "I'm hungry for pizza." Forgetting about the SUV, Lana started up the staircase.

"Maybe you'd allow me to take you both to Bella's," suggested a familiar voice from behind her.

She turned to see Todd grinning up at her. He looked fantastic in a leather jacket and snug jeans, making her painfully aware of her old slacks and lack of makeup. Automatically her hand went to her hair, fastened into an untidy knot. "What are you doing here?" she blurted.

"I knew you'd come back!" Molly exclaimed, darting past Lana.

Todd patted Molly's shoulder. "I couldn't call," he told Lana. "You're unlisted."

"I know that." Her hand gripped the metal railing tight enough to leave prints as she tried unsuccessfully to think of something clever to add.

Molly had no such problem. "Mommy, let's go to Bella's with Mister Todd," she begged. "If you don't have enough money, maybe he'll buy us a pizza."

Lana's cheeks went hot, but she couldn't blame Molly for repeating her standard excuse for not doing things.

"You can call me just plain Todd," he told Molly. "How about it, Mom? If I pay, will you lovely ladies join me?"

* * *

Todd had dreamed of escorting the most popular girl in school into the best pizza place in town, but he'd never believed it would actually happen. Now here he was, seated in a booth with Lana and her daughter. As usual, the place was busy and the aromas were to die for. Bella's granddaughter had just taken their order.

"Just plain Todd?" Molly asked. "Do you live at the North Pole with Santa and his elves and his reindeer?"

"Nope," he replied, "I live near you, in a condo."

"What's a condo?" she asked.

"It's like an apartment, except that you own it instead of renting like we do," Lana explained. She smiled at Todd, but her green eyes seemed guarded. "How did you know I didn't want to cook tonight?"

"I was afraid I'd have to knock on doors until I found you, but I drove up and there you were." His timing couldn't have been better. Was that a sign from the matchmaking gods or just a dumb break for a dumb guy?

"Molly stays with a neighbor after school until I get off work," Lana explained as the waitress brought their drinks. "I had just picked her up."

"Where do you work?" He wanted to know everything about her, but he didn't want to scare her with too many questions.

"I work at the senior center." Instead of elaborating, she turned the question back on him.

"I was a small fish in a large architectural firm in Seattle, but I wanted more control over the projects I take on," he explained. "Gary Perkins and I went into partnership a few months ago." Todd didn't want to bore her with the details, so he didn't go on.

"We're divorced," Molly announced cheerfully. "I'm going to fly on an airplane to California."

So she was going to be gone for Christmas. Todd wasn't sure how to respond to what must be a sensitive subject for Lana. "That sounds like fun," he said, thinking that it sounded like anything but fun for Lana.

A flash of something like pain crossed Lana's face. "Mike's coming up on business, so we're meeting him at the airport."

The arrival of their pizza was a good excuse to change the subject. After they filled their plates and their glasses, Todd lifted his in a toast. "To the two prettiest girls in the room."

"That's very sweet of you," Lana murmured, touching her glass to his and then Molly's.

"And to just-plain-Todd." Molly tipped her glass when she raised it, spilling some of her soda onto the table.

When he and Lana both reach out to mop it up, their hands bumped. The accidental contact sizzled up his arm. "No harm, no foul," he said with a grin.

"That was fun," Lana told Todd when they reached the apartment stairs. She had been surprised by his invitation, but he'd seemed to enjoy himself, despite the spilled soda. He had even headed off Molly's tears with a little story about Rudolf. From what Lana could remember, in class he had been quick and clever, even though he was shy. Now he seemed more relaxed, more confident. She wished that she could say the same, but Mike's betrayal had rocked her foundation.

Was the reason Todd had shown up tonight because he hadn't made a lot of friends since he'd come back to town? It didn't seem likely, but it was possible. I*s that why you gave him your number?* asked a tiny voice inside her head. *Because you thought a hunk like Todd Elsoe was lonely?*

"When are you taking Molly to the airport?" he asked. "Maybe I could drive you." His offer surprised Lana. The trip over to Sea-Tac involved a long ferry ride to Seattle and a longer drive through heavy traffic.

"Can we, Mommy?" Molly asked, clapping her hands. "He could meet Daddy."

"We're going Wednesday afternoon," Lana told Todd. "I appreciate the offer, but I don't think it's a good idea." No way did she want someone else involved in what was always a stressful situation for her. "Good night."

"But Mommy—" Molly protested.

Lana shook her head. "Come on, honey. Don't argue." Firmly she grabbed her daughter's hand and headed upstairs. She could feel Todd watching them, but she didn't look back. Molly, on the other hand, turned and waved.

"He's nice," she exclaimed well before she and Lana were out of earshot. "Don't you like him, Mommy?"

"Of course I do," Lana hissed, key in hand. She did like Todd. He was attractive and smart. Obviously he was kind, too, but she wasn't going to let her emotions run away with her common sense, not this time around.

CHAPTER SIX

TODD didn't know why he kept setting himself up for rejection, but he couldn't persuade himself to give up on Lana. Perhaps it was because she'd stood up for him once back in school when her boyfriend was bullying him, an incident Todd figured she wouldn't even remember. Not only was she gorgeous, but she intrigued him. Who was the real Lana MacDonald?

"I know it can't be easy letting Molly leave right before Christmas," he said when he called her on Tuesday afternoon. "I get why you don't want a near-stranger with you, but I thought you might want some company when you get back. We could meet for a drink or coffee, anything you want."

Now that Uncle Hank had recovered from the flu, he was ready to take over as Santa once again. Not only did he grow out his white beard ever year, but he'd even had a new Santa suit tailor-made. As much as Todd had enjoyed filling in, he was ready to reclaim his evenings.

For a moment Lana didn't reply, making his hopes plunge. What had he expected, that she would suddenly realize he'd evolved into a real catch?

"I don't know," she murmured. "I probably won't feel like socializing."

"Come on, you don't have to entertain me," he wheedled. "I'm just offering a friendly shoulder, nothing more." *Nothing more?* Who was he kidding?

There was another silence, during which he was tempted to bang his head on the nearby door jamb. At what point did a man cross the line between being pathetic and a stalker?

"That might be nice." Her words caused him to almost drop his phone. "Could I let you know on my way back? I'm not sure which ferry I'll catch, but I could call you."

"Heck yes, that's totally fine. I'll be waiting." To stop the gush of words, he clamped his teeth together, nearly biting his tongue.

"Thanks," she said, voice like warm brandy. "I'll talk to you later."

Before he could pry open his clenched jaw and babble his gratitude, she hung up, sparing him further humiliation.

Through a blur of fresh tears, Lana saw the sign welcoming her back to Crescent Cove. The tight knot that always formed in her chest whenever she had to say goodbye to her daughter had barely begun to ease. Seeing Mike at the airport had left her emotionally wrung out. She no longer loved him and sometimes—most of the time—she didn't even like him. Her brave face was for Molly, who had loved her doll and given Lana a Christmas tree pin she had made at school.

On the way home Lana had just missed the ferry, so she'd been stuck in line for a half-hour waiting for the next one. All she wanted was to go home and burrow under the covers until the holidays were over and Molly was home again. Instead she'd given in to temptation and called Todd from the ferry. Nervously she touched the tree she'd pinned to her collar. What was she getting herself into?

She drove herself to the Crab Pot, a cozy tavern on the waterfront. After they ended up staying for the area's best fish and chips, Todd insisted on following her home.

"You wouldn't want me to lie awake all night worrying, would you?" he teased when she pointed out that it wasn't late and she'd be perfectly fine.

How did one argue against that kind of persuasion?

A little while later, Todd stood facing Lana beside her parked car. Lightly he touched her hair with his hand. "You're probably tired, so I'll say goodnight." Lana had been ready with reasons for *not* asking him up, so his comment caught her totally off guard. Maybe she had talked too much or not enough at the Crab Pot, she thought, and now he couldn't wait to get away. "It seems as though I'm always thanking you."

"No problem." His face was in shadow, his expression unreadable and his hands planted firmly in his pockets.

The grounds were deserted. Even the street was empty of cars, but obviously there was no need for privacy.

"Well, good night." Vaguely disappointed, she started to leave. Before she could take two steps, Todd touched her arm.

"Lana." His husky voice sent shivers down her spine. "Wait."

Slowly she turned back to face him, her heart tripping in double time. She could no longer deny, at least to herself, how strong the attraction she felt was. The more she saw him, the more it grew.

When he closed the space between them, she was almost afraid to breathe, to spoil the moment. He lifted his hands, cupping her face as though she were a fragile glass ornament. "I've wanted to kiss you for so long," he murmured, thumb caressing her lower lip.

Lana slid her hands up the front of his jacket, the leather soft and smooth beneath her palms. "Show me," she whispered daringly. She hadn't been with a man, hadn't even been kissed, since her divorce.

With a groan Todd wrapped her in his arms and bent his head. The first touch of his lips felt cool on hers, but then heat flared between them, threatening to burn her right up.

Lana clung to his wide shoulders as sensation swept through her like a prairie fire through dry grass. It felt so good to be pressed against him, to feel the response he was unable to hide.

Todd changed the angle of the kiss, murmuring something against her mouth, coaxing her to yield. She forgot everything except the feel of him. Then a car horn blared from out on the street. Like a blast of arctic air, reality came roaring back. Shivering, Lana pulled free of his arms. "I've got to go," she exclaimed.

"Lana, I didn't mean—"

"Good night," she said, cutting him off. As she hurried toward her building, she wondered if he thought her a tease. She hesitated at the stairs, tempted to go back, to explain. To say what? That she was afraid of getting hurt?

Before she could figure out what to do, she heard his car start up. She turned in time to see the headlights sweep across the lot as though he couldn't escape fast enough. She hoped it was because he, too, had been unprepared for the sparks between them, but she didn't think that was very likely.

"Way to go, Elsoe," Todd muttered as he drove away. The poor girl had expected a friendly goodnight peck and instead he'd acted as though he wanted to devour her. No wonder she'd leaped away like a scalded cat.

Frustrated, embarrassed, mad at himself, he slapped the steering wheel hard enough to make his palm sting. Did he have to make that lame comment about waiting so long to kiss her? There was nothing sexy about desperation. She probably figured once a geek, always a geek.

He wasn't inexperienced, but when he had felt her response, his control had shattered like a cheap vase. Shaking his head, he pulled over to the curb and picked up his cell phone.

CHAPTER SEVEN

"I WANTED to make sure you're all right," Todd said into his phone when Lana answered.

For an achingly long moment, she didn't reply. "I'm fine, thank you." Her voice was distant, as though they were a thousand miles apart, not just a few blocks.

"There's a basketball game at the high school on Friday," he said, swallowing hard. "Would you like to go?"

"I'm pretty busy with the holidays and all. I'd better pass."

What had he expected, that she would magically realize she was crazy about him? This was real life, not a fairy tale. "Well, good night, then." He'd barely choked out the words when he heard the click of her phone in his ear.

Lana sat behind the desk in her cramped office at the senior center across from two members of the Women's Auxiliary. Since Lana had begun working here as an aid right after Mike left, she'd advanced steadily until she was now a combination activities director, scheduling coordinator and event planner. Today she was meeting with the co-leaders of the volunteer group who put on an annual Christmas party for area seniors. Perhaps she could stay busy enough to stop missing Molly—and Todd.

Better to be disappointed now than hurt later. Too bad that knowing she had done the right thing in discouraging Todd's

attention didn't make it any easier. The bright coral poinset-
tia plant left on her doorstep yesterday hadn't budged her
resolve and she hadn't thanked him, hadn't even picked up the
phone when he'd called later. Let him think she was rude
while she tried to forget how much she'd enjoyed being with
him, how attracted and how terrif ied of getting hurt she was.

One of the other women cleared her throat. Hastily Lana
glanced up from the list she'd drawn up for the party. "Re-
freshments?"

"The caterer's confirmed, complete with cookies provided
by our baking committee," replied Mavis Board.

"Sounds wonderful." Lana checked off the item. "Decorations?"

"Already bought. The high school pep club is putting them
and the donated tree up this weekend."

Pleased, Lana moved quickly down her list. The entertainment, music, a small gift for each senior and transportation
for those who needed it had all been arranged. Her pen was
poised over the last item as she ignored the lurch of her heart.
"Santa Claus?"

Neither woman spoke up.

Lana glanced at Mavis in time to see her exchange glances
with her co-chair, Ginny Sullivan. "Didn't you take care of
that?" Mavis asked her.

Ginny shook her head. "I thought you said you'd talk to Hank."

"Oops. I'll call him right this minute." Mavis dug her cell
phone from her purse and stepped out of the room.

"Who else would have Santa on speed-dial?" Ginny said
dryly. The two women had been in charge of the party for
years. Since Lana had begun working with them, this was the
first glitch she could remember.

As she and Ginny waited, they could hear Mavis talking on
her cell. When she finally reappeared, she looked concerned.
"Hank's already booked. If we can't find someone else, we
might have to change the date."

"The party's next week and most of the flyers are already up," Ginny protested. "It's too late to reschedule."

Mavis pushed her glasses back up her nose. "I'm sure we'll find someone, but it might be harder tracking down a suit and a beard, I suppose. I'll get right on it."

"I'll call around, too," Ginny offered while Lana remained resolutely silent.

Two days later, Mavis contacted Lana. "I found three men and a woman who are all willing to play Santa, but there isn't a red suit to be found from here to Bremerton. Quite frankly, I'm stumped."

What was a Christmas party without Santa Claus? It was time for Lana to put her personal feelings aside. "I may know someone," she told Mavis, stomach fluttering with nerves. "He comes with a borrowed red suit."

Would Todd agree? After the way she'd acted, would he even talk to her?

Drumming his fingers, Todd stared out his office window at the steady rain running down the glass. The weather matched his mood. When he'd first seen Lana again and heard her daughter's wish, his hopes had soared. He'd thought that maybe, finally, after all this time, he had a second chance. Bah humbug.

His odds of winning the state lottery were better. His high school crush had grown into something more. A lot more. After seeing her only a couple of times, he had fallen like a skydiver whose chute didn't open. He had crashed and burned once again, a pathetic heap at her feet.

With a sigh, he turned his attention to the current design project on his computer, a waterfront condo complex he and Gary were developing. At some point, the sound of knocking broke his concentration. Glancing up, he realized that his assistant was standing in the doorway and the afternoon was nearly over.

"You've got a visitor," Gail said quietly. "She doesn't have an appointment, but she promised to take only a few minutes."

Drop-in clients were unusual, but Todd didn't have anything scheduled. "What's her name?" he asked, getting to his feet. You never knew where the next commission might come from.

"Maybe you know her," Gail replied. "Lana MacDonald?"

Each year Lana decided that the party at the senior center was the best one yet. This time, as she mingled with the elderly guests, she was sure of it.

The pep club had done an excellent job on the decorations, including a huge Douglas fir covered with multicolored balls and twinkling lights. The catered buffet was outstanding. Even the entertainment, made up of local volunteers, had been well received.

Best of all, Todd had excelled as Santa Claus. He'd proven to be as adept with his oldest fans as he'd been with Molly. He'd flirted gently with the women and traded jokes with the men. More than once Lana had seen him listening intently to a veteran's war story or exclaiming over a proud grandma's photo gallery. Except for a brief exchange when he'd first arrived, Lana hadn't talked to him all afternoon.

Finally the party started to wind down. The caterering crew had already packed up the leftover food, most of the guests had gone and a few volunteers picked up the party clutter. Lana stood by the door, thanking everyone for coming and watching for Todd.

CHAPTER EIGHT

AS THE HALL cleared, Todd was still seated at a table with Henry Crow, an old man with no family. The two of them had been deep in conversation, but finally Todd helped Henry to his feet.

After they shook hands, Henry bade Lana goodbye. "I can't

remember when I've enjoyed myself more," he said with a smile on his lined face. "It's not often someone is willing to listen to an old man's stories."

"I was fascinated," Todd told him. "I hope we'll get a chance to talk again."

Henry leaned toward Lana, eyes twinkling behind his thick glasses as he poked his thumb out at Todd. "Did you know he's still single?" Henry asked. "You'd be smart to grab him."

Lana had to laugh at Henry's obvious matchmaking. "I'm already spoken for," she joked, no longer sensitive about Molly's comment. "My daughter asked Santa to bring me a boyfriend for Christmas."

Henry laughed and slapped his knee. "Keep me posted." With a final wave, he left with one of the volunteer drivers.

"Want some coffee before you go?" Lana asked Todd, hoping to stall his departure until she could figure out if there was a chance he might still be interested despite the way she had acted. "There's some left in the kitchen."

"Let me peel off my beard and I'll meet you back here," he replied, raising her hopes. At least he hadn't bolted while he had the chance.

When he reappeared, face bare of the fake beard and red jacket unbuttoned to reveal a snug white T-shirt, Lana remembered the attraction she'd felt the first time she saw him and didn't realize who he was. Despite her attempts to resist, her feelings had grown amazingly fast. Now her hands tightened on the arms of the overstuffed chair. She had kicked off the uncomfortable high-heeled shoes she wore with her dark green dress and tucked one bare foot beneath her.

"Forget the coffee," he said. "You've earned a break after all your hard work."

She wouldn't feel right taking the credit. "The volunteers did almost everything."

He sat down across from her, booted feet stretched in front

of him. "How did you end up working here?" he asked. "If today was an indication, you must love it."

Before she realized it, Lana had told him everything, from her unsuccessful job search after Mike left to juggling her job here as an aid with being a single mother. By the time she'd finished and glanced guiltily at her watch, she was shocked to see how much time had passed. "I've talked your ear off." She shot to her feet, embarrassed. "It's time I locked up here and said goodnight."

"We'd better make sure that coffee's turned off." He draped his arm across her shoulders and led her toward the kitchen while she basked in his nearness.

After they'd gone through the doorway, he stopped her. "What have we here?" he asked, looking upward without letting her go.

She stared at the bunch of mistletoe tied to the overhead light fixture. "That wasn't here before."

Todd grinned down at her. "According to the Santa handbook and my Uncle Hank, I can't ignore tradition as long as I'm wearing the suit."

The quick kiss he gave her was both a surprise and a disappointment. Had she managed to stomp out whatever spark of attraction he'd felt? Then why didn't she feel relieved that temptation had been removed from her path?

On Christmas Eve, Lana sat alone on her couch, staring at the flames in the fireplace. Molly's phone call earlier had been the bright spot in her day. In defiance of her own dark mood, Lana had changed into a stretchy velvet track suit with snowflakes embroidered on the jacket. She'd used the perfume the staff at the center had given her and she was even wearing her jingle bell earrings.

Two days ago she had, against her better judgment, left a present with Todd's receptionist. She had no idea whether he liked the small Santa statue carved out of wood. She hadn't heard from him.

She was about to turn off the music and watch TV when there was a knock on her front door. She looked through the peephole and had no idea what to think. Fastening the chain, she opened the door and peeked out. A Santa Claus complete with red hat and white wig stared back at her through the eye holes of his full face mask.

"You're my very last stop," said a muffled voice. "Then I can go home to the North Pole and Mrs. Claus."

Was this someone's idea of a joke? "Who are you?" she demanded.

Santa lifted up the mask, the hat and the wig, all in one motion.

"Todd!" she exclaimed with a burst of delighted laughter. "What are you doing here?"

His grin was the most welcome sight she could have asked for. "Invite me in and I'll tell you."

Quickly she freed the chain and opened the door. "Can I offer you some cider and cookies?" she asked, heart pounding as he stepped inside and firmly shut the door behind him.

He shook his head, smile fading and his gaze locked on hers. "Not right now. I came to deliver Molly's present."

Lana hoped he hadn't been able to tell how she'd completely misread his visit. "She won't be back until next week."

"Your daughter doesn't need to be here," he said, gaze unwavering. "Don't you remember what she asked for?"

Lana did remember. The intensity in Todd's eyes stirred an unfamiliar feeling in her. Anticipation.

His voice grew surprisingly husky. "I've looked and looked, but I couldn't find anyone who's just right for her mommy."

Lana swallowed hard. "You can't disappoint a little girl on Christmas Eve, so what are you going to do?"

Todd rested his hands on her shoulders. "I know it hasn't been very long, but when something feels as right as this, time isn't important."

She couldn't speak past the sudden lump in her throat. She could only nod.

"Lana," he said gravely, "what I want for Christmas and for every Christmas to come, is you. I'll give you all the time you need, but please, please, give me a chance to make a family with you and Molly."

Lana swallowed hard. "How could I turn down Santa Claus on Christmas Eve?" Her eyes filled with happy tears as she slid her arms around his neck. "I can hardly wait to see what you'll bring me next year," she whispered. And then she kissed him.

* * * * *

EVIDENCE OF DESIRE

Debra Webb

At the age of nine, **Debra Webb** began writing stories for the characters who lived in her too-vivid imagination. By eighteen she had turned wife, mother, and career woman, leaving her writing behind. But those imaginary characters just wouldn't go away.

For the next eighteen years she did everything from managing a Captain D's seafood restaurant to holding an executive secretarial position at NASA, while the characters and their stories continued to traipse around inside her head. Eventually they just had to come out and Debra began the journey that would take her to where her heart had been all along – writing romance.

Debra was born in Alabama, but now lives in Tennessee. Her journey, however, wasn't a simple trek northward to the Volunteer state. First, Debra, her husband, and oldest daughter did a little traipsing of their own. From Texas to Berlin, Germany, Debra followed her husband's military assignments. Finally landing in Tennessee, they had their second daughter and settled in a small community they fell in love with on sight.

Debra Webb is the creator of one of Mills & Boon® Intrigue's most popular mini-series, THE COLBY AGENCY. Don't miss her next edge-of-your-seat instalment in February 2010, *Small Town Secrets*. THE COLBY AGENCY is back!

EVIDENCE OF DESIRE

Six days 'til Christmas

KENNER CITY and the Four Corners area where Colorado, Utah, New Mexico and Arizona collided were a world away from Boston.

Olivia Perez stared out the window of her tiny one-bedroom apartment overlooking the mountain ranges beyond the city. At five on a Monday morning Kenner City was barely awake. It was December 19 and the temperature was about forty degrees. The only snow she would likely see would be atop those mountains that framed her view.

Nothing like home.

What Olivia needed was a cup of coffee and a shower. After all, *she* was the one, much to her family's dismay, who'd decided to leave Boston. After several years as a biochemist for a New England medical research company, she'd ditched her parents' dream and headed west to work as a forensic scientist in law enforcement.

But the last few days she'd begun to have her doubts about her decision. It was almost Christmas and she was lonely.

What she needed was to put up a Christmas tree. That would surely lift her spirits. Today, after work. No more putting it off. She was going to dive in to the holiday spirit.

Two hours later she parked her aging Volvo in the rear lot of the annex building on the outskirts of the city. The building wasn't impressive—a halfhearted effort on the part of the powers-that-be at providing space for the new crime lab. Though the third-floor facilities were far from cutting-edge, Callie McBride, the lead scientist, had put together an outstanding team.

Olivia was early as usual. Callie, who seemed to live in her office, was already on the job. The only other person who consistently arrived early was Jacob Webster, the most experienced member of the team. Olivia's pulse skipped at the thought of those precious few minutes she would have alone with him before the rest of the lab personnel filtered in.

It was silly. Truly it was. Olivia tucked her purse and jacket into her assigned locker and shouldered into her lab coat. She just couldn't help herself. Maybe it was because she was so far from home. Or the fact that it was almost Christmas. Whatever. There was just something about the man that made her foolish heart react in a wholly uncharacteristic way.

She took a breath and braced for the impact of seeing him. He was several years older than her thirty—forty or forty-one, maybe. His hair was still dark, no sign of gray. But it was his eyes that really got to her. She melted each time she had the pleasure of peering into those deep, rich brown eyes. He was tall, obviously worked out and he had that movie-star classic profile. Strong jaw, perfect nose. Olivia shook her head as she moved to her station. She had to stop this. The man scarcely knew she was alive.

Still, she glanced across the lab to where he worked, fully engrossed—completely unaware of her presence.

Maybe this silly crush had nothing to do with being so far from home or the holidays…maybe it was that ridiculous concept of a woman's biological clock. After all, Olivia was barreling toward thirty-one. Never married, hardly any past relationships to speak of.

Whatever it was, she had to regain her perspective. After two months, it was clear Jacob Webster wasn't interested.

"Olivia, I need a word with you."

Olivia jumped. Too preoccupied with adolescent adulation, she hadn't realized Callie was right behind her. "Sure." She offered her boss a bright smile, but the frustration etched across the other woman's face dragged Olivia's lips into a frown. "Is something wrong?"

"Why don't we talk in my office?"

If Jacob had looked up from his work when she came in, he wasn't looking now. Olivia was glad. Any time Callie McBride had that look things were far from good.

In her office, Callie took a seat, as did Olivia, and got straight to the point. "I'm very pleased with your work so far. However, when I give you an assignment with a deadline, I expect that deadline to be met. At the very least, I expect to be kept abreast of any reason that can't happen."

Confusion joined the anxiety twisting away at Olivia's insides. "I'm sorry. I don't understand. All my assignments have been completed. In exactly the time frame I was given." This made no sense at all.

Callie's eyebrows lifted in surprise. "I asked you to have the Tanner case results in by five *yesterday*, so that I would be prepared for my eight o'clock briefing this morning."

Now Olivia was utterly dumbfounded. "I e-mailed the complete file to you. Just as you instructed."

Callie gave her head a little shake. "I don't have it. And I need it—" she glanced at the clock on the wall "—in less than half an hour."

Olivia stood. "There must have been a glitch in the e-mail system last night. I'll resend it now. Or print you a hard copy."

"Just resend it." Callie looked even more flustered as she shifted her attention to the mound of paperwork on her desk.

Olivia hurried back to her station and logged on to her computer. A few clicks later and she searched her e-mail's Sent box just to set her mind at ease. Then a new wave of confusion furrowed her brow. "That's impossible." She *had* sent the file. But her Sent box indicated otherwise.

Olivia shook her head and prepared to resend. She clicked the necessary keys. Strange. *File does not exist.*

Fear detonated in her chest. What the hell? She searched her system. Nothing.

Hours of work gone. Poof!

The file had vanished.

CHAPTER TWO

OLIVIA scrambled through her notes. She had twenty-eight minutes to pull her results back together and e-mail them to Callie for the second time. Her hands shook. She could do this.

"Want some help?"

Olivia's heart thumped against her sternum. "Jacob." *Breathe!* That made twice this morning that she'd been so caught up in her own thoughts that someone had sneaked up on her. Only this time it was him. *Jacob.* "I—" she cleared her throat of the lump lodged there "—I have to reorganize the results on the Tanner case and give it to Callie again."

He smiled.

Her heart jolted again. He never smiled! Not for her, anyway.

"I know. Callie asked me about them before you got here this morning. I assumed something had gone wrong."

Focus. "I e-mailed her the file, but it has…disappeared."

He moved in next to her, hip to hip. The air evacuated her lungs all over again. "Let's try this." His fingers flew across the keys. "What time did you send it?"

Olivia blinked. Answer the question! "Four-fifteen, four-thirty yesterday." She had to stop staring at his mouth…his jaw. And, God, he smelled so good. Something subtle and earthy. Very sexy. She wondered if he understood that the cologne or aftershave he selected was so enticing. He certainly didn't give off any availability vibes.

"Let's take your system back to five p.m. yesterday. That should give us what we want."

She desperately needed to find that file. But right now what she *wanted* had nothing to do with her job. The realization startled Olivia. She'd worked hard to get through Harvard. She'd been at the top of her pay grade in her former position. All because she was focused, driven. How had meeting this man suddenly diverted a significant portion of her attention to…sex?

"There it is."

Relief flooded her, washing away those forbidden desires. "I should have thought of that." She'd been so shocked when Callie questioned her that she hadn't been able to think straight. "Thank you, Jacob." She knew the file had to be there somewhere. "I'll run a virus check on my system. There must have been a glitch."

"Callie's under a lot of pressure right now." Those dark eyes studied Olivia closely as he spoke. "We all have to be on our toes."

Olivia was glad he returned to his station without a backward glance. Her face had gone beet red. The heat scalded her cheeks. She'd foolishly stood here, gawking at him in all her schoolgirl adoration, when he hadn't been helping her—he'd been helping Callie.

Olivia mentally added a bottle of wine to her list of things to pick up after work. She was definitely going to need it to shed the day's stress.

At five-thirty she shut down her system, locked up her station and gathered her things. Besides Jacob, she was the last to leave.

The temperature had dropped significantly with the sinking sun. She glanced longingly at the snowcapped peaks in the distance as she trudged across the parking lot to her Volvo. In Boston, there would be lots of white stuff by now. Her family would be preparing for the big Christmas feast and exchanging of gifts.

No looking back. Olivia had done the right thing. She'd needed to prove herself. To strike out on her own instead of always following the parental master plan. Each of her siblings had done exactly that. She was the youngest and the first to go after her own dreams.

"Not such an easy task," she muttered as she climbed into her car. She shoved the key into the ignition and gave it a turn. Something under the hood growled then sputtered to a grinding halt.

She gave it another try. That weird sound again. The engine failed to crank even after a third attempt.

She dropped her head against the headrest and blew out a weary breath. What was the name of that mechanic shop one of her coworkers had said he'd used?

Max's or Lex's… She didn't have a clue.

Olivia started to dig through her purse in the hopes of finding a note to herself with the name and number when Jacob exited the building.

She tried starting the car once more. *Nada.* She gazed at the man walking toward his SUV.

Maybe he wouldn't mind rescuing her twice in one day.

CHAPTER THREE

JACOB hesitated before unlocking his SUV. He was no mechanic, but even *he* recognized the grinding noise coming from Olivia's Volvo as a problem with the starter.

He surveyed the parking lot. Empty. Other than the evening-shift security, the place was completely deserted. He sighed. It wasn't that he minded helping out a colleague—or a stranger for that matter. The problem was that every time he got close to Olivia Perez, he regretted it. Take this morning, for example. He'd known she was panicked. One look at her face had told him she was in crisis. So he'd given her a hand. He enjoyed the sweet sound of her voice, the way she stared at him with such admiration. What man wouldn't be flattered...tempted?

But the next hour afterward had been spent attempting in vain to refocus on his work. He was forty years old and not a single woman he'd ever known had possessed the ability to distract him to this degree.

From the moment she'd joined the lab's staff, he'd been struggling with keeping his mind off her. He'd gotten his heart tanked back in Durango, and he'd promised himself then that it would never happen again. Who needed a wife or children? He had his work.

That had been enough.

Until now.

What was it about this young woman that distracted him so?

"Jacob! Hey!"

He watched as she dashed across the parking lot in his direction. Dark hair flying behind her like a cape of silk. Hazel eyes wide with worry. Already his body had reacted to her distress.

Or, more likely, her coming nearer.

"Sounds like your starter has gone bad on you." He could make a call to a mechanic he used. But the chances of getting the automobile fixed tonight were slim to none. She would need a ride home.

He could give her a lift. It was the right thing to do. Truth was, being close to her for a few minutes more...alone... wouldn't be a bad thing.

"Do you know a good mechanic?" She bit her lip, staring up at him hopefully.

Jacob fished in his jacket pocket for his cell phone. "I haven't had any complaints with the guy I use. I'll give him a call."

"Thank you." The worry lifted from her face. "I owe you big-time for this morning. Now this. You're a real lifesaver."

"Thanks is quite enough," he said as he pulled up the number of the shop from his contact list.

A few minutes on the phone with the mechanic and a tow truck was on its way.

"So I just leave the keys under the floor mat?" she confirmed.

He nodded. "Security will let the tow truck into the lot. You'll get a call sometime tomorrow about when your car is ready for pickup."

"Great." She grabbed her purse and closed the car door. "It's very sweet of you to drive me home."

She chatted away as they loaded into his SUV and headed for town. He got the distinct impression she was nervous. He'd never known her to talk so incessantly about nothing at all. Usually she was quiet and focused on her work. He acknowledged once more how very much he enjoyed her voice. As well as her brilliance.

"Oh, darn," she said suddenly.

He glanced at her as he braked for an intersection. "Did you forget something?" Being alone with her was playing havoc with his ability to breathe normally. But this wasn't smart. He wasn't the type of man to evoke desire in a young, beautiful woman like Olivia. Hadn't he learned that lesson already? She admired him, yes. But he doubted her feelings went beyond that.

She turned and stared back at the store they'd just passed. "I'd planned to pick up a Christmas tree this evening." She sighed. "It's only a few days before Christmas and I…" She turned to him and smiled. "This is my first Christmas alone. I guess I'm a little homesick."

He took the next right and doubled back. How could he resist? She'd sounded so forlorn.

"You didn't have to do that." She beamed at him. "I really do appreciate it, though."

"No problem."

Yes, he argued silently. It was a problem.

She was a problem.

The last thing he wanted to do was set himself up for a fall.

Unfortunately, it felt like he was already falling.

CHAPTER FOUR

"MAYBE it would look better over here." Olivia hurried to move the chair from the corner.

Jacob patiently relocated the six-foot tree and its stand to the corner she'd cleared.

She smiled. "That's perfect." The scent of evergreen permeated her tiny apartment, and just seeing the naked tree standing proudly next to the window made her heart glad.

Not to mention the handsome man so generously lending his aid.

She was suddenly starving. It was nearly eight o'clock. Good grief! She hadn't even offered him anything to drink. "I didn't realize the time. I absolutely have to make you dinner." She made a quick mental scan of the offerings in her pantry.

He held up both hands as if pushing away the idea. "That's not necessary."

"I insist." She'd had to ask twice for his coat when they'd first arrived before he'd grudgingly shed it. Enticing him to stay for dinner would likely take an act of Congress. "I won't be able to sleep tonight if you don't let me do something to make up for your patience and kindness." Before he could say no, she added, "You really went above and beyond the call. Please. It's just dinner."

He plowed his hand through his hair. "I suppose that would be…okay."

She couldn't hold back a grin of victory. "Great."

In the kitchen, she checked her fridge. Thank God. She had salad dressing. A quick salad with last night's leftover chicken would be perfect. She made coffee and poured her guest a cup. "Cream? Sugar?"

"Black is fine."

She placed a steaming cup on the counter for him. He sat on the living room side of the bar, probably using it as a boundary between them. She hoped her jittery excitement wasn't coming off as juvenile. It was just so nice to have company.

"You have family in the Four Corners area?" she asked to break the silence.

He cradled his coffee mug as if his hands needed warming. She thought of all the ways she could warm those long-fingered hands…. Stop! If she kept thinking like that it would show on her face and he would be out of there in a heartbeat.

"My family's in Durango."

"Are you going home for Christmas?" The thought had her heart sinking.

A quick shake of his head sent her hopes rising again.

"Then you absolutely must have Christmas dinner with me." She gave the fridge door a shove with her hip to close it. "If you don't already have plans, I mean."

It would have been nice to see his eyes, to maybe get some take on what he was thinking, but he stared into his coffee. "I don't usually bother with the whole Christmas thing."

"No tree?" Christmas was…well…Christmas. Not having a tree was positively Scroogelike.

"I can't remember the last time I had a tree."

There was something in his voice when he made the statement that told her there was a story behind that decision. She didn't dare ask.

Thankfully she had the good sense to let silence settle between them. She busied her mind with the presentation on the plate. For some reason getting it exactly right was immensely important. She held up two bottles of salad dressing. "What do you want? Ranch or Caesar?"

When he looked up at her question, there was no way to disguise the grimace. He wasn't comfortable here…with her. She had been too forward. Darn it.

"Whatever you're having is fine."

"Ranch it is." She drizzled the dressing over his salad and placed it in front of him, then quickly prepared her own. "Water?" When he nodded, she poured two glasses of water and freshened his coffee.

Opting not to crowd him, she pulled up a stool on the kitchen side of the bar. If she hoped to be friends with Jacob Webster, patience was going to be key.

She paused, fork halfway to her mouth. Who was she kidding? She didn't want to be friends with him…she wanted *him*.

As if her thought had reached out and tapped him on the shoulder, he lifted his gaze to hers. There was no time to wipe the desire from her mind or her eyes.

"This is…" his gaze dropped to her parted lips "…very good."

She licked her lips. Couldn't help herself. "Thank you."

He aimed his attention back at his plate.

That moment was the beginning of the end. He rushed through the rest of his meal and fled as quickly as possible.

Olivia sagged against the closed door.

How was she ever going to reach that man?

CHAPTER FIVE

Five days 'til Christmas

THE NEXT DAY Olivia recognized the magnitude of her mistake. She should never have insisted Jacob stay for dinner. Now he wouldn't even look at her, much less speak to her.

Not that he spoke to her on a regular basis before, but typically he at least said good morning. Plus, the lab wasn't that large; usually they barely missed running into each other around one piece of equipment or another. He would smile and say, "excuse me"—but not today. He kept to his station without so much as a glance in her direction.

She'd probably screwed up any chance of getting closer to him.

It was likely for the best. Coworkers weren't supposed to date. Friendly get-togethers were acceptable. In fact, the whole staff operated very much like a family. A strictly platonic family.

Her gaze wandered across the room. Jacob Webster was far from the most outgoing member of the staff. He was considerably older than Olivia. Why was he the one she longed to know more intimately?

Just like back in college, she reminded herself. Then, too, she'd picked a guy who was way out of her league, and it had cost her. She'd gotten his attention all right. He'd gotten what he wanted and then split.

End of story.

Jacob evidently wanted nothing from her, either, because he avoided her very carefully. Obviously, he'd only taken her home last night because there hadn't been anyone else.

"Hey, Olivia."

She jerked her attention back to her own station. Bart Flemming had stopped next to her, a file in his hand. She produced a smile. "Hey, Flemming." He was young—twenty-five, she thought. Light brown hair, a little long for Olivia's taste. He liked teasing her because she was new. She got the distinct impression that he was the competitive type.

"Webster says you had a little trouble with your computer yesterday." He cocked his head in that I-got-you-covered way. "You want me to have a look?"

"That would be great. I need to check on some of the tests I started yesterday, so I'll get out of your way."

He grinned. "Yeah, I wouldn't want you to learn any of my secrets."

Olivia's smile was genuine this time. Bart was one heck of a smart guy. Kind of a jack-of-all-trades. Any time there was a computer glitch, he could usually figure it out. Not to mention he was an outstanding forensics tech as well.

Olivia pulled up the analysis for her samples. *Sample insufficient for testing.* What in the world? She checked each one. They all said the same.

That was impossible. She never made that kind of mistake. Her pulse lunged into hyper mode. Those test results were due this afternoon. She glanced at the clock. She could try to rerun them, but she'd be damned lucky to make it happen by her deadline.

She stopped and pressed the heels of her hands to her eyes. What was wrong with her? Sure she'd been a little lonely lately, wasn't sleeping well. But none of that was bad enough to interfere with her job.

She had no time to worry about it now. As quickly as possible, she prepared new samples and prayed they would finish in time.

When she returned to her station, Flemming shrugged. "Didn't see a problem, Olivia."

Her hand shook as she swiped her hair back behind her ear. "Thanks for checking. I guess I did something wrong."

He held up both hands. "Now I didn't say nothing like that."

She managed a smile. Her stomach was churning. As Flemming walked away, she considered him and the others working diligently at their stations. Was there something going on that she didn't know about? A joke? On her? Someone testing her grace under fire? Flemming certainly possessed the expertise to mess with her electronic data and files.

Maybe she was just growing paranoid because she'd screwed up? Not once, but twice?

She opened the next case that required her attention. Maybe she was making too much out of this. Everyone had an off day. Maybe yesterday had been hers.

It would be nice if she had someone to talk to about her feelings. Her gaze wandered across the room to Jacob.

She was the newest member on staff. She had no friends outside work. Well, except for the one neighbor.

Maybe she had no friends here, either.

There it was, another of those "I'm lonely and no one likes me" moments. She had to get over these silly feelings.

Just work, Olivia. Everything else will fall into place.

Unless…someone was out to get her.

CHAPTER SIX

A GROCERY BAG in each arm, Olivia dropped her keys twice before she managed to unlock her apartment door. Nothing about the day had gone right.

Jacob had avoided her the entire shift. And because of the erroneous test results first thing that morning, she'd been behind all day.

Running late made the lab look bad, made her look bad.

As she twisted the key, she lost her hold on one of the grocery bags. It plopped to the floor and burst like a bomb, sending cans and produce in every direction. She bent down and her purse slid off her arm, hit the floor and vomited its contents. "Damn." Olivia fell to her knees and raked up her scattered belongings. She was beyond ready for this day to be over.

"Let me help you with that."

Olivia looked up to find Gerald McKay rushing toward her. "Hey, Gerald."

"You should try making two trips." He nodded to the tumble of groceries.

"Yeah, I know." She shook her head as she gathered the last of her personal belongings. She snagged her badge. If she lost that she would just cry. She'd already lost one.

Gerald gathered the final can of soup and pushed to his feet. Arms full of groceries, he waited while she opened the door.

"Just dump it all on the table." She tossed her purse on the sofa and took a breath. The day was done. *Let it go*. "How's your new job going?" she asked Gerald.

"Great." He stacked the last of her purchased items on the table. "I didn't think I would like working in a medical lab, but it's growing on me."

"Sometimes I wish I'd taken your advice and signed on with MedTech." She'd only been in Kenner City a couple of days when she'd met Gerald. He lived on the opposite side of the hall, two doors down. He'd told her about an opening at MedTech, but she'd been all gung ho to start at the crime lab. That was the reason she'd made the move from Boston; she'd wanted to stretch her horizons, do something that mattered on a different level—one where results were more readily seen. Medical research sometimes required years, if not decades, of work before results were gleaned.

"Bad day, huh?" He grabbed an armful of apples and followed her into the small kitchen.

"Really bad day." She shivered. It wasn't that cold outside, but with everything else, she felt cold inside. "Want some coffee?" She wasn't in the mood to be alone right now and Gerald was good company. Recently divorced, he'd come to her more than once needing to talk.

"That would be grand."

Olivia set the coffee brewing and between the two of them they put away her groceries. She couldn't talk about her work, but she could commiserate with him about the feeling of not fitting in.

"Olivia…" Gerald began slowly "…I don't really know any of the people you work with, but I've heard rumors around MedTech that the guys at the crime lab are ruthless when it comes to promotions and such. Maybe you should watch your back."

Olivia really hoped that wasn't true. "Thanks," she said with a pathetic attempt at a laugh. "That really makes me feel better."

"Sounds like you need chocolate."

"Chocolate?" She was pretty sure she had absolutely nothing chocolate in the apartment.

He held up a hand. "I'll be right back."

She peeled off her jacket, hung it in the closet and set her hands on her hips. Only five days until Christmas. She needed to get that tree decorated. She inhaled deeply, loving its smell. That was something nice to come home to. After toeing off her shoes, she shuffled back to the kitchen and poured two steaming cups of black coffee. Maybe the caffeine would give her a boost. She placed Gerald's cup on the coffee table and curled up on the sofa with her own.

"Here we go." Gerald breezed back into her apartment, a plate of brownies in one hand. He held them out for her viewing pleasure. "This is just what the doctor ordered." He kicked the door shut behind him.

"Are you serious?" The treats smelled as if they'd just come out of the oven. Brownies were her favorite. "Did you make those?"

"As soon as I got home today." He sat the plate on the table and settled into a chair across from her.

"You're a good neighbor."

"So," he said as he picked up his mug, "tell me about *him*."

Olivia rolled her eyes. She should never have mentioned in a weak moment that there was a guy at work she was attracted to. "He still doesn't know I'm alive. Not in that sense, anyway."

"Then we'll have to do something about that." Gerald sipped his coffee. "Have you thought about inviting him over for dinner?"

Olivia told him the story about her car troubles. That was another thing that had made today suck. A new starter, the labor for replacing it and the towing had set her back considerably.

"It's your turn to go to his place," her neighbor suggested.

"What?" He had to be out of his mind. She knew where Jacob lived, but only because each staff member's name, telephone number and address were on the personnel roster.

"Make up an excuse." Gerald shrugged. "Bring him a gift in thanks for rescuing you. Just show up at his door."

"What if he has company? He could have a girlfriend or something."

Gerald shook his head. "You told me that one of your coworkers said he was a loner. No attachments."

True. She laughed. "How do you remember that?" Even she'd forgotten.

"Just do it," her nosy neighbor insisted. "Show up at his door with a gift and—" he grinned "—dressed for seduction."

It had been so long since she'd tried, Olivia was pretty sure she had forgotten how to seduce a man.

CHAPTER SEVEN

Four days 'til Christmas

ONLY FOUR more days until Christmas and Olivia was at home alone. Except for the two bags of newly purchased Christmas decorations sitting at her feet.

The only good thing about today was that none of her test results had gotten lost or otherwise corrupted. Work had actually gone fairly smoothly. Maybe because she'd slept like the dead the night before. She couldn't remember when she'd been out cold like that.

After leaving the lab, she'd stopped to buy decorations, come home, given half a minute's consideration to Gerald's suggestion and promptly decided her neighbor was nuts.

Showing up unannounced and uninvited at Jacob's door was completely and utterly out of the question.

He would think she was insane. Like her neighbor.

Don't think about Jacob. He'd ignored her all day, just like the day before. Clearly strong-arming him into dinner the other night had been a big mistake.

Office romances were not a good idea, anyway, even when there wasn't an unwritten rule about them. When Callie had interviewed Olivia she had mentioned that avoiding that kind of relationship with colleagues was preferred. Considering all the strange mishaps with her work lately, Olivia didn't need anything else to put her on Callie's bad side.

Why was it that having a boyfriend suddenly mattered so much? Back home in Boston, she'd rarely thought about her social life. Now she obsessed on it.

That wasn't true. She obsessed about Jacob. He was... handsome. Extremely intelligent. And she loved the way he talked. His voice was deep, his words always chosen carefully.

Stop. "Decorate the tree, Olivia."

The distraction worked for about an hour. She wound the strands of lights and the glittery strands of pretend snowflakes. Then she hung four different types of glass ornaments. Last but not least, she topped the tree with an angel.

When she plugged in the lights and stepped back, she beamed in satisfaction. It looked nice.

Jacob had said he didn't have a tree yet. Hadn't bothered with one in a long time. She wondered about that. Had he lost his heart once and decided it wasn't worth the pain, like she had?

The telephone rang. "Saved by the bell." She'd been about to go off on another long analysis of the man. One glance at the caller ID screen and she smiled. Her mother.

The conversation lasted nearly an hour. Both her mother and her father updated her on things in Boston—from different perspectives, of course. They were so funny. Outwardly they never appeared to agree on anything. But where no one could see, they were completely in tune with one another. The perfect couple. That was what Olivia wanted.

She heaved a big, loud sigh. She could go for a run. But running a few miles wouldn't help. If talking to her parents for the better part of an hour didn't do the trick, nothing would.

There was only one thing to do.

Bring Jacob a thank-you gift and see what happened.

The only question left was, what kind of gift? She chewed her lip, thought about something sweet like a cake or pie. But he was a health fanatic, or so it seemed. His lunches were always the good-for-you kind.

A grin stretched across her lips. She knew just what to get him.

Something he hadn't bothered with in a really long time.

CHAPTER EIGHT

JACOB set the newspaper aside. He mulled over the offerings on television. Scanning the channels would be a waste of time. Holiday movies and television shows. Even the news would focus on the holidays.

He surveyed his living room. Small, utilitarian. He'd bought the modest bungalow after relocating here permanently from Durango. Traveling back and forth as he helped Callie McBride set up the new Kenner City crime lab hadn't been so bad. But once the lab was operational and he'd decided to stay on, moving had made more sense.

What little family he had left—a brother and an aunt— were back in Durango. But each had a large family to keep them busy, so he didn't go back often. Besides, he was occupied here. Callie needed him. The lab needed him.

What else did *he* need?

Nothing to speak of.

Jennifer had taught him well. He'd loved her for five years and lived with her for four of those. Then she'd left him. Simply came home from work one day and said she'd met someone new. Someone who didn't spend all his time at work. Someone who wanted to start a family *now*. Someone completely opposite from Jacob.

That had been eighteen months ago. The last he'd heard, she was married. Her first child on the way. He was happy for her.

Work fulfilled him as nothing else could, even Jennifer. Jacob stood and walked to the front window. Darkness had fallen and the streetlamps had awakened. Yes, he had loved Jennifer. But not the way she had needed him to. He wasn't sure he was capable of that depth of emotion.

His mind drifted to Olivia Perez and immediately his heart rate reacted. A frown furrowed his brow. What was it about the woman that got under his skin? He'd known her scarcely two months. She was a colleague, for heaven's sake. Not once in his career had he been attracted to a coworker. Even Jennifer had not possessed the ability to distract him from his job. She would be the first to say so. But Olivia... The dark hair that hung nearly to her waist made him want to run his fingers through it. Jennifer had worn her hair short. She'd always said it was more practical. There was nothing practical about Olivia's long mass of silky tresses.

He fisted his hand at the thought of touching her hair. He had once. Accidentally. His fingers had tingled, his pulse had raced. The whole concept was ludicrous. As if that wasn't bad enough, her big hazel eyes tugged at him. Made him want to reassure her whenever she looked stressed or frustrated.

The whole scenario was utterly foolish. He was not a schoolboy, far from it. Yet when she came near he felt exactly like one.

Perhaps it was time for a change. He certainly wouldn't go back to Durango. But there were other places in the Four Corners area. Places where he wouldn't have to see her every day. Where he wouldn't hear her soft, velvety voice, or the sweet sensual laughter that pulled at his senses.

Something to think about.

A car pulled to the curb up the street, just past his driveway. He couldn't quite determine the make since a well-shaped spruce lay atop its roof. A Christmas tree, he realized. Most of his neighbors already had their trees. The lights twinkled nightly from the windows.

Someone visiting a neighbor, he supposed.

The car door opened, but the brief light from the interior prevented him from seeing if it was a man or woman.

He started to turn away but then the figure, tree in tow, stepped into the pool of light near his sidewalk. For one second he was certain his errant thoughts had prompted a delusion.

But, no, it was *her*.

Olivia Perez marched up the sidewalk to his door, lugging a Christmas tree.

CHAPTER NINE

OLIVIA RANG the bell twice. No answer. She was certain she was at the right house. His SUV sat in the driveway. There were lights on inside. The glow filtered through the drapes.

Nice place, she decided. Classic bungalow with a generous porch for summer evenings. The stucco was painted a rich earthy brown with tan trim. The door was a mellow gold with a distinctive Spanish flare. *Very* nice place.

If he wasn't home, she would just die. She could leave the tree and a note on his porch, she supposed.

The door opened.

She held her breath.

"Olivia?" He looked from her to the tree she'd broken her back heaving off the top of her car and hauling to his door.

"Merry Christmas, Jacob." She managed to suck in a lungful of air. "I wanted to repay you for giving me a ride home the other night—"

"You made me dinner," he countered. "This—" he gestured to the tree "—wasn't necessary."

She shrugged, almost losing her nerve. But she was here, by God. She was going to do this. "It is necessary. We work together. We're friends. It's almost Christmas and I wanted to…to show how much I appreciate all the times you go out of your way to make me feel at home…at work." The more she said the worse it sounded. He must think she was an idiot!

He stared at the tree a moment before meeting her eyes again. "I suppose…" He stepped back, opened the door wider.

As soon as she had crossed the threshold he took charge of the tree. "Whew," she said. "That thing is heavier than it looks."

"I don't have—"

"Don't worry." She'd figured as much. "I have everything you'll need. I'll be right back." She rushed out to her car, got the bags of decorations and the tree stand. She'd also picked up some hot cocoa for him and another tin for herself. Snow or not, she could sit by the tree with her cocoa and pretend.

When she returned from the car, he was still standing right where she'd left him, looking completely dumbfounded. "Pick a spot," she ordered.

He settled the tree on the floor, closed the front door and looked around the room.

Impatient, she suggested, "How about by the front window. It won't be in the way there." Not that he had that much furniture. He actually had several good spots for locating the tree, but the big window would allow his neighbors to enjoy the lights. She missed that in her apartment.

"Sure," he said.

Olivia took the lead. She set up the stand and guided the trunk into it as he positioned the tree upright. Once they'd secured it and added water, she grabbed the packages of lights. Jacob's movements were a little stilted and awkward at first, but by the time they got to the glass ornaments, he was moving along quite efficiently. She'd even coaxed him into conversation.

"You have a large family, Olivia?"

Olivia hid her smile. He'd just asked her a personal question. He never did that. "Yes. Two sisters, three brothers. We're all either lawyers, doctors or law enforcement."

"Impressive." He smiled—just a little but she noticed.

"You?"

"A brother and an aunt in Durango. He's a university professor, she's a retired nurse."

They were making progress. The last item she pulled from one of the shopping bags was instant hot cocoa mix. "Now we have to celebrate with hot cocoa."

She could tell he wanted to decline. But then he surprised her again and agreed.

Ten minutes later they were sitting on his sofa enjoying the cocoa. If she had known chocolate would relax him like this she would have brought Godiva to the lab weeks ago.

He regarded the decorated tree for a moment. "It looks pretty."

"More?" She reached for his cup.

He held up a hand and shook his head.

"I'll take care of this." She picked up his empty mug and stood.

"That's okay."

She just smiled and kept walking toward the kitchen. He joined her.

"I have a dishwasher," he reminded her as if the appliance tucked into the cabinet next to the sink wasn't visible.

"I can see that." She rinsed the cups and spoons and stacked them into the dishwasher. He hovered nearby. This domestic scene made him nervous. She picked up on his tension immediately. She shouldn't press her luck.

She dried her hands. "I guess I should go. This was nice."

He stared at her mouth. Five seconds, then ten. She considered saying something else but she was afraid she would break the spell. He wanted to kiss her. She was sure of it.

Afraid to give him too much time to think, she went up on tiptoe and kissed his jaw. "Good night, Jacob."

She didn't give him an opportunity to analyze what had happened before she got out of there. By the time she pulled away from the curb, she'd managed to catch her breath again.

She'd kissed him.

Now she was scared to death what his reaction would be.

Tomorrow she would find out.

CHAPTER TEN

SHE'D kissed him! Actually stepped right up to the plate and done the deed. Second thoughts warred inside her. Was her move too forward? Would he tell her to never come to his house again?

She couldn't think about it. Olivia turned onto Fourth Street so she could stop by Ferguson's for a bottle of celebratory wine. She'd intended to pick up wine the other night but she'd forgotten. This was the first time in two months—since moving west, actually—that she'd felt like celebrating. And quite possibly she shouldn't be feeling that way. Jacob might be infuriated that she'd been so bold.

Enough. *Just put it out of your head and wait and see what happens.* Shortly before making the turn she noticed the dark sedan in her rearview mirror. If there had been any traffic to speak of she might not have noticed. But there wasn't. The car had followed her every turn since leaving Jacob's house.

She made the right into the Ferguson's parking lot. Going inside would provide the opportunity to prove that the car wasn't following her. The idea was a bit over the top. She might not have thought anything of it if the training for her job hadn't mentioned the possibility she could become a target in certain high-profile cases.

None of the cases she'd worked on so far had fallen into that category, but there was no need to take the chance.

The car drove past slowly as she emerged from her Volvo. She didn't recognize the make or model. There was a dent in the trunk area as if the driver had backed into something. The important part was that he or she had driven on. Olivia relaxed.

Inside the grocery store, she strolled the aisles looking for something chocolate she could munch on. Chocolate was defi-nitely her weakness. She craved the stuff whenever she was nervous or stressed. It was a flat-out miracle she hadn't gained twenty pounds since moving here. She'd recently made it a point not to bring chocolate home. But it was practically Christmas. Like the hot cocoa, chocolate was just a part of the holiday.

She picked out her preferred white wine—something sweet and a little bubbly. Finding nothing chocolate in a bag or box that tempted her taste buds, she moved onto the bakery section. Right there in the aisle in front of the bakery case, she melted. Chocolate cake with fudge icing.

Exactly what she needed. Thankfully it was one of the small cakes, more likely meant for two. In her case, it would amount to *two* servings. One for tonight, one for tomorrow night.

Almost as good as sex.

Yeah, right. Even she hadn't done without for so long that she would presume to substitute chocolate for sex and come out satisfied.

Cake and wine in hand, she made her way to the front registers and paid. As she climbed into her car, she found herself scanning the street for the sedan that had been following her. Or the sedan she'd *thought* was following her. The latter was far more probable.

About seven minutes more and she would be safely tucked into her apartment, anyway. Security was good at her place. That had been one of the key selling points when she'd taken the lease.

If she remained in the area she would eventually need to buy a house. Something small and cozy…like Jacob's. But she would make it a home. His still looked and felt like a house—not a home. No doubt a bachelor thing.

Lights flickered in her rearview mirror. The vehicle roared up behind her—too close for comfort. She couldn't be certain it was the same car. Same color, it seemed. She hadn't had a good look at the driver before. She peered into the rearview mirror, tried to make out what he looked like as she slowed for an intersection. Definitely looked like a he. Was he wearing sunglasses?

At night?

He was.

A shiver danced up her spine.

That was officially weird.

She drove to her block but didn't turn into the parking lot. Instead she moved into the left turning lane as if she intended to maneuver into the lot of the building across the street. The car cruised by.

Her heart skipped a beat.

The same car. The dent in the rear end was exactly the same.

As soon as the car had driven past, she checked her rearview mirror and cut across the lanes to the garage beneath her building.

When she'd entered the code and gotten into the garage she breathed a little easier.

She'd definitely been followed. The only question was why.

CHAPTER ELEVEN

Three days 'til Christmas

Olivia had slept fitfully the night before. Not even the wine and the chocolate had relaxed her nerves.

The car had been following her. She was certain of that. She'd considered reporting the incident to Callie, but her boss hadn't appeared to be in a very good mood this morning so she'd scrapped the idea.

Olivia would watch when she left work. If she saw the car again she would call the police then tell her superior. It wasn't totally outside the realm of possibility that the whole event was coincidence. The car hadn't made any aggressive moves. The driver hadn't even looked at her.

It just felt…odd. Had her instincts on alert.

There were people who had light sensitivities who wore protective eyewear at night. She may have made too much of that part.

Bottom line, there was really no reason to get paranoid. Yet.

She had a bigger problem today, anyway. Jacob was avoiding her again.

He hadn't said good morning. Hadn't looked her way once. She shouldn't have kissed him.

Even now her face heated at the memory. The move had been a mistake. If she'd needed any confirmation, his actions today had given her all she needed.

Just do your work, Olivia.

She could sit in the corner wearing a dunce cap when she got home tonight.

Bart Flemming and another of the lab's forensic analysts, Bobby O'Shea, returned from a meeting in Callie's office. Olivia had been a little worried when the meeting hadn't included her, but Jacob hadn't been at the meeting either. Meetings with Callie were usually about whatever case one was working. Olivia knew that, but she was feeling extra sensitive these days considering the mistakes she'd been making.

And that was another thing—she'd never made mistakes before. She'd always been one hundred percent. A lead analyst at her former job. Maybe this whole distraction with Jacob was interfering with her work. She would need to think long and hard about that. Or maybe it was the holidays. Or a combination.

"Olivia," Bobby said as he passed her station, "Callie wants to see you."

"Thanks." Olivia shut down her system, something she'd started doing whenever she left her station. She refused to believe anyone here would sabotage her work, but she wasn't taking any chances.

Ruthless. That was what Gerald had heard about the guys here. Olivia thought of her coworkers and honestly couldn't bring herself to believe that rumor was grounded in any sort of reality. Probably just jealousy on the part of the MedTech personnel. But then, Flemming *was* a genius with computers.

Olivia shook off the idea and tapped at Callie's door; her boss motioned for her to come on in. "You wanted to see me?"

"Have a seat, Olivia."

Callie looked tired. Olivia had noticed an additional layer of weariness about her for a couple of weeks now.

"We have a problem."

Those instincts that were already in overdrive started to hum. "What sort of problem?" This couldn't be happening again.

"The file you sent me this morning," Callie explained, "was empty. I checked the system and apparently you failed to follow through on the program before leaving yesterday and all your data was lost."

That was impossible. Olivia had double-checked her work before sending the data to Callie. "That can't be right. I—"

Callie shook her head. "Olivia, I'm not accusing you. Yet," she qualified. "But something's going on here. A glitch in your access code, maybe. I'll have Bart check on things. Meanwhile, why don't you print hard copies for me from now on? At least until we clear up this...situation."

"Of course."

Olivia moved blindly to the ladies' room. She couldn't go back to her station. Not yet. She had to pull herself together.

Did Flemming and O'Shea know? Had Callie voiced her concerns to two of her more trusted staff? Were they all suspicious of Olivia? The new girl? The outsider?

This was wrong.

Very wrong.

CHAPTER TWELVE

It WAS past eight o'clock before she finished.

Everyone else had gone already. Except the security personnel in the lobby.

Olivia stretched her neck and rolled her shoulders. It'd taken her all this time to catch up with today's work after redoing yesterday's tests. But now, as Callie suggested, she was printing hard copies of everything. A copy for herself, which she locked in her station, and a copy for Callie, which she put in a large envelope and slid under the door of her office. She wasn't about to leave anything lying around...to disappear.

Jacob had left at six. He'd said good night to Olivia but he'd rushed to get away after that.

She really had gone too far last night. He must think her a complete fool.

Maybe the whole problem—work, Jacob, all of it—was with her. Olivia wasn't herself. Clearly.

She pulled on her jacket and retrieved her purse. She, apparently, was forgetting things. Her focus was easily distracted. But that was only because she had increasing difficulty keeping her mind off Jacob.

She took the stairs down to the lobby. Okay. Time to get her stuff together. She had to stop this whatever-it-was with Jacob. The distraction. The obsession. And she had to pay extra attention to her every step at the lab. Maybe she would even start a second log, one of her own that had nothing to do with the official system.

Good plan. She felt better already.

As she waved to the security guard, a thought she'd been mulling over entered her mind once more. She was grasping at straws...but there was only one way to be sure. She hurried over to the security desk and presented a smile to the guard on duty. She would never know if she didn't ask.

"Can I help you, Ms. Perez?" he asked. The Rudolph the red-nosed reindeer pin on his shirt glowed.

Olivia smiled. "I like your pin."

"Thank you. My granddaughter insisted I wear it."

"I believe I was the last to leave last night." She held her breath and took the plunge. "Did anyone from the lab come back after that?"

The guard turned to the computer on his desk and tapped a few keys. "No one except Bart Flemming. He returned around ten for half an hour." The guard shook his head. "That young man is a go-getter."

"Thank you."

Dazed, Olivia wandered to the exit and pushed out the door. The wind was a little brisk. Instinctively, she pulled her coat tighter around her. This couldn't be right. There was no way one of her colleagues would do this....

She took a breath. Made a decision. If her work was tampered with again, she would mention this to Callie. Otherwise, she would give Flemming the benefit of the doubt.

Maybe she just needed a break. That idea of trying to get a last-minute flight to Boston Friday evening was suddenly sounding a lot more appealing. Monday was a holiday. She could spend a long weekend surrounded by family and clear her head of everything here.

Including Jacob Webster.

She drove home slowly, pondering the idea of packing a bag and putting it in the trunk so she would be ready to go straight to the airport after work on Friday.

If she decided that was the thing to do. There went the second thoughts.

Going home would be good, she reminded herself. She would be too far away to think of anything or anyone here.

She noticed a pair of headlights behind her as she made the turn onto her street. Her heart rate sped up even as she told herself she was only being paranoid.

Still, she opted not to turn in at her building. Instead she drove farther up the street. She waited long enough to make it seem like she was headed someplace else, then she whipped into the lot of a convenience store. She jerked to a stop and stared after the sedan, which had no choice but to continue on.

Her heart surged into her throat.

It was the same car.

CHAPTER THIRTEEN

JACOB opened his front door to find Olivia standing on his porch. Her hazel eyes were wide with…fear. Her breathing was ragged, as if she'd run all the way to his house instead of driving. But her Volvo sat at the curb.

"Olivia, what's going on?"

The reality that she had kissed him last night abruptly kicked him in the gut.

"Someone's following me," she said in a rush.

He glanced at the street. No traffic. No unfamiliar cars. "Who?" If anyone had followed her here, they were gone now.

"Please." Her eyes pleaded. "Can I come inside?"

Whatever had happened, she was terrified. "Of course." What was wrong with him? She'd obviously had a scare. He stepped back to let her pass, then closed the door. "Start at the beginning and tell me everything."

She started to shake. Not little shivers but big, body-quaking shudders.

"Maybe you should sit down." He took her by the arm, riding out the instant electrical charge that touching her elicited, and guided her to the sofa.

Once she was seated, he moved to the chair directly across from her. "What happened?"

She described the dark blue sedan, particularly the dent in the area where the trunk closed. The evasive maneuvers she had taken to clarify whether the vehicle was actually following her were adequate. Judging by her experience, he had to agree she was being followed.

"Have you received any strange phone calls? Hang ups? Heavy breathers? Anything like that?"

She shook her head.

"You haven't seen any strange cars hanging out around your apartment complex?"

Another shake of her dark head.

Disturbing. "Have you reported this to Callie or the police?"

"No. I…I thought…I wasn't sure." She hugged her arms around herself. "But now I'm certain. The man is definitely following me."

"He wears sunglasses and a baseball cap, you think?"

She inhaled a long, shaky breath. "I'm not positive about the cap but I'm absolutely positive about the sunglasses."

This needed to be brought to Callie's attention, as well as to that of the chief of police. "Tell me about the cases you've worked recently." Though the work they did was not anything like what one saw on television, their analysis helped law enforcement bring criminals to justice. Those criminals, at times, targeted the ones they felt were ultimately responsible for their arrests. The forensic analysts.

She listed the cases she'd performed various tests to support. None struck him as particularly high profile or intense investigations. "Are you certain you haven't made any enemies since moving here? A jilted boyfriend? Or an admirer you've offended somehow?" The idea of Olivia with another man burned deep in his belly.

She shook her head. "I've been busy with the lab. I really haven't made any social connections."

Which meant she was like him. Alone. His chest tightened at the thought.

"Let's get you calmed down." That was the first priority. "Then we'll call Callie and discuss the situation with her."

Olivia nodded. "Okay."

He remembered how much they'd enjoyed the hot cocoa last night and he amended his plan. "Let's have some more of that hot cocoa first."

The hint of a smile touched her lips. "That would be great."

"I'll put the water on."

Jacob went into the kitchen and filled the kettle. His logic warred with his emotions. He shouldn't be encouraging this thing between them.

But...

But nothing.

He was tired of being alone.

Taking a risk on Olivia would be worth the potential pain.

CHAPTER FOURTEEN

OLIVIA CRADLED the hot mug of cocoa in both hands. Logically she knew she was warm now, but somehow her brain failed to deliver that message to the rest of her. She couldn't stop shivering. Couldn't stop wondering why anyone would be following her.

Or why everything was going wrong for her at work.

She lifted her gaze to Jacob's. He'd been watching her closely since her arrival. He was probably afraid to look away for fear of being attacked. She closed her eyes and pushed away the embarrassing memory of kissing him the way she had.

Poor man. She was like some crazed fan.

Callie would likely regret hiring her when she heard about this latest drama. What was going on with her life? Had she ticked off some god or spirit?

Drink the cocoa. Calm down.

Until then she hadn't noticed that the lights on his Christmas tree were twinkling. He'd bothered to turn them on. A genuine smile slid across her lips. Maybe she'd done one thing right in all this.

Evidently he'd followed her gaze. "I turned the tree on when I got home. It was the least I could do after all the trouble you'd gone to."

"It looks nice. Homey." It was true. The evergreen scent and the classic lights made the place feel more like a home.

"I don't do much to promote that, I'm afraid."

Had she made him feel guilty for his lack of a festive spirit? "I didn't mean it that way. I just meant—"

He nodded. "I know what you meant." He glanced around the room. "I've lived here for more than a year and I haven't really made it my own."

Was that because he was single? Was he missing someone from the past? The idea twisted her already knotted stomach. "It takes a while sometimes." The chitchat was awkward. She knew the reason why. That stupid kiss was dangling between them like a black cloud. "Maybe you can give me some pointers on the market when I start house shopping."

"Gladly."

Their gazes held long enough to make her pulse react. She should leave. She didn't need Jacob to call Callie for her. Olivia was fine now. The last thing she wanted to do was make him think she was incapable. She set her cup on the coffee table and stood. "I'm feeling calmer now. I should go."

He looked surprised, but pushed to his feet as well. "What about Callie?"

"I'll call when I get home. I shouldn't have bothered you." She made it as far as the door before he stopped her. He took her by the arm and pulled her around to face him. Another of those full body shivers rippled through her, but this time it had nothing to do with being cold.

"Olivia." He searched her eyes, seemed to struggle with what to say. "This is real. You were frightened. You can't just leave like this. Let's call Callie and then I'll follow you home."

Every word he said made perfect sense. "I..." It was time to be totally honest here. "I feel bad about last night." She forced her gaze to meet his, as hard as that was. He had to think she was a fool. "I shouldn't have...kissed you. It was unconscionable of me. I apologize."

He was staring at her mouth again. She couldn't say another word. Couldn't breathe. *Please don't look at me that way,* her mind begged.

"You didn't do anything wrong," he finally said softly. "I..."

He was still looking at her mouth. Her heart fluttered like a butterfly trapped in her chest.

And then he kissed her. Softly, so very softly. His lips felt so good against hers. When he stopped, which was all too soon, he pressed his forehead to hers.

"We really have to figure this part out. That's why I'm so careful at work."

Her lips stretched into a smile. "I thought you were avoiding me."

"Hardly."

And then he kissed her again.

CHAPTER FIFTEEN

Two days 'til Christmas

OLIVIA could scarcely contain herself at the lab that morning. Jacob had smiled at her when she'd arrived. Not the usual manufactured smile that he tossed at whoever spoke to him, but a real smile that reached his eyes. Whatever was happening between them she wanted it to continue.

Callie had filed the incident report with Kenner City's chief of police. Both the chief and Callie had insisted that Olivia had been right to report the activity. Callie also agreed that none of Olivia's cases were the kind that would prompt such a reaction. Still, one could never be certain.

Olivia had decided not to go to Boston after work today. She was hoping against hope that she and Jacob would spend Christmas together. But she was getting ahead of herself. He'd kissed her. Twice. That was true. And he'd followed her home. He'd even come into her apartment and checked that all was clear. Then he'd called her before he went to bed just to be sure she was really okay.

That was a beginning. Wasn't it? They hadn't discussed where this was going. But one thing was certain—no one could know. Callie wouldn't be happy. And they could not allow their personal feelings to interfere with their job.

Those were the rules. Simple enough.

Olivia took a breath. Anything but simple.

Now, if she could just get through the day without any incidents. Callie had gotten the hard copies of her data from yesterday. So all was well on that front. Olivia would do the same today. Better safe than sorry. The last thing she wanted to do was be here alone the day before Christmas Eve—or worse, on Christmas Eve. The lab was supposed to shut down for the weekend.

Of course, if any high-priority requests came in someone would have to work. Depending on the nature of the analysis needed, that would likely be Olivia since she was lowest in seniority.

"Olivia, do you mind working at my station for the rest of the day?" Flemming leaned on her table and rested his head in his hand. "Callie wants me to go through your computer. When I ran a routine check this morning of all the systems, there appeared to be some discrepancies in your access. Some appeared to be remote, as if you'd worked from home."

"I don't work from home," she said. Her suspicions about him rose again even though she'd thought she had put her worries aside where Flemming was concerned. "I usually stay here until I'm finished or come in early the next day."

"Yeah, that's what I thought, but something isn't right." He straightened. "We all remote-access the system when we're out of the lab on a case, but you haven't traveled on one yet. Maybe it's nothing, but I should look into it."

"All right." She considered asking him if he thought the problem could be related to her stalker, but she wasn't sure if Callie intended for anyone else to know at this point. Maybe she should just ask him if he had something against her.

But she had no proof. Just…nothing.

"Log in from my station and I'll see what I can find."

"No problem."

When she'd settled in at Flemming's station, Jacob joined her. Her pulse skipped.

"Is everything okay?"

She liked that he worried about her. There she went, making too much of things again. "Flemming thinks there might be some glitches in the access of my account. He's checking it out."

"I'm glad they're taking seriously whatever is going on." He hesitated as if he had more to say.

She held her breath.

"I hoped we might have dinner tonight." He searched her eyes, his own uncertain. "There's a very nice place in town."

"That would be awesome." She knew she was grinning like an idiot. She couldn't believe it! They had a date!

He touched her arm before walking away and it warmed her all the way to her toes. *Slow it down, girl.*

Too late. She was running with it.

Unfortunately, the day went downhill from there.

A multiple homicide sent Callie, Flemming and O'Shea to the scene. Callie called in and warned Jacob that it was going to be a long one and that he should join them. With the rest of the lab staff already on location at other scenes, that left only Olivia to hold down the fort.

It was going to be a long night.

CHAPTER SIXTEEN

As IF she'd needed anything else to go wrong, the lights in the lab had started to blink half an hour ago.

Security had called up and warned her to brace for the coming storm. It was promising to get ugly. Spotty power outages were being reported around town.

Olivia reminded herself that the generators would kick in if the power went out. She didn't have to worry.

But she did anyway.

Callie and her team hadn't returned. They were trying to get a second sweep of the scene in before the storm hit the area too hard.

A little more data compilation and Olivia could call it a night anyway. The drive to her apartment might be a little hairy, but she was more than ready to get home.

Anticipation welled in her chest. She and Jacob had a date. God, she should hurry home to change. What if he was held up?

No, she wasn't going to think that way.

She printed her hard copies and took them to Callie's office, which wasn't locked. Odd. She always locked her office when she left the lab. Olivia shrugged and pulled the door closed as she left. Maybe Callie had just been in a hurry.

One final test check and Olivia was out of here. She would compile the data Monday morning since it wasn't a high priority.

She'd just started back to her station when the lights went out.

Olivia froze. No need to fall over anything or bump into a door. Just stay still until the generators brought the power back on.

She checked her cell phone. Watched the minutes tick off. First one, then another. Okay, the generators should have kicked in by now.

Using the meager light from her cell, she made her way to the nearest station and reached for the phone. No dial tone. She checked all the lines, including the intercom. Nothing. That wasn't supposed to happen.

Fine. She would call security on her cell.

Except she didn't know the number. If she needed to contact security there was a button for that on each phone in the lab.

"Dammit."

She would just have to make her way down the stairs to the lobby. If she took her time, she could make it with her cell phone as a poor excuse for a flashlight.

The corridor leading from the lab to the reception area was pitch-black. She kept having to hit a button or reopen her phone to keep its dim light glowing. As little help as it was, it was better than nothing.

It was so damned quiet.

Creepy quiet.

When she reached the stairwell door she relaxed marginally. Three flights down and she would be in the lobby. Security would be there and they would have flashlights. There were flashlights back in the lab, but she felt better heading straight for the lobby rather than feeling her way to where they were stored in the lab.

Truth was, she was spooked.

Second floor.

First floor.

"Thank God."

She opened the door into the lobby and found it wasn't much better. The wall of windows facing the front parking lot revealed that the cloud cover had obscured the moon. She tried to open one of the exit doors but it was locked. Strange.

Okay. All she had to do was get to the security desk.

She was halfway across the lobby when she realized that there was no one there.

"Hello?"

No answer.

Fear crept over her.

"Hello?" she repeated.

Nothing. Not a sound.

Her phone's screen went black again.

That was when she heard it.

A footstep somewhere behind her.

CHAPTER SEVENTEEN

OLIVIA didn't turn around.

She ran.

If whoever she'd heard coming had been a member of the lab staff or security, he or she would have called out to her. Every instinct urged her to run.

Her phone slipped from her fingers. Hit the floor and slid God-only-knew where. She couldn't go back for it. He could be right behind her.

Sheer luck and a good memory was all that prevented her from running headlong into a wall or piece of furniture.

She found the rear exit and slammed her weight against the door.

Nothing happened.

What the…?

The door wasn't supposed to be sealed. What if there was a fire? The front doors had been locked, too. This was wrong.

Running footfalls whispered against her eardrums.

He was coming.

She flattened against the wall, unsure of herself now. Struggling with the effort, she slowed, quieting her breathing.

She couldn't get out. Her only choice was to make her way back to the stairwell door and head back up to the lab. She could lock herself in Callie's office.

Listening for sounds, she felt along the wall, making sure there were no obstacles before she moved.

If she made a single sound…

She didn't want to think about it.

Just move.

Almost there.

A few more steps and she would reach the stairwell door. Her fingers encountered the cold metal knob and she froze.

Where was he?

She hadn't heard a sound in several minutes. It could have been only one or two, but it felt like an hour had passed. Her heart strummed against her sternum. *Don't listen to the sound of your fear…listen for the threat.*

Silence.

If she hadn't dropped her phone this would be a good time to call for help.

But she had.

There was nothing else for her to do. The lab was her only resort. She had to go for it.

She turned the knob. The sound echoed in the silence. She winced. The door would probably creak, too.

Screw it. She jerked the door open and moved into the stairwell. With the door pressing against her back, she listened.

Nothing.

Slowly, holding her breath, she let the door close. The click reverberated like a rifle shot.

Still no sound to indicate whoever was in here was close by or even following.

Holding the handrail like a lifeline, she moved up the stairs. Slowly, trying her best not to make a sound. Her soft-soled shoes were a blessing to her feet on a daily basis but even more so now.

Second floor.

One step at a time. Don't breathe too loudly. Don't allow your lab coat to brush against the metal railing. Silent as the proverbial mouse.

Third floor.

She stood outside the lab for a full trauma-filled minute.

Once she entered the third floor there was no place left to go. The fourth floor was a storage room for the city, and there was no access from the lab.

If he—whoever he was and if he was a he—had come to the third floor in anticipation of her going back there or to steal files from the lab…she was in deep trouble.

Brace yourself.

Take a breath and open the door.

A creak echoed from below.

Door. First floor.

He was coming.

CHAPTER EIGHTEEN

IT TOOK every ounce of courage she possessed, but Olivia opened the third-floor door with the same painstaking effort as she had the others. No need to give away her position.

She allowed the door to close as noiselessly as was humanly possible.

Then she ran. Down the corridor. Into the lab.

She grabbed for the door to Callie's office and twisted the knob.

It didn't budge.

How could it be locked?

Her whirling mind recalled her steps as she'd placed her report in Callie's office. She'd closed the door behind her.

Had it been set to lock?

Never mind.

She had to hide.

Picking her way carefully between the stations, she rushed through the mental list of other places to hide. She needed to be able to barricade herself away from the threat.

He would be reaching the lab any second.

Maybe he already had.

She had to hurry!

Something hard stopped her forward momentum. Strong fingers clamped down on her arms.

Her survival instinct erupted inside her.

She kicked. Screamed.

He twisted her body around and flattened her back against his chest. Definitely a he, her mind analyzed.

"Scream one more time and I'll shoot," he growled.

The cold, unyielding muzzle of a weapon bored into her skull.

She stopped flailing even as her mind raced to rule out the names and faces that didn't go with that voice. She knew it, even though he had whispered roughly, obscuring the tones…but there was something familiar about him.

As he dragged her backward, she tried to assess his height and build. Tried to inhale his scent. Anything that might help her identify him.

Where was he taking her?

Then she knew.

The door that led to the fourth floor and roof access.

But that door was locked.

When he reached the fourth-floor entrance, he shoved her

face-first into the wall and jammed the muzzle into the back of her skull. "Move and I will kill you."

He didn't whisper this time. The voice was clear…hard…

Keys rattled. A lock turned. He opened the door, grabbed her around the neck once more and hauled her into the stairwell.

The smell of disuse filled her nostrils.

Her mind was replaying his last statement over and over. The words had been void of any emotion. Blank. Dead.

They moved up another set of stairs. He was taking her to the roof.

The urge to fight roared through her. But the metal tip of the weapon's barrel kept her submissive.

The icy air hit her as he dragged her through the final door. Cold rain fell, making the flat rooftop slippery. Lightning lit the sky, followed by the boom of thunder.

He pushed her away from him, but kept the muzzle pressed to her skull. "Now get down on your knees and keep your mouth shut. You make a move and you're dead. You do exactly as I tell you and everything will be just grand."

Realization sucker-punched her.

"Gerald?" She resisted the urge to turn around, to allow her eyes to confirm what her brain had told her. "What're you doing?"

Why would Gerald do something like this? Was he responsible for one of the crimes she was evaluating evidence on?

This was insane.

"I said keep your mouth shut!"

She dropped to her knees the way he'd told her, kept her mouth closed.

"You've made this entirely too difficult." He circled her.

She dared to look up at him.

"Keep your head down!"

She lowered her gaze.

"Every time I fouled up your data, that idiot McBride just let it go. I even did it from your apartment so they would think it was you." He laughed. "Surprised, aren't you? Not only am I a magnificent scientist, I'm a wizard with computers." He paced and paced, the weapon trained on her. She didn't have to look to know. "You should have been fired the first breach they discovered. But they just kept you around. I ran out of options. So I made a new plan. I took your badge, took care of the security guard and set the security system to total lockdown—full dark mode. No one goes in or out. And here we are."

"I don't understand."

He slammed the gun against the side of her head. The blow knocked her off balance, and she scrambled to get back into a kneeling position.

"This job was supposed to be mine. McBride had already interviewed me. She promised to call me back. Then you showed up. You know that bitch never even called me to let me know I wasn't getting the job? I needed it. I had plans for tapping into certain opportunities."

"Gerald, I'm sure it was all just a misunderstanding." Olivia's head was spinning. She had to calm down, think of the right things to say. She had to keep him talking.

"Oh, it was a misunderstanding, all right. I wanted her to see what a mistake she'd made. Then you would be fired and the job would be mine."

Olivia closed her eyes, ordered her head to stop spinning. Didn't help.

"But she didn't fire you." He suddenly stopped pacing. "I just can't deal with any of it anymore. Now I'll have to kill you."

CHAPTER NINETEEN

JACOB had been trying to call Olivia for half an hour. He'd called her cell phone and her apartment.

Something was very wrong.

He'd driven like a bat out of hell, ignoring the angry weather, and now he couldn't get into the lab.

The doors were locked. The lights were out.

She was in there. Her Volvo was in the rear parking area.

Every instinct warned that she was in trouble.

He'd already wasted time going around the building to every single access door. All were locked up tight.

He wasn't wasting any more time.

He raced back to his SUV, started it and pulled the gearshift into Drive. He pulled on his seat belt and floored it, pointing it toward the wall of glass.

The crash exploded around him. The airbag deployed, knocking the breath out of him. He shook himself. Unfastened his seat belt and scrambled out of the damaged car. Glass crackled beneath his shoes.

The fact that the security system didn't sound sent off another set of alarms inside him. He punched 9-1-1 into his cell.

"This is Jacob Webster. I'm at the Kenner City Crime Lab. There's been a break-in." He glanced around the lobby. "Security personnel are down. Send help." He didn't stay on the line to answer any of the dispatcher's questions.

He had to find Olivia.

He double-timed it back to his SUV for a flashlight, then headed at a full run to check the first floor.

By the time he completed his round of the second and third floors, panic had started to set in.

The echo of a gunshot from above sent ice splitting through his veins.

The roof.

He ran for the fourth-floor access, made it to the top of the stairs and hesitated. He needed two things. The element of surprise. And a weapon.

On the fourth floor he found one item that could loosely be called a weapon—the ax located next to the fire alarm. The alarm was dead, too; he'd tried it in an effort to startle whoever had Olivia on that roof.

Ax in hand, he headed for the stairs to the roof. He moved more slowly now. Listening for screams, cries, anything.

As he moved cautiously onto the roof, he did one more thing he hoped would help. He prayed.

His heart stumbled at what he saw when he cleared the final obstacle between him and the wide-open rooftop.

Olivia was on her knees. Some scumbag had a handgun pressed to the back of her head. He was ranting at her.

Moving a scarce inch at a time, Jacob eased closer and closer, the ax ready to swing.

Sirens abruptly split the air.

The creep with the gun jerked his head toward the highway. The distant throb of lights confirmed that the police were closing in.

Jacob had to act now.

Olivia suddenly twisted at the waist, hitting the man at pelvis level. The gunman stumbled back. Olivia dived for his right leg.

The weapon discharged into the air.

Jacob slammed the broad side of the ax square into the middle of his back. The gunman flew forward, stumbling over Olivia. Jacob dived onto him, crushing him with his full body weight. The gun slid across the roof. The perp went crazy, bucking, screaming profanities. It was all Jacob could do to hold him down.

"Stop!" Olivia shouted.

Jacob looked up. She had the gun. Jacob didn't know what kind of marksman she was, but he wasn't taking any chances. He scrambled up and backed out of the crazy bastard's reach.

The fool made a dive for Olivia.

She squeezed off a warning shot in the air. He cowered on the ground.

The sound of running footsteps announced the arrival of backup.

Jacob's and Olivia's gazes met for the first time.

And he suddenly understood that deep, emotional connection he'd never quite gotten before. It had taken him two months to understand the feelings growing inside him, but now he knew.

He couldn't ever lose her.

CHAPTER TWENTY

Christmas

OLIVIA SNUGGLED more deeply into Jacob's arms. He hadn't let her out of his sight since Friday night…except for those few hours on Christmas Eve when they had done their shopping. He'd driven her to town and they'd gone their separate ways until the job was done.

It was Christmas, she was with Jacob and all her worries were behind her.

She shuddered when she thought of her former neighbor. The police had discovered that Gerald had been diagnosed as bipolar with violent tendencies years ago. Somehow he'd managed to keep it out of his official records. The guy had been bullying his way through life since he was sixteen. He'd gone completely over the edge with his obsession with Kenner City's crime lab.

He'd drugged Olivia with a light sedative the night he'd brought over the brownies. He'd done it more than once so that he could access her home computer at a time when she was also home. He'd wanted to make her look incompetent or perhaps even like a traitor.

Callie and Flemming had been suspicious for several days,

but they'd had no proof or clear-cut conclusions on what was going on. So they'd waited and watched.

Olivia was glad the whole thing was over. She'd called her parents and wished her family a merry Christmas. Jacob had done the same.

Other than that, they had been simply enjoying each other's company. And the tree they'd decorated together.

"We should eat that amazing dinner we prepared," he suggested.

Something else they'd done together, but she didn't want to move. She liked it right here in his arms.

Her body warmed, melted as she thought of all the kisses they had shared. Lots of slow, lingering kisses. She smiled against his chest. She loved the way he kissed.

"I'm not hungry," she confessed. She wanted to sit here like this, in his arms, until one of them had to move.

They'd talked about their pasts, their hopes and dreams. Everything. It was like fate had had this plan all along. She understood in the deepest, farthest reaches of her soul that this was the man she'd been waiting for.

The man who would treat her with the respect and admiration with which her father treated her mother.

Who could ask for more?

"There are ways to work up an appetite," he suggested.

Another smile pulled at her lips. "We could take a walk."

"There is that."

"Or we could open those presents under the tree." She'd bought a very special gift for him. One she hoped would show him just how much she wanted to get to know all of him. She had bought him a scrapbook for their mementoes, a framed photo of her to sit on his bedside table and a duplicate of the key to her apartment. For him. His own key to her place. And a slinky negligee for their first night together.

Which just might be tonight. Excitement whirled beneath her belly button.

"We could," he agreed, "but then you'd only get distracted with your gift."

She raised her head to look at him. "Just give me one hint."

He shook his head. "You have to wait."

He'd been saying that all day.

She sighed and collapsed against his muscled chest once more. "In that case, I can't think of a thing else to do."

"Actually." He wiggled free of her, stood. "I can think of lots of things." He picked her up and carried her to his room.

He kissed her in that slow, sweet way of his and she forgot all about the negligee. She just wanted him to keep kissing her.

Frantic hands tore at clothes until they were skin to skin. She couldn't catch her breath. Didn't care. She just wanted to be with him…in every way.

Hours later, as they lay completely sated on his tousled bed, she announced, "I'm starving."

He rolled onto his belly, propped up on his arms and smiled down at her. "Shall we have dinner in bed?"

"That would be amazing."

He kissed the tip of her nose. "Promise me you won't move."

"Promise."

He was gone long enough to make her want to break her vow. When he finally returned, he carried a tray laden with the exquisite dinner they had prepared together.

"Dig in." He backed toward the door. "I just have to get one more thing."

She nibbled on a slice of turkey breast. He was back in a flash, the elegantly wrapped gift in his hands.

He sat it on the bed in front of her. "Open it."

Anticipation searing through her veins, she bit her lips, searched his eyes for some hint.

"Open it," he urged.

She released the silky red ribbon, let it fall around the box. She lifted the lid and frowned at the mounds and mounds of paper inside. "What's this?"

"You'll see."

She dug through the paper, finally found a long, slender box. Her heart bumped hard. "You shouldn't have," she warned.

"Just open it already."

She opened the box. Inside was a dazzling diamond necklace. She gasped. "Jacob, you really, really shouldn't have."

He pressed a fingertip to her lips. "Look under the necklace."

She pulled the velvet liner from the box. Another gasp stole her breath.

A shiny brass key.

"My home is your home."

That dark gaze meshed with hers and in that instant she knew that their future together was set.

But, for now, it would be their secret.

It would be better if no one at work knew. Plus, there was just something wickedly sexy about the forbidden.

She tugged him down onto the bed. Forgot about the food. And her presents for him.

She hugged him, silently thanking her lucky stars she had found him.

* * * * *

LETTING GO

Karen Martyn

Karen was born in Malvern, Worcestershire. One of six girls, she moved to Ontario with her family as a baby and then to California for five years.

On their return to England, the family moved to Kent in the "garden of England" and apart from four years at Hull University reading American studies, Karen has lived there ever since, the last twenty-two years spent in the Kentish countryside with her commuter husband Steve, raising their five children.

Apart from some part-time book-keeping, Karen has devoted the last thirty years to motherhood. She has always enjoyed reading romantic fiction including Mills & Boon® books, which, with their uplifting stories of love and romance, have helped see her through the difficult times of caring for their autistic son.

She has always nurtured dreams of being a full-time writer and hopes this year will see two major productions, the completion of her first Mills & Boon® story and the birth of their first grandchild! When not writing and looking after the house and thirteen-year-old daughter, Karen enjoys walking, cycling and visiting National Trust houses. She looks forward to travelling more widely in the future, for research purposes of course!

Mills & Boon teamed up with *Women's Weekly* to run a short story competition – and Karen's story, *Letting Go*, was the winner! If you'd like to write for Mills & Boon, why not visit our website? There's tons of information at http://www.millsandboon.co.uk/aspiringauthors.asp! ★

LETTING GO

WITH a final burst of effort, Millie plunged the spade into the soil and levered the root free from the earth. She'd been digging for nearly three hours—rising at six and throwing on a pair of old jeans and a sweatshirt to get the job done before Billy came down for breakfast.

'At last,' she groaned, dragging the lifeless tree from its home of six years, and feeling a surge of mixed emotions at the sight of the brown withered branches against the vivid green of the grass. She knelt to touch a papery leaf, closing her eyes against the sting of tears at the memory of their second anniversary.

'You can look now,' Nathan had said on that bright spring morning, leading her to the kitchen window, one-year-old Billy perched on her hip.

'It's beautiful!' she'd gasped, taking in the sight of the newly planted magnolia, with its dark, glossy leaves and tiny furled buds.

'To give you something gorgeous to look at when you're washing up…and when I'm not around, of course,' he'd added cheekily, dropping a kiss on Billy's downy head and encircling them both with his arms.

A few weeks later Millie had watched with delight as Billy toddled unsteadily beneath its spreading branches, pointing a chubby finger at the starry white flowers above him. In the spring after Nathan had died, he'd crouched in the grass, catching the dropping leaves in his small outstretched palms, too young to know or understand why the frostbitten buds would never unfurl their waxy petals.

'So you've done it at last.' Dan's soft, deep voice startled her back to the present.

'Sorry we're a bit early for football training,' he said, helping Millie to her feet. 'Only this little pest wanted to show Billy his new game. Is it OK if he goes in?'

Before she could finish nodding, Harvey had pulled off his shoes and was racing up the stairs to find his best friend. Millie laughed shakily, touched as always by the eagerness of the two seven-year-olds to share everything in their lives.

Shy, freckle-faced Harvey who had never known his mother—according to Dan, she'd quickly grown bored with marriage and motherhood and moved to Canada when Harvey was just six months old—and her own tough little Billy, often boisterous and noisy, sometimes lapsing into moments of quiet sadness, but always kind, with a maturity beyond his years.

'I'm sorry,' she told Dan, brushing her teary face with the back of her hand.

'What for?' he asked, pulling a clean tissue from his pocket and gently wiping the mud smears from her cheek. 'I like my women dirty sometimes.'

Millie smiled wanly at Dan's friendly, weathered face, with its dimpled chin and twinkly blue eyes that crinkled at the corners when he laughed. Kind, patient Dan—always there with a smile that just lately had tugged insistently at her heart.

'For this,' she said quietly, gesturing at the tree. 'For not letting you help with this stupid thing.' She gave a weary sigh. 'It was really hard. I shouldn't be so stubborn.'

They both looked at the deep hole in the lawn.

'Yup.' Dan winked. 'You're right about that bit—just wanting to prove you've got bigger muscles than me.'

He stepped forward and drew Millie into his arms with an affectionate hug. 'Look, I completely understand,' he said, brushing her cheek with a light kiss.

Millie sighed, wanting to stay in the reassuring warmth of his arms, to rest her head against the comforting bulk of his chest. Tell him she was sorry for everything—not just the tree. Sorry for all the times she'd pushed him away, afraid he might want more than she was prepared to give. Sorry she hadn't been able to let their friendship deepen into a love she wasn't ready for. *I think I might be ready now,* she wanted to say, but knew it might already be too late.

The noise of the boys bumping down the stairs in their football kit, clamouring for breakfast, was a welcome distraction from her painful thoughts. Millie collected things together for their packed lunches, watching as Dan poured cereal and orange juice for the chattering boys, fielding their eager football questions while still managing to calm them down.

She looked up from buttering the bread to catch Billy's rapt expression as he chomped on his cereal, watching as Dan moved about the kitchen with an imaginary ball. He loves this man like a father, she thought with a stab of concern. If… No, *when* he finds another partner, goes on to marry again… She shivered at the notion. Would they still share the school run, Saturday football, picnics together in the park? Her heart sank at the thought.

Ten minutes later they donned football boots and clattered off to the car, and Millie was left in the deafening silence of the kitchen with only her thoughts for company.

She was tired, she told herself, turning on the radio and humming tunelessly along to a song she didn't know. She washed up the few dishes, trying not to notice the empty space outside the window or give in again to the tears that pricked behind her eyes.

After she'd showered and eaten, she sat at the table and tried to sort out some overdue paperwork—make the most of a day on her own. It was no use. The letters and numbers swam and merged before her eyes, blotted out by vivid images of the day she'd first met Dan. After half an hour she gave up on the papers and made herself a coffee, carrying it outside to sit on the garden bench.

Millie fondly remembered the day, three years earlier, when she'd opened her door to a tall, smiling man and his tiny sandy-haired son. He had explained that they'd just moved in across the way, and that Harvey was due to start school at the same time as Billy.

She'd been a widow for two years by then, and with no family nearby to support her had quickly grown a tough new skin of independence, combining a part-time job in the library with raising a boisterous four-year-old. Millie managed, with joyless pride, to do tasks that had automatically been Nathan's: changing tap washers, topping up the oil in the car, trimming the hedge, even constructing and creosoting a simple garden shed by herself.

Gradually the raw edges of her grief had softened to the dull ache of missing Nathan's company and his part in their lives. She'd learnt to cope on her own. But Millie knew she would never get used to the searing loneliness of long evenings on the sofa or dark, endless nights in an empty bed, yearning for the warm, loving touch of another.

'A penny for them?' Millie looked up to see Dan.

'Sorry for startling you again. That's twice in one day.'

Millie's stomach gave an odd lurch. 'Is everything OK?'

'Yeah, fine,' he said reassuringly. 'Jim's the coach today. He's going to keep an eye on the boys for a while. You've been very brave, you know,' he said gently, sitting down and taking both her hands in his own

Millie felt her heart skip a beat at his closeness and his soft words of concern.

'It's been a tough few years…for us both,' he added flatly. 'But we've got through, haven't we?'

Millie nodded, smiling, her heart swelling with gratitude for this wonderful man.

'That silly thing with the tree. Yes, it *was* silly,' she insisted, seeing that Dan was about to protest. 'I know I should have got rid of it years ago.'

'It was your way of saying a final goodbye.' He stroked soothing fingers across her cheek. 'Only you knew when that time would come.'

'I just wanted to tell you…to let you know…' She faltered, searching for the right words.

'I couldn't move on—wasn't ready for anything more.' She looked at Dan and their eyes locked. 'But I am now,' she said faintly.

'I'm so happy to hear that,' Dan said quietly, his voice heavy with emotion. 'We have all the time in the world—but right now…'

He stood up and reached behind a shrub.

'I have a present for you—to mark the start of your…*our* new life. It's called "Especially For You",' he said, lifting up a rosebush smothered in a mass of butter-yellow blooms.

'It's beautiful…thank you,' Millie said simply, watching as Dan placed it where the magnolia used to be.

Dan pulled Millie into his arms, gently holding her face between his big hands.

'I've replaced the tree,' he said, looking intently into her misty eyes, 'but I'm not trying to replace Nathan. You know that, don't you?'

'Shhh…' she said softly, tilting her mouth to meet his, their lips touching in a lingering kiss that was as deep and sweet as their love promised to be.

* * * * *

LOVING ELEANOR

Natasha Oakley

Natasha Oakley told everyone at her primary school that she wanted to be an author when she grew up. Her plan was to stay at home and have her mum bring her coffee at regular intervals – a drink she didn't like then. The coffee addiction became reality, and the love of storytelling stayed with her. A professional actress, Natasha began writing when her fifth child started to sleep through the night. Born in London, she now lives in Bedfordshire with her husband and young family. When not writing, or needed for "crowd control", she loves to escape to antiques fairs and auctions. Find out more about Natasha and her books on her website www.natashaoakley.com

Natasha says…

"I write romance mainly because I like happy endings. I think life is tough enough without reading something depressing."

LOVING ELEANOR

LUKE BURNETT lay flat out on the sand, one arm shading his eyes from the sun. Susanna rolled over and looked at him. He was so sexy. So perfect. And hers.

In two days they'd be married. A lifetime ahead of them. A bubble of pure happiness seemed lodged in the middle of her chest.

His arm moved and his sinful blue eyes opened and glinted across at her. She stirred.

"Where are you going?"

"Nowhere."

He moved swiftly, pinning her beneath him. "I should think not." And then he kissed her. "I'd miss you."

Susanna reached up and smoothed his dark hair back from his forehead. "Would you? And the baby?"

His mouth twisted into the kind of smile that turned her bones to liquid. "What do you think?"

And then he was kissing her again…and she couldn't think. Her fingers curled into his dark hair and she forgot about everything except how much she loved him. How much she wanted to be with him.

For a few blissful hours while she slept, everything in Susanna's world had been perfect…but now she was back in reality.

She opened her eyes and felt the familiar sense of despair return. As it always did. Day after day.

Eleanor was dying.

Her little girl. Her baby. The knowledge thumped through her head with each beat of her heart and every morning it was the same.

While she slept she had a few hours respite. A brief interlude where she could make-believe she had a life like any other mother of a thirteen-month-old little girl.

But it *was* make-believe and, in many ways it made it worse when she woke. As soon as she opened her eyes the bleakness closed in around her with fresh impact. She was back in a long dark tunnel that stretched out endlessly before her without the slightest glimmer of daylight.

Today would be like yesterday…and tomorrow like today. She would sit beside Eleanor's tiny bed and try to ignore the tubes that connected her daughter to the ventilator that kept her alive. She would reach out and hold the perfectly formed little hand and pray.

Susanna rubbed at her eyes trying to erase the spike of pain that had settled in the center of her forehead.

Necrotising Enterocolitis.

Before Eleanor was born she hadn't known such a condition existed. Now she couldn't imagine a day where she didn't think those two words and understand exactly what they meant to her daughter.

They were a death sentence. Probably.

Susanna rolled over and looked at the luminous hands on

her alarm clock. There was never any need to set it. She woke with depressing regularity in the early hours of the morning.

"What time is it?" Luke asked beside her, his voice heavy with sleep.

"Just after three."

She heard the slow exhale of breath, his determination to keep calm.

"I'm sorry I woke you." She was always sorry she woke him. There was nothing she'd like better than to be able to sleep through until morning. But…

She rolled out of bed and padded across to her dressing gown, wrapping the long robe around her body.

"What time did you say it was?"

Susanna looked over her shoulder. "Just after three. I'm going to make a cup of tea. Do you want one?"

She watched him struggle to sit up. "Susanna, come back to bed. Get some sleep."

They'd played this scene out over and over. She knew it irritated him but she couldn't just lie there. The thought of Eleanor, so many miles away, tenaciously fighting for her life, crowded in on her. It made her restless.

"I'll sleep better after I've had a hot drink." Which was a lie. She never slept better. Susanna watched the lines furrow his forehead and turned away not wanting to hear anything else he had to say.

"Susanna—"

"I'll be fine." She pulled tight the final knot in her dressing-gown sash. "Go back to sleep."

Luke pushed back the duvet and she caught a glimpse of the athletic physique that had first attracted her. It seemed a lifetime ago now. So much had happened since then; it hardly seemed worth remembering. Their marriage had never stood a chance.

"I'll have a cup of tea."

"What?"

He reached out and picked up his own dressing gown from the rail of the footboard. "If you're making tea, I'll have some."

Susanna looked across at him, shocked. This wasn't the way they played this game. He never said "yes." He always rolled over in the pale blue covered duvet and went back to sleep. "I could bring it up."

She saw the faint shake of his head. "Put the kettle on. I'll come down."

It amazed her how much she resented him joining her. This was her private time. A time she desperately needed.

She was used to the steady tick of the clock, the creak of the floorboards and the sense of peace. In the quiet of the night she always felt she could think. She could remember everything about Eleanor's short life, from her traumatic birth at twenty-eight weeks to the severe liver failure that threatened her now.

In the morning she would need to be strong. Every atom in her body focused on willing their daughter to live. She needed the night to grieve.

"Okay." It didn't seem worth arguing. Luke would do what he wanted to do—he always did.

Susanna hit the landing switch and let the harsh light illuminate the sweeping mahogany staircase. Her bare feet were silent on the thick carpet as she made her way downstairs.

Luke Burnett had been all she'd ever wanted. She'd idolized him since she'd been fourteen. Loved him since her eighteenth birthday party. It was strange, now, to know there was such a chasm between them. Such a gaping hole that now she even resented his company.

Luke had been the golden boy. Handsome, clever and rich. He'd succeeded at anything and everything he'd turned his hand to.

And he'd married her.

She'd thought she'd struck gold. That some mythical fairy had sprinkled some stardust and answered her secret dreams.

Luke…and a baby. Their baby. How good could it get? She'd built such dreams around the birth of their first child. The first of three, maybe four.

She'd hoped.

Every foolish daydream mocked her now. She'd skipped into this nightmare, never dreaming of what lay in store for them.

Susanna filled the kettle.

"How long have you been awake?" Luke asked, his hair tousled and his face sleepy in the kitchen doorway.

"Not long."

The silence stretched out between them, awkward and uncomfortable.

Luke walked farther into the room, resting his hand on the granite worktop. "Did Dr. Lane say anything about the search for a suitable liver donor when you spoke to her yesterday?"

"No." Susanna reached for the teapot.

She'd been told what she already knew—that her daughter was a very sick little girl. With infinite care, Susanna knew she was being prepared for the day when they would tell her Eleanor had died.

She knew, without a transplant, it couldn't be long. Day after day, sitting beside Eleanor, with a tiny pink teddy bear she was too ill to notice tucked in at her daughter's side. White tubes pushed up her daughter's nostrils and another taped to her mouth. How could she not know?

"No progress at all?"

"No." She poured in the boiling water.

"I wondered if she'd said something that…upset you?"

"No." There was nothing the doctor could say that would upset her more than the fears already existing in her head. Nothing worse than sitting beside Eleanor, her little face swollen and yellow and her life hanging by a thread.

Susanna turned in time to see Luke rub a hand against the back of his neck.

Just fifteen months after they'd married each other and there was really nothing left to say. It was as though they'd each become locked inside separate worlds and there was no bridging it.

But then Eleanor was all there'd ever been that had connected them. Once Susanna might have tried to convince herself differently, but deep down she knew. Luke would never have married a girl like her if she hadn't been pregnant with his baby.

In the handful of months they'd had together before Eleanor's birth, he'd been incredible. Her knight in shining armor. Everything a husband should be. There was just one thing missing...

He didn't love her. Had never loved her.

CHAPTER TWO

DURING their short engagement and the early weeks of their marriage, Susanna had allowed herself to hope Luke loved her. He was so passionate and exciting.

She'd told herself no one got married for the sake of a baby, anymore. She'd tried to imagine the night they'd created Eleanor was the result of a mutual and overwhelming desire. Something magical.

But you could only go on lying to yourself for so long.

He'd never once said he loved her. Not on their wedding day. Or during Eleanor's premature birth. Not even when they'd first heard the words Necrotising Enterocolitis.

He'd married her because she was pregnant with his baby. Because he was too good a man to leave her to cope with the consequences alone. Deep down she'd always known that, from the very beginning when he'd slipped the wedding band on her finger.

But she'd hoped and dreamed of the day when he'd realize he'd loved her all along. Only that hadn't happened. Instead, they'd been locked into the nightmare of Eleanor's illness, a huge wedge between them.

Susanna lifted the lid of the teapot and stirred the contents, acutely aware of Luke watching her. "I think I'll pack a bag and stay at the hospital for the next few nights."

Luke's fingers moved on the worktop. "You're supposed to be getting some rest."

She shrugged. "I find it easier if I can see her."

"Susanna, she's getting the best possible care. She's—"

"In the best place. I know."

It was what everyone said, but she didn't believe that. The best place would be home with her, well and happy. At thirteen months, she should be getting into everything, starting to walk, making sounds they could both pretend were words…

Susanna focused all her attention on what she was doing. She poured the milk into two cobalt blue mugs and carefully added the tea.

"You'll be ill yourself if you don't pace yourself."

Susanna wanted to scream at him that he didn't understand. That her world had shrunk to the hospital where Eleanor spent her days tied to a ventilator, whereas he still spent his in the outside world pursuing a lucrative career as an investment banker. It was only on evenings and weekends that he touched the agony that was her day-to-day existence.

She said nothing. Instead, her fingers closed around her warm mug and she sipped the hot tea.

"You could get more involved in the campaign to try and find a donor," Luke suggested, reaching out for his own drink. "Do something practical. The local paper is going to run a story on Eleanor and the hope is it'll be picked up by the nationals. They want to print a few pictures—"

"No." The word shot from her mouth.

Luke looked across at her. "What do you mean?"

"I don't want Eleanor's face plastered all over the paper. I don't want people seeing all the tubes and..." She covered her face with a hand and tried to fight back the tears.

Luke watched helplessly. He understood what Susanna was really saying—that she didn't want Eleanor to be ill. But she was...and the best chance, the only chance, Eleanor had was for a liver donor to be found.

"It's an excellent opportunity," he said carefully. "I contacted them last week and I had a phone call yesterday from one of the reporters. I meant to tell you...but you came back from the hospital so late. The idea is to appeal directly to bereaved families. The wider the net, the better our chance of finding a compatible match."

She looked up, her eyes rimmed red. "But why do they need photos?"

"To make it feel personal. It's a difficult decision for anyone to make, and they have to make it at an impossible time."

Luke had struggled with that thought himself. For Eleanor to live, someone else would have had to have died. Another man's child.

But he was desperate. His love for his daughter meant that he'd do anything. Ask anything. He'd happily donate his own liver if it would mean Eleanor could live.

What he couldn't cope with was standing helplessly by, watching her fade away. He hated the feeling of powerlessness, of events being so far outside his control. It was better to focus on the positive, on what could be done, rather than spend hour upon hour, like Susanna did, watching each assisted breath.

It was easier, too, not seeing Susanna cry. He hated that. Her face was red and blotchy from tears and lack of sleep. She looked like someone who was merely existing...which he supposed she was. And there was not a damn thing he could do about it.

"They want to do a real 'tug on the heartstrings' piece. Perhaps, have you looking down at Eleanor?"

Susanna's mouth moved in a soundless "no."

He reached forward to take hold of her hand, but she pulled

it away. She tried to make it look as though she needed it to hold her mug. It didn't fool him.

Susanna couldn't cope with him touching her. Not for comfort. Not for anything. Her attention was focused entirely on their daughter. Everyone else had been pushed away and shut out. The only thing that mattered to Susanna was Eleanor. And Eleanor was dying.

"They think a headline like Mother's Vigil might reach the parents of potential donors," he continued tonelessly. "Touch their emotions and make them want to bring something good out of their own tragedy."

"I—I can't."

Susanna's voice was a whisper but he heard it. "We can talk about it later. I haven't said we'll do it." He drained the last of his tea. "I'm going to try and get some sleep. You?"

She shook her head—as he'd known she would. "I'll read down here for a bit."

Luke knew she wouldn't. She would curl up in the brown leather armchair and cry. Racking sobs that tore into him and made him hurt with an intensity he hadn't imagined existed.

And there was nothing he could do. Not for Eleanor. Not for Susanna. He set his mug down on the worktop. "I'll leave the landing light on."

"Thanks."

It was easier to pretend. He watched her turn and carefully place her empty mug in the dishwasher, then his own, and knew she didn't want him to see her face. She'd shut him out.

She always shut him out. Her grief was so overwhelming…so all encompassing. She made him feel guilty when he came home and he hadn't thought about Eleanor for several hours.

There were moments in his working day when he could forget the lead weight settled in his heart. It wasn't like that for Susanna. Whole swathes of her time were spent at the hospital and when she was prized away her mind was still there.

Some days, God help him, it took everything he had not to stay in the car and keep driving. He felt trapped. Angry.

For the first time in his life there was nothing he could do that would change things. He could work on raising the profile of organ donation, but it felt like he was chipping away at a mountain.

It changed very little.

He paused at the doorway, wanting to say something that would help her.

"Eleanor's a determined little thing—"

"She's dying."

He felt like she'd slapped him. "I know."

Susanna turned away, her blond hair dull and lifeless. The soft highlights that had streaked her hair when they'd gotten married had grown out and her layers were overlong.

It was months of not caring. So different from the bright, vivacious woman he'd married.

Not that he'd had much choice. Five months pregnant with his child, he'd felt it was the only thing he could do.

Twenty-six years old, midway through a law degree, Susanna had told him the news. She was pregnant and she was keeping the baby.

His baby.

Her brown eyes had been completely fearless, but he'd known she couldn't have been feeling like that. Both her parents had died, an only child...

There'd been no choice. He'd taken a deep breath and asked her to marry him. And then she'd smiled. It had started in her eyes and spread out from there. Her face had lit up as though a light had switched on inside her...and he'd felt great.

It wasn't what he'd planned. He hadn't felt ready for marriage or children. But making a final commitment was always going to be difficult and, he'd told himself, it might even be better this way.

He hadn't understood what he was doing.

"Go to bed, Luke. I'll be fine." She wrapped her arms about her body. "You need to get some sleep if you're going to work tomorrow."

"What about you?"

Her face twisted. "I'll survive."

CHAPTER THREE

EVEN IF Luke hadn't been called into the hospital, Susanna would have known it was bad news when Dr. Rosemary Lane shut the door of her office. Susanna glanced across at her husband, glad he was with her if only because it meant she wouldn't have to tell him what had been said.

He stood with his hands in the pockets of his jeans, a small muscle pulsing in his cheek. It was the only sign he gave of any sort of inner turmoil.

It angered her that he could remain so calm. It made her feel so alone. Her mind was pulsing with fear at what the head of the liver transplant unit might be about to tell them, but when she looked at Luke, she saw...nothing. Just that tiny muscle clench and unclench.

"Eleanor is an incredible little girl," Professor Lane said as she sat down. "Mr Burnett...Luke, would you like to take a seat?"

Reluctantly, he sat where she indicated. Susanna tried her best to swallow the hard lump that had settled in her throat as she waited for what would come next.

"Eleanor's a real fighter..."

Susanna heard the scrape of Luke's chair as he pushed it backward, the sound of feet in the corridor outside.

"But...I'm afraid she's also one of the sickest children we've seen in the unit for a very long time." Dr. Lane looked from one parent to the other. "The infection she caught two weeks ago has led to a dramatic deterioration in her condition and I think—" she paused again, her voice kind "—I think we're at the stage where we must now consider using a liver from a different blood type."

Susanna nodded because she knew it was expected. Her eyes fixed on the other woman's as though they were a lifeline.

"Is that possible?" Luke asked beside her.

Dr. Lane turned to look at him. "It's possible, but not ideal. As you know, Eleanor's rare AB blood type is only found in approximately two percent of the population and she is running out of time. If successful, a transplant now, albeit using a less-than-perfect match, will keep her alive until a more suitable donor can be found."

The words were stark in their simplicity. Susanna felt the explosion in her head, the panic and the screaming fear.

Each time, every time, she'd thought she'd heard the worst. It was like facing the sea, with wave after wave crashing down upon her. Unstoppable.

Luke cleared his throat. "There doesn't seem to be any choice."

"Very little," Professor Lane agreed. "We need a donor very quickly. Eleanor is struggling to stay alive. Every day we wait is a risk."

"What are the chances of one being found in time?"

Susanna sat in numbed shock. All she'd really heard was the fact that her baby was running out of time. She'd known that, but hearing the words sent ice coursing through her veins. Then she felt the pain. Long fingers gripping her heart and squeezing tight until she thought it would have to stop beating.

A shadow passed over Dr. Lane's face. "Parents whose children have just died are naturally reluctant to donate the organs of their loved ones and it's difficult for health professionals to approach them."

"So, it's not likely?" Luke's voice sounded overloud in the quiet confines of the small office space.

Susanna glanced across at him, but Professor Lane answered calmly, "We have to hope that there are some very special people out there who can use their own tragedy to save Eleanor."

Luke sat back in his chair and raised a hand to shield his eyes.

"Would you like a cup of tea? A moment together to discuss what I've told you?" A moment together? Susanna didn't know how to answer that. How did other parents manage in a situation like this? Did they cling to each other, united in their grief?

Their marriage wasn't like that. Had never been like that. She didn't even know how Luke was really feeling. They didn't talk about things like that. Their conversations were entirely practical. If she cried he turned away.

What would it be like now to have Luke hold her? Loving and supportive? Her throat was sore with the effort of not crying, her eyes were smarting and her head ached…and she couldn't tell him how she was feeling.

Couldn't tell him because he didn't seem to care. Or didn't want to care.

Luke let his hand fall. "We've got to go to the papers. If the story gets taken up by the nationals there's a small chance it will hit someone's doormat at the right time and they'll act with their hearts. Susanna?"

Her mind seemed like it was full of fog. She couldn't think quickly. Didn't really understand what he was talking about.

"A nationwide appeal would certainly be helpful," Professor Lane said, standing up. "I'll leave you alone to discuss it. Perhaps, you'd like to take a walk together outside in the sunshine? We've a couple of tests we need to run on Eleanor in the next few minutes."

Her shoes clicked against the hospital floor and the door shut with a quiet thud.

"Susanna?"

She turned to look at him, her eyes blind with grief.

"I need to call the local paper now. They need to do the story straightaway."

His words shot at her like bullets from a gun. There was no escape. She nodded.

"Did you hear what I said? We need to do the story now."

Susanna stood up and brushed a hand across her eyes. "Whatever."

Her arms felt heavy and her legs no longer seemed to want to take her weight. She just wanted the night to close in on her so she could shut all of this out. Every hateful moment. The pain was too much. Far, far too much.

Luke caught her as her body swayed, his hands holding her arms and forcing her to look at him. "Susanna, we can do this. *Eleanor* can do this. Don't give up on her now."

His eyes were bright blue, startling against the dark brown of his hair—and strong.

Why could he do this and she couldn't?

She felt like a shaken rag doll, so punch-drunk she could scarcely stand. Susanna felt the first tear fall, hot against her cheek. "I'm scared," she whispered.

His right hand slid up her arm and gently held her face, his thumb stroking away the trail of moisture. "I'm scared, too."

His admission surprised her, as did the warm feeling of his fingers against her skin. Susanna ached to curl in against him. Have his strength wrap itself around her. She wanted so much to believe Luke would one day love her. That their marriage might become something beautiful.

"E-Eleanor might die."

"I know." She heard the tremor in his voice and then felt his arms close around her. Her heart hammered against her chest. Nothing had changed. She still wanted him. Loved him. "Eleanor hasn't lost yet." His fingers threaded through her hair and his hand cradled her head.

He hadn't held her for so long. She closed her eyes and let her body relax against his. She'd almost forgotten how wonderful this felt.

The subtle scent of a masculine body spray mingled with

something that was entirely Luke. The steady beat of his heart beneath her fingers as they rested against his chest. It felt like she was standing in the eye of the storm. Right here, right now, she was at peace.

It was a dangerous feeling. He made her feel cared for, loved even—but she knew it had no basis in reality. Luke was a good man, a passionate man, a man who would have loved her if he could.

She had to remember that the only reason he was with her was because of Eleanor. And if their daughter died…he would leave her.

CHAPTER FOUR

SUSANNA made herself pull away from the comfort of being held by Luke. It would have been easy to let herself rest against his chest, to feel his arms around her and imagine he really wanted to hold her.

But, it was an illusion. She knew she'd trapped Luke into this marriage. She hadn't meant to. Her pregnancy had been a shock—even the night Eleanor had been created had been a surprise.

She'd loved him for so long…and when he'd kissed her she'd been lost. No part of her mind had thought of anything but how it felt to have his lips on hers, his hands moving over her body.

It might have been a sin, it was certainly wrong, but she'd wanted him…whatever the consequences.

Eleanor was that consequence. And because he was a fantastic man he stayed. She wasn't a fool. She knew she was his second best. Not the woman he would have chosen.

And if Eleanor died…he would be free. Had he thought of

that? Susanna turned and brushed away the tears on her face. "I'm sorry. I shouldn't have done that."

"I don't know why!"

"I need to be strong for Eleanor."

She heard the soft expletive he muttered under his breath. "You are strong for her. You're bloody amazing."

He stretched out his hand and she couldn't do anything but hold out her own. His fingers threaded through hers, so dark against the paleness of her skin.

"Let's make the call to the newspaper. It might not work, but at least we'll know we tried everything we could."

There was no choice. Eleanor's life hung in the balance. "Okay."

"We need to go outside. I can't use the cell phone from here."

Susanna nodded.

He led her out of the office, along the corridors painted in soothing pink and out into a bright May morning. Cocooned inside the hospital walls she'd almost forgotten there was a world outside.

Luke let go of her hand and Susanna sat on the nearest bench. Somewhere on the third floor medical staff was seeing to her baby, replacing tubes and giving her injections they didn't want her to see.

She watched Luke take his cell phone and a crumpled piece of paper from his pocket, and then key in the number he had written down. Even hearing just the one side of the conversation, she understood it all.

Luke's crisp voice explained Eleanor's condition. He talked about timescales and locations. He gave directions to the ward Eleanor was on and agreed to meet a man called Brian in the reception area at three o'clock.

As he ended the call, he glanced across at her. "It's settled."

Susanna nodded, and knotted her hands together in her lap.

"They're coming today. This afternoon."

Again she nodded.

"Brian Hartman and a woman called Veronica Lewis. She's the photographer." Susanna felt the tears well up behind her eyes and bit down hard on her lip.

She'd seen articles like this many times over the years. She'd looked at the pictures of desperately ill children and anguished washed-out women and felt an abstract kind of sympathy. She'd never taken the time to imagine the heartache behind the pictures.

And now she was to be the anguished washed-out woman—and Eleanor the child.

Luke sat down beside her. His eyes fixed on her profile. "Do you want to get a coffee?"

"No."

He glanced down at his wristwatch. "We ought to give them a few more minutes with Eleanor before we go back up."

Susanna nodded and then turned to look at him. "Do you think she's going to die?"

She saw the sudden movement of his throat and watched his eyes skit away. "Luke?" she prompted.

He turned back to look at her. "I don't know."

"Perhaps, we ought to ring your parents? Ask them to come to the hospital?"

Luke shook his head. "I've telephoned them. They know what's going on…but she's our little girl. She needs us."

Us. Susanna let the word swirl about her mind. Luke had married her because he believed their child needed a mother and a father.

She'd married him because she'd needed *him*. "Do you remember the day I told you I was expecting Eleanor?"

"I remember." His eyes scanned the sky.

"What did you really think? Honestly?"

Think? He turned back to look at her, trying to understand the question. Think? He wasn't sure he knew what he'd thought.

She was pregnant…and it was his baby.

Susanna leaned over and picked a single stem of lavender.

"I nearly didn't tell you. It didn't seem right, though. To just have your baby and not tell you anything about it."

God, no. He swallowed painfully. "What made you change your mind?"

"Arlene Peacock. Do you remember her?"

He nodded.

"She used to help out at the post office on Tuesdays. I felt sick one day and she got me a glass of water. She guessed…"

Luke frowned with the effort of trying to understand where his wife was going with this. Her eyes were fixed on a small spot in the distance, her mind far away.

"Not about you." She glanced across at him, a wavering smile touching her lips. "Just about the baby. She asked me if I'd told the father."

"And you hadn't?"

Susanna shook her head, her fingers picking at the lavender. "Would you have preferred not to know?"

"Of course not." Or would he? Sometimes, during the past few months he'd thought about what it might have been like if Eleanor hadn't been born. If Susanna hadn't cried that night, when their daughter was conceived…

She seemed to read his mind. "I shouldn't have married you." Her eyes turned back to look at the shredded lavender stalk. "I always knew you didn't love me." And he couldn't speak. His mind, usually so sharp, couldn't think of one single intelligent thing to say.

"I was wrong to do that to you."

Luke swallowed hard. "We made the baby together."

"Yes, but I knew I wasn't taking any precautions."

"So did I."

She shook her head, but then she said, "I was so glad not to have to do the whole baby thing on my own. When you asked me to marry you, I just said yes. I shouldn't have done that."

"Susanna—"

"No, let me finish." She threw the shorn lavender stalk on

the ground and plucked at another. "Whatever happens now with Eleanor…" Her voice wavered. "Let's stop pretending. We made a great little girl, and we love her…"

Luke couldn't bear to hear any more. He watched the trembling of her lips and the shimmer that covered her eyes. "This isn't the time—"

"I know. I just wanted you to know…well, for you to know that I know you don't love me."

And Luke felt like he'd been punched in the solar plexus. Hard—with a fist as solid as a cannonball.

CHAPTER FIVE

LUKE WANTED to find words to reassure Susanna. In an ideal world he would have put his arm around her and told her to stop talking nonsense. Told her that, of course, he loved her. That their marriage wasn't a mistake.

But …

She wanted him to know that she knew. Simple. Dignified. Just as Susanna always was.

She smiled, her eyes honest and brave. "We'd better go back in. Are you coming?"

He swallowed. "I-In a moment."

For a second he thought she was going to say something else, but she nodded and turned away.

His wife.

His.

The woman who said she knew he'd never loved her.

Luke's eyes clouded over as he thought about that. He'd been married to Susanna for fifteen months and he'd never known she'd nearly not told him about Eleanor.

He didn't even know why she'd decided to sleep with him that night. The need to be close to someone? Anyone?

He didn't know.

How was it possible you could share your life with someone and know so little about them? Why hadn't he asked those questions?

He'd blithely assumed this was his life. He'd resented it, but he'd never really questioned it. And, there'd seemed to be so much time.

Luke glanced up at the third story window where Susanna and Eleanor were. It was all changing now.

Eleanor was dying, and Susanna...

What?

Susanna had chosen the difficult path. She always did.

She'd chosen to keep their baby when many other women would have terminated the pregnancy without anyone knowing. She'd brought Eleanor home and given her five special weeks. She'd shelved the final year of her degree to care for their baby.

She'd told him she knew he didn't love her...

Who *was* she, this woman he'd married?

Luke stood up and twisted the wedding ring on the third finger of his left hand. There was so much he wanted to know.

How did she feel about him?

In the beginning there'd been moments when he'd wondered if she loved him. If she had, he'd done nothing to foster it.

And suddenly it mattered. He had to know what he'd thrown away so carelessly.

Veronica Lewis, the photographer, knew what she was doing. She waited until Eleanor was sleeping and positioned the small pink teddy bear so its face peaked out of the hospital blanket.

"Mrs Bennett, if you would look down at Eleanor. Perhaps, rest your chin on your hands?"

Susanna leaned forward on the hospital chair and overlapped her hands. It was all so orchestrated and artificial. Luke hated it.

"Can you think about how Eleanor might be feeling now?"

He wanted to shove the photographer aside for such a crass remark. He watched the flicker of pain pass over Susanna's face as she schooled her features to give what was wanted.

Her chin rested next to the narrow wedding band he'd given her. No engagement ring. There hadn't been time.

And he hadn't thought.

Had she wanted one? Had she dreamed of a large white wedding with a four-piece band?

"That's beautiful. Thank you." Veronica Lewis straightened and looked across at her colleague. "I have everything I need."

Brian Hartman nodded and smiled at Luke. "That's it. We'll try and get the pictures in the paper this weekend."

"Thank you."

"No guarantees, of course, but a human interest story… anything we can do to help," he said, stretching out his hand.

Luke went through the motions. Out of the corner of his eye he watched Susanna stand up, her fingers stroking lightly across Eleanor's bare chest. Almost an apology.

He saw the dark smudges beneath his wife's eyes, the exhaustion that hung about her frame.

Veronica packed away her camera and turned to Susanna. "I hope your little girl pulls through."

Susanna's smile wavered, the tears she'd kept back until then slowly formed in her eyes and softly tumbled over.

Luke moved. His hand snaked around her waist and he held her tight against his body.

"I'm sorry," she murmured, her voice muffled.

"You did great." He felt her shudder and heard the first heartrending sob. Luke gathered her closer.

He saw Veronica wave a hand in goodbye, but he kept his arms tightly around his wife. There was nothing more important than this.

Her fingers clutched at his shirt and her tears wet the thin cotton fabric. There was nothing he could do but hold her.

Every sob, every heartrending gulp, tore into him. He felt so helpless, so…impotent…to do anything. His hand moved through her hair feeling the long blond silkiness and he closed his eyes and prayed. He hadn't prayed since he was a child, but everything seemed so overwhelming.

Gradually, her sobs quietened and she stood exhausted in the circle of his arms. Her cheek lay warm against his chest and he felt how right it was she should be there.

It had always felt right. The first time, in his parents' home…

An amazing, sexy night. Beyond anything he'd ever experienced before. It had felt…cosmic. As though the heavens had shifted and, suddenly, everything was right in his world.

Luke rested his chin on the top of her head. What would it have been like if he hadn't left for New York the weekend after? If he'd rung her up and they'd gone out to dinner? Talked?

What if…

Her body felt warm and soft. He let his fingers move across her back, hoping that she would understand what he was trying to convey, even though he wasn't sure of what it was himself.

Susanna sighed and then pulled away, her fingers wiping at her eyes. "I'm sorry to cry all over you."

"It's been a long time since you have." Her eyes flicked up to his and back to Eleanor. Luke moved closer, his hand resting lightly on Eleanor's crib. "Why?"

"Why what?"

"Why did you stop crying in front of me?"

Susanna looked up, her eyes enormous in her white face. "It was all I was doing." It wasn't the real answer—and she knew it.

Luke reached down and stroked the top of Eleanor's head. "I love her, too."

She didn't doubt that. Had never doubted it. "I know that."

"Then why, Susanna? Why couldn't we have cried together?"

She looked up into his face. Luke's eyes were a murky blue, like a troubled sea. He really didn't know.

That seemed unbelievable to her. There were so many reasons, but, perhaps, the main one was the shuttered look on his face when he walked through the front door. A masklike control.

And she'd never felt so lonely. She'd poured over photographs of Eleanor and ached for her little girl. She'd suffered with each and every operation her daughter had undergone.

If Luke had loved her, perhaps, they'd have drawn closer. Instead, she'd been alone. Isolated.

"We began wrong," she said gently, aware of the nurse sitting quietly in the corner.

CHAPTER SIX

SUSANNA saw the whiplash effect her words had. She hadn't meant to hurt him. Luke must have known they'd begun badly.

He must have felt it.

The nurse stood up and checked the monitors. She paused and smiled. "Eleanor is very peaceful. Why don't you take the opportunity to get something to eat?" Susanna couldn't imagine eating. Everything tasted like cardboard these days. She glanced down at Eleanor's sleeping face.

"If she needs us we can be fetched," Luke said quietly.

Susanna looked from Eleanor to Luke and then back to the nurse. Annie's solid good sense radiated from every pore—and Eleanor liked her.

"I'll be here all the time," Annie said. "And your husband's right. I'll have you called if there's the slightest change."

Reluctantly, Susanna nodded. "I'll be in The Swannery." The sandwich shop was a great alternative to the main cafeteria, as it was a lot quieter.

Vaguely, she was aware of Luke behind her. She went to the locker and pulled out her handbag. She turned to face him.

"It's probably a good idea to get some food. It's going to be a long night."

He nodded.

Susanna knew her way to The Swannery blindfolded. She'd spent so many hours there over the past year. It was bright and clean, with emerald green trelliswork trying to give the impression you'd stumbled into a bistro.

"What do you mean 'began wrong'?" Luke asked as soon as they were out in the corridor.

Susanna kept her eyes focused on the double doors ahead. "I'm not a fool. I know how much you gave up for Eleanor."

"I've never said that."

"No." He hadn't. Perhaps, it would have been better if he had.

He'd been twenty-six. The world had been opening up before him. Luke could have done anything. Gone anywhere. Instead, he'd tied himself to a woman he didn't love for the sake of his baby.

It had taken her a while to understand that. She'd wanted to believe the fairytale. Most of her still did.

"But you can't *pretend* you married me because you wanted to be with me...can you?"

She saw his eyes flick away and then back again. He couldn't say that. Susanna strode on through the double doors and paused at the elevator. She reached inside her handbag and rummaged inside for a pack of tissues.

"Why did you sleep with me that night?" Luke asked abruptly.

The elevator doors opened and Susanna stumbled inside. To answer that question was to bare her soul. She'd slept with him because it was everything she'd ever wanted.

She looked up at him. It had been like being transported from the slums of Calcutta to Buckingham Palace. "I don't know."

"I don't believe you."

The lift doors closed. Susanna stepped forward and pushed the ground floor button. The lift shuddered and started its decent.

Luke laid a hand on her arm. "Susanna, I need to know."

Perhaps, he did. They'd gone from being almost friends...to being lovers...to being parents far too quickly. And Eleanor was his child, too.

"It just happened," she said huskily. Her fingers trembled as she searched for the string that would open the packet.

"That's no answer. I don't even know why you were at my parents' house."

"I was their cleaner. It was my part-time job."

Luke shook his head. "Not at nine o'clock at night. Susanna?"

His blue eyes seemed to bore into her soul. Everything he said was true. She shouldn't have been there so late. In fact, she shouldn't have been there at all. Marilyn and Robert had flown to Barcelona for a week's holiday. The house had been left spotless.

But she'd had a key, and Marilyn had told her to use the house as her own. Susanna pulled out a tissue and fiercely blew her nose.

That night she'd really wanted to escape the well-meaning sympathy of friends. It had seemed like such a good idea. If she'd known Luke was going to be there she wouldn't have gone.

Or would she?

"The telephone kept ringing at home. Really nice people wanting to say really nice things about Dad...but I'd got tired of hearing them."

"So you went to escape?"

Susanna nodded. "Your mum said I could. If it all got too much. My aunt had gone back home that morning. She'd stayed for a couple of days after Dad's funeral..."

"I remember. You said."

Susanna pushed the door of The Swannery open. "I really missed her when she left. I hadn't realised quite how much she'd been shielding me."

"So you went to my parents' house." Luke picked up a tray.

She glanced across at him, then back at the counter. "Then you came home." Luke knew that part of the story. He'd opened the front door and had heard a noise. His first thought had been that he'd disturbed burglars.

Only it hadn't been. It had been a beautiful blonde. She'd been dressed in jeans and an oversized sweater that kept slipping off her shoulder. It had been classic student dress, but he'd found it amazingly sexy.

He remembered that.

She'd seemed almost as shocked as he was when he'd walked in, but he'd persuaded her to stay. He'd opened a bottle of wine and they'd sat and talked. Endlessly. She'd told him about her law degree, her ambition to become a lawyer and her failed French 'A' Level. He knew her favorite flowers were lilies of the valley and she'd told him why. It had been the only flower her mother had let her pick in the garden as a child.

He'd forgotten that.

It had been a wonderful evening. He hadn't wanted it to end. When she'd looked at her watch and suggested she ought to leave he'd persuaded her to stay the night. There were plenty of bedrooms…and he'd opened another bottle of wine.

"I just want a coffee," Susanna said at his elbow.

He looked down at her, and for the first time in months he saw the woman he'd met that night. "I'll bring it over. Do you want to pick somewhere to sit?"

She nodded. Luke watched her walk across to a table by the window. She put her handbag on the floor and leant forward with her head in her hands, elbows on the table.

This couldn't be the life she'd planned for herself. He felt like he'd been struck over the head with a bat. He'd been so focused on doing the right thing, on how he was feeling…he'd scarcely thought about Susanna.

About how much she'd given up.

He put two coffees on the tray and selected two plastic wrapped sandwiches—one ham, one cheese—and then he lined up to pay.

Luke caught sight of Susanna as she ran her fingers through her hair and fixed unseeing eyes on the view outside.

He'd never asked her how she'd felt when she first discovered she was pregnant. By the time she told him he was going to be a father, all the important decisions had been taken.

The consequences of deciding to keep her baby had been as far-reaching for her as him. Her law degree had been abandoned; all her hopes of being a barrister had been put aside.

And she'd done it freely. It made him feel ashamed at how much he'd resented the changes in his own life.

Luke set the tray down on the table and waited until Susanna looked up. He sat in the chair opposite. "Now tell me why you slept with me?"

CHAPTER SEVEN

LUKE'S choice of words jarred. He wanted to know why she'd *slept* with him. Susanna would never have described it like that. As far as she'd been concerned, she'd made love. With every fiber of her being. It had been like coming home.

Susanna reached out and tore open a sachet of Demerara sugar. She watched as the brown crystals sank into her coffee and then she picked up her spoon.

"Susanna?" Luke prompted.

She looked up at him. His eyes were fixed on her face. There was obviously going to be no escape. Slowly, she stirred the dark liquid. "Do you remember the summer you came home for your parents' silver wedding?"

"Y-yes. No." He looked confused. "What's that got to do with anything?"

With meticulous care she laid the spoon on the tray. "I was

fourteen. My mum was ill by then, but she managed to come to the garden party. We were all there."

He nodded.

"You'd come back from university specially."

"I remember."

Susanna smiled. It had been a beautiful day and the Burnett's garden was a stunning place to spend a summer afternoon.

"I watched you play tennis. You won."

Luke pulled his coffee nearer. "I don't understand…"

"No. Well." She reached out and picked up the cheese sandwich. Without thinking she pulled back the plastic cover. "You were with some girl who had long red hair."

"Kim Grantham."

Susanna looked up. "Was it? I never knew her name. She was the most glamorous person I'd ever seen." She paused while she took a bite of her sandwich. "And I thought you were gorgeous. I spent months imagining what it would be like to be her."

"And that's why you slept with me?"

Susanna hesitated. To say "yes" would be the easy answer. End of interrogation and they could go on as before. It wouldn't be the truth, though. The silver wedding party had been the beginning.

She'd been fourteen and he'd been twenty. She'd not been in love with him then—but it was the first time she'd noticed him. He'd seemed almost godlike. Perfect.

She hesitated. "Not exactly. Why is this so important?"

Luke picked up the ham sandwich. "Because I don't know the answer."

"It doesn't matter."

"It does to me."

Susanna let a beat of silence pass and then she asked, "Why did you…make love to me?" She chose her words carefully, but Luke didn't seem to notice. His long fingers pulled back the cover on his sandwich and he took it out of the wrapper.

"Because you cried." And then, "I think. I think that's why it happened."

It wasn't the answer she'd been expecting. "Because I cried?"

"I think so."

Not because he'd wanted to. Not because he'd been overcome by passion. Just because she'd cried.

Because he'd felt sorry for her. His words twisted a knife inside her.

Susanna felt angry with herself. Even now, after all the heartache, she still allowed herself to hope. There'd been a tiny chink of…something that made her dream of a different answer.

It was time for all this to be over. Past time. She placed her half-eaten sandwich back in the plastic triangle it had come in and pushed it away.

Luke put his own sandwich down. "So you fancied me at fourteen? What happened then?"

Susanna looked up and met his eyes for a moment. She saw in them a confusion that didn't match his voice or the words he was using.

Her fingers played with the rim of her mug. This was the moment of no return. If she told him she'd fallen in love with him at her eighteenth birthday party, dreamed about him every night since, she could never unsay the words.

He would know. Always.

But did that matter now? She'd already decided that whatever happened their marriage needed to end. For both of them.

There was something about telling him Eleanor had been made out of her love for him that really appealed to her. A child *should* be made out of love.

"When I was eighteen…" I fell in love with you. She even remembered the moment. The exact second when she'd looked across the room at him and known she'd never feel like that about anyone ever again.

Luke frowned. "Your birthday?"

"I had a party. Your mum had arranged it because my

mum had died by then, and she wanted to look out for her friend's daughter."

He nodded. "You were home for the Christmas holidays."

In his face she saw the first trace of real understanding. As though he remembered the mistletoe.

"I kissed you."

Susanna kept looking at him. She watched his eyes. They seemed to change color, from gray to blue. In the end it was easy to say the words. They'd been locked up inside her for so long it was almost a relief. "I fell in love with you then." His mouth moved, but he didn't say anything.

"It was as simple as walking from one room to another. One moment I was suffering an adolescent passion and the next…well, the next I knew I was in love. That I'd met the man I wanted to be with."

Luke brushed a hand through his hair. In some distant recess of her mind, Susanna felt sorry for him. He'd obviously had no idea. He'd started this conversation with no inkling of what she'd say.

"The trouble was, you didn't feel like that."

"I—"

"Don't." Susanna stopped him. She didn't want him to feel bad. It wasn't his fault he couldn't love her. "That night…the first night…I slept with you because I loved you."

She saw the flush hit his cheekbones, the uncertainty in his eyes. "It doesn't matter. Not now. Whatever happens with Eleanor…if she lives or…" She couldn't bring herself to say the words. "Whatever happens now, it doesn't matter. Eleanor will always be your little girl. Our baby. Always."

Susanna reached out and took hold of his hand across the table. His fingers closed around hers. "That's why I said, it's time this all stopped. You tried. Really, really hard."

"No. I—"

"I shouldn't have let you marry me. I always knew you

didn't love me. You're a kind, passionate, wonderful man…but it's not enough. I want more. Whatever happens, I think we should get a divorce."

Luke's hand gripped hers. "Susanna, I—"

"You're unhappy…and so am I." Gently, she disengaged his fingers. "I ought to go back up and check on Eleanor. I don't like to think of her on her own."

Luke sat as though a tranquilizer gun had hit him. The mother of his child had just told him she loved and wanted a divorce in the same breath. He knew he nodded and he saw her leave. She glanced back at him once, just as she pushed open the double doors.

He didn't understand how he felt. He didn't understand anything. Susanna had slept with him because she loved him.

All those vague suspicions crystallized into something tangible and real. Susanna loved him. *Had* loved him.

And she wanted a divorce.

His daughter was dying and his wife wanted a divorce.

CHAPTER EIGHT

TWENTY-FOUR HOURS and Luke hadn't been able to see Susanna alone. She'd said she loved him—once—and he hadn't seen her alone since to talk about it.

Or about anything.

Luke spread the newspaper out on the white plastic table in the waiting room. They'd made the nationals. Just as they'd hoped. There was his little girl, her life slipping away.

And his wife…gazing at Eleanor with such love in her eyes. The softness in her face made her look incandescently beautiful. Luke reached out and traced Susanna's cheekbone, the shape of her jaw.

He was about to lose them both. One because she wasn't well enough to live…and the other through carelessness. There'd been a time when Susanna had looked at him that way. With love. He wanted that back.

The photograph was haunting. There was Eleanor. His daughter. Eyes tightly shut. Tubes everywhere. The pink teddy bear his parents had bought…

He swallowed painfully. And Susanna. Bone weary and emotionally drained. Her eyes focused on the precious life they'd created together…because she'd loved him.

Memories of that night streamed through him. She'd said "they'd begun wrong," but that wasn't true. They'd begun *right*.

It was just he hadn't recognized how right it was. He'd been young and selfish, fixated on the opportunities New York would bring him. He hadn't seen how precious the pearl he was leaving behind was.

Susanna had always been there. So close, he'd not noticed her. Six years younger than him, but so much more mature.

He'd told her he'd slept with her because she'd cried, but that wasn't true. He'd made love to her because he hadn't been able to do anything else. When she'd cried it had seemed the most natural thing in the world to hold her. And when he was holding her it had been the most natural thing to kiss her. And when he'd kissed her…

It still felt natural. Every time he was with her, every time he touched her, something deep inside him responded to her.

Because he loved her.

How could he have missed that? Images passed through his mind. He saw Susanna standing before him telling him she was expecting his child. He saw her laughing at a joke, sun streaming through her hair. He saw her eyes clouded with passion. For him.

"Luke?"

He turned to look at Susanna. Her hand was splayed out on the waiting-room door, her face tired but calm.

"Dr. Lane wants to see us."

She looked so beautiful that he was almost too frightened to speak to her.

"Now?"

She nodded. "I don't know why." She raised a hand and brushed away a tear. He wanted to hold her. To tell her he loved her. That she was the woman he wanted to walk through the rest of his life with—whatever trials and tribulations it might bring.

Luke stood up and stared at her as though he was seeing her for the first time. He wanted to be there for all her good times. Comfort her in the bad. He wanted to help her scale every mountain and stand looking at the view together. He wanted to see her get her law degree. Become a lawyer. Have other children, maybe.

Tears swelled behind his eyes. He'd never wanted anything so fiercely as Susanna in his life. He'd been such a fool. He'd taken her love and screwed it under his foot. And now she wanted to walk away. She wanted a divorce.

She was bright and beautiful, honest and caring. In many ways she deserved a new start with someone better than him…but he loved her and without her he'd be nothing.

Luke felt the first tear drop down his face. It burned across his cheek like acid.

"Luke?" Susanna moved forward, her face full of concern. Her hand reached out, then hesitated, not quite touching him. That killed him. She didn't feel she had the right to touch him.

Dear God.

Luke reached for her and he hid his face against her hair. It smelled of vanilla and summertime. His body throbbed with pain. He felt like he'd only just come alive.

Susanna's arms held him tightly. "It might not be bad news," she said softly. "There's been no change in Eleanor."

Every sense he had was screaming out with a desire to keep this woman close. To have, and to hold, for as long as they both should live.

And he didn't know where to begin.

He didn't know how to find the words to tell Susanna he loved her. How did he start to heal the pain he'd caused her? How could he make her believe in them? Luke pulled back and moved to hold her face between his hands. He stared down at her. "I love you."

He saw the confusion hit her brown eyes. Perhaps, he should have led in more gently, perhaps…

But they were the words of his heart and they spilled out. He forced her to keep looking at him, his blue eyes pleading for her to understand and see what was deep within him.

"Luke, you don't—"

"I love you," he repeated, his voice stronger. "I don't want you to leave me. Or divorce me."

Susanna's eyes took on a new vulnerability. "Eleanor will always be your daughter…whatever happens between us," she whispered.

He nodded and let go of her face. "I know that." He reached out for her hand and held it gently between his own. His thumb moved against her palm. "You know the moment you looked at me and knew you loved me?"

She nodded, her hand still in his.

Luke swallowed. "I just had that moment. Susanna…" He searched for the words. "Susanna, I want to do all the things I should have done before. I want to take you to dinner. I want to sit up late talking. I want to know every thought in your head. I want to fill our garden with lilies of the valley so our children and grandchildren can pick them." His voice deepened. "I want to go to sleep every night knowing you're going to be beside me when I wake."

Susanna felt the first whisper of hope.

Slowly, so slowly, giving her every opportunity to pull away, Luke kissed her. His lips touched hers. Hesitantly, like a first kiss. Then, as he felt her hand twitch, he pulled back to look in her eyes.

"I love you."

"You love me?" she whispered brokenly.

His mouth twisted into a wry smile. "I left it a bit late to tell you."

Susanna stared up into his face. "A little."

"I'm sorry."

It was all there in his blue eyes. All the love she'd dreamed of seeing there—one day. She reached up and stroked the side of his face. The man she loved. Had always loved. The moment felt surreal.

"I love you, too."

Luke pulled her in close; so close she could feel the beat of his heart. His arms locked about her as though he would never let her go and Susanna felt the fear recede.

With Luke beside her she could do anything. Cope with anything. "We need to go," she said softly.

The door banged open and one of the nurses from the night shift rushed in. "There's been a phone call from London. They have a near perfect match for Eleanor."

Susanna turned within Luke's arms to look at her. "A liver?"

She nodded, her eyes glowing. "It's on its way. Dr. Lane has just called in a team of three surgeons. She needs to speak to you."

"We're coming," Luke said behind her. The young nurse nodded and left.

For a moment Susanna was too scared to believe what she'd heard, then relief started to flood through her. She knew there were no guarantees. That it would be a long seven- or eight-hour operation, followed by an agonizing wait to see if the organ had taken.

"Eleanor's got a chance," she said brokenly.

Luke smiled. The kind of smile that made her heart feel like it would burst from happiness. "A good one."

He laced his fingers between hers and led her out through the doors, toward their daughter.

* * * * *

A FOOL FOR LOVE
Susan Mallery

Susan Mallery is the *New York Times* bestselling author of over one hundred romances and she has yet to run out of ideas. She has written series romances, as well as single titles, historicals, contemporaries and even a lone time travel. Always reader favourites, her books have appeared on Walden's bestseller list, along with the *USA Today* bestseller list and, of course, the *New York Times* list. She has won awards for everything from "best single title contemporary," to best "Special Edition of the year," and recently she took home the prestigious National Reader's Choice Award. As her dgree in accounting was not very helpful in the writing department, Susan earned a Master's in Writing Popular Fiction.

Susan makes her home in the Pacific Northwest where, rumour has it, all that rain helps with creativity. Susan is married to a fabulous, hero-like husband and has a six-pound toy poodle, who is possibly the cutest dog on the planet.

Susan says...

"I've always believed the true measure of a people is who we love and who loves us. My characters are looking to belong. Along the way, they fall in love, which is pretty fun."

Susan's gorgeous, sexy, emotional romance, *Sizzling*, will be out in March 2010 from M&B™!

A FOOL FOR LOVE

"AND the last bachelor up for bids is…"

Alex tuned out the auctioneer's voice and wondered for the millionth time how he'd gotten roped into this. A bachelor auction was definitely not his style—even on Valentine's Day. But, he reminded himself, this was for a good cause.

Tugging at the collar of his uniform, he shifted uneasily as the auctioneer continued his sales pitch. Should he smile? Pose? He just didn't feel comfortable up on stage with a blinding spotlight shining on him. He hoped he didn't look as nervous as he felt.

The auctioneer was driving up the bids—but all Alex could hear was the roar of the crowd as women yelled out numbers and cheered each other on. Squinting into the lights, he tried to make out who was bidding on him, but to no avail.

Then, before he knew it, the gavel sounded. He'd been sold! But to whom…?

He'd given Deena specific instructions to outbid anyone

else, but with the Parker deal about to reach critical mass, she could have been on the cell phone arranging a last meeting. His efficient assistant might be capable of keeping his chaotic business affairs in order, but even she couldn't arrange his schedule and bid at the same time.

"Congratulations," the auctioneer said with a grin. "You went for the most money. Things got pretty heated there at the end." The older man glanced at Alex's dark blue jacket. "Women have a thing for men in uniform."

Alex didn't want to think about the scratchy nineteenth-century British naval officer costume he'd been forced to wear. A bachelor auction hadn't been enough for the charity organizers. Instead they'd offered a chance to bid on "Military Men through Time." He consoled himself with the thought that a heavy jacket and too-tight pants were far better than the toga he'd seen one poor guy in earlier.

Alex stepped off the stage and into the crowd of women. He ignored them as he searched for a petite redhead with a cell phone in one hand and a PalmPilot in the other. He found her by the side of the stage. As he approached, she tore off a check and handed it to the woman in charge.

He grinned in relief. "I thought you might be on the cell setting up the Parker meeting and miss the auction."

Deena accepted the receipt and tucked it into her large shoulder briefcase. "I took that call while we worked our way through Christopher Columbus and Henry the Eighth. You're flying out to see John Parker first thing Monday morning. I've arranged for Legal to review the initial offer and I've put off the press conference until Tuesday. If the meeting goes well, we'll have it. If not, there's plenty of time to cancel it."

She rattled off the rest of the arrangements she'd made while he'd been busy preparing to be sold to the highest bidder.

As always, her efficiency impressed him. When his assistant of ten years had retired nearly nine months ago to spend more time with her husband and grandchildren, he'd doubted she could be replaced. But Amanda Smith's last act had been to find him Deena. At first he'd balked at the idea of a pretty woman in her twenties sitting in the office next to his. His assistant had to travel with him, be available seven days a week and generally keep his life in order. Foolish young women only interested in the latest fashions or finding a man need not apply.

But despite his misgivings, Deena had proved herself to be even better than he'd thought possible. Without her keeping his life running smoothly, Thornton Industries would not be on the verge of closing a multibillion-dollar deal.

He glanced at the well-dressed crowd. "Let's get out of here before they rope us into staying for lunch."

Deena nodded and led the way to the waiting limo. As she walked, she stuffed her PalmPilot and cell phone into her briefcase. She was shaking so much that she thought she might drop them.

What had seemed like a really cool idea at the time had instead turned into a nightmare. Knowing she only had herself to blame for the situation didn't make the knot in her stomach go away.

She could still get out of it, she told herself. All she had to do was tell Alex that she'd used her own money instead of the company's and all would be made right. He would reimburse her and life would go on as before. Except then she might never get a chance at what she really wanted—to be seen as a person by the only man she'd ever loved.

Alex held open the rear door of the limo, then climbed in after her.

"How much did you have to pay?" he asked as he began to unbutton his costume jacket.

"Eight thousand dollars." Money that had just about cleaned out her savings account.

He raised his dark eyebrows. "Eight thousand for twenty-four hours? Not a bad living." He shrugged out of the jacket. As he moved, his muscles clenched and released.

Tall, lean and strong, Alex played as hard as he worked.

Three mornings a week he spent an hour in the company gym. Deena knew, because she was usually there with him, going through her own exercise routine, with a small tape recorder tucked in her pocket. She took verbal notes, sometimes breathlessly, depending on her level of exercise and whether or not Alex took off his shirt.

"Set up a brunch with the lawyers for Sunday," he said.

Nine months and fourteen days after she'd walked into his office for her initial interview and had been struck by lightning, Deena was finally prepared to do something about her completely foolish, completely inappropriate feelings. Because she couldn't go on like this anymore. Because she had to know if there was chance. Better to find out the truth, even if it was bad, than spend the rest of her life wondering.

"No," she said quietly.

"And then you can—" Alex stared at her. "What did you say?"

She squared her shoulders. "No. You won't be having brunch with the lawyers on Sunday. You'll be with me. I didn't use the company check you gave me, Alex. I used my own money and bought you myself. Starting Saturday at noon, you're mine for twenty-four hours."

CHAPTER TWO

ALEX couldn't have been more surprised if the limo had spoken. "You what?"

Deena's steady gaze never left his face. "I bought you myself. You're mine. I can schedule the brunch for Saturday, if you'd prefer." She reached for her cell phone.

Saturday would work, he thought, then mentally stumbled. *Deena* had bought him? "Why?" he asked.

He'd seen his assistant go without sleep when helping him close a big deal. She'd worked with the flu, through holidays and during an earthquake. He'd shown up at her apartment in the middle of the night, where she'd accepted the invasion with good grace and an offer of coffee. But he'd never seen her blush or look away.

"You don't have a life," she said. "There is nothing for you but Thornton Industries. You have no family, no social life. I want to show you that there's a whole world out there you need to acquaint yourself with."

He had a life. A good life. Yes, work consumed him, but what else was there?

"A nice thought," he said, "but not necessary. I'll reimburse you for the money."

"No."

No argument, no persuasion, just a simple refusal. He'd known Deena long enough to understand that when she dug in her heels, she couldn't be budged. That was one of the things he liked about her. She wasn't afraid to push back when she thought he was wrong.

"Deena, this is a busy time for me."

"It's always busy. That's how you like it. It's just twenty-four hours, Alex. It's the weekend, and the markets are closed. Everyone else is going to be taking it easy, so you don't have to worry about the business."

"What if I promise to take a vacation in a few months?"

She shook her head. "We both know you'd be lying. I'll pick you up tomorrow at noon. Dress casual."

Los Angeles was home to enough of the rich and famous that nearly everything amazing was available to rent. Which was why Deena pulled up in front of Alex's building with her own—for the weekend anyway—sleek silver BMW convertible.

She'd moved from simply shaking to feeling nauseous—definitely not an improvement. Her Aunt Amanda might applaud Deena's tactics, but she would take her to task for lying.

"But I couldn't tell him the *real* reason I bid on him," Deena murmured as she waved at the doorman and made her way to the elevator. "Alex sees me as a piece of office furniture, not a woman. Telling him I care about him would be as interesting to him as if the fax machine declared its affection. Telling him I'm doing this for his own good is better. Really."

Had Aunt Amanda been there, the old woman would have looked disappointed, even though she wouldn't have said anything. Her aunt was a firm believer in unconditional love.

Deena exited the elevator on the top floor and made her way to Alex's penthouse. She was still rationalizing the decision to keep her feelings to herself as she pushed the bell.

She half expected him not to be there. After all, he'd grumbled under his breath the entire previous afternoon, complaining about all the work he would be missing. But he'd never actually refused. She tried to tell herself that was a good thing.

When the door opened, she braced herself for more complaints. Then she was glad she was braced because while Alex in a suit made her heart beat faster and Alex in workout clothes made her want to throw herself in front of him, Alex in jeans and a snug-fitting polo shirt took her breath away.

Soft worn denim hugged strong thighs and narrow hips, while the deep red shirt emphasized broad shoulders. Her gaze rose to the set of his square jaw, to his firm mouth that smiled ever so slightly. Finally she looked at his eyes—dark, mesmerizing and today filled with questions. As usual, his dark hair was short and layered, with a single lock drifting onto his forehead.

How many times had she wanted to lean close and push that wayward strand back into place? How many times had they worked late, pouring over schedules, planning meetings, all the while sitting shoulder to shoulder, his masculine scent invading her body and making it nearly impossible to stay rational?

"Right on time," he said. "You told me casual. Does this work?" He lightly brushed the front of his shirt.

She nodded because speaking was more than she could manage. She'd been planning this day since Alex had walked into her office and tossed the charity request for the bachelor auction on her desk and announced his intention of having her buy him so he could be charitable but not lose time. So much rode on these few hours. If Alex could finally see her as a person rather than a machine—as a *woman*—then maybe there was a chance. If not she would have to find a way to collect the bits of her broken heart and move on.

"So what's the plan?" he asked as he stepped into the hall and closed the door behind him. "I've been thinking about this and figured you'd want to get back at me for all the nights I made you work late. Are you going to have me wax your car? Paint your living room?"

She thought of the elegant and expensive day and evening she'd arranged. "Not exactly."

Not exactly was right, Alex thought as they pulled up at the marina and Deena led the way to a beautiful seventy-foot yacht.

On board the captain greeted them. The boat was theirs for the next five hours. Where would they like to go?

"How about cruising up the coast?" Deena asked. "All right with you?"

As she spoke, a crewman opened a bottle of champagne and poured them each a glass. Alex took in the luxurious cabin, the elegant furniture and the tray of hors d'oeuvres beside the champagne and frowned.

As he'd already told Deena, he'd expected her to force him into hard labor for their twenty-four hours together. He'd never thought she would come up with something like this.

"Alex? The cruise?"

"Whatever you'd like."

He accepted the glass of champagne then followed Deena

onto deck where they watched the crew cast off. It might be winter everywhere else, but Los Angeles was balmy and clear.

While their yacht moved through the maze of boats at Marina del Rey, Alex found himself more interested in the woman standing next to him than in the spectacular view. She looked different. For once her long hair was loose, rather than up or in a braid. She wore tailored cream slacks and a matching blazer, while her silky shirt exactly matched her dark-green eyes.

Had she been anyone else, he would have done the math. One yacht, one bottle of champagne and an entire night together. It equaled seduction to him. But that wasn't Deena's style…was it?

He realized he knew nothing about her personal life. Nothing about her, save the fact that she made his world rotate smoothly.

If she had seduction in mind, did he want to participate?

She turned and caught him staring at her. One corner of her mouth curved up in a smile.

"What?" she asked.

"You're a surprise," he said.

"You mean the boat and everything."

"No. I mean you."

CHAPTER THREE

ALEX'S VOICE rubbed against her like warm velvet. Deena had to consciously hold in a shiver, while she attempted a cool, sophisticated expression.

"I'm who I've always been," she told him.

His dark gaze never left her face. "Funny, I didn't notice."

Hardly news. "I'm like one of those multifunctional printers. Except I do more than print, copy and scan." Sad but true.

He chuckled. "If you're trying to make me forget work, you're doing a great job. All right, Deena, now that you have me here, what do you plan to do with me?"

She hated that her mind instantly flashed to the large master suite she'd seen when she'd toured the yacht before reserving it. The bed was large, and the amenities impressive enough to dazzle a prince...or a tycoon.

But she'd never been one to make the first move, and buying Alex for the day had used up all her moxy.

"I plan to show you a good time."

"What does that involve?"

"A few hours here on the water. You told me once you used to crew on sailboats in the summer and that you missed it."

He frowned. "How could you remember that?"

Because she remembered everything he said, everything he did. He was her world. Either she evened the score and became his world, too, or she had to make a clean break and start her life over. That was the other reason she'd carefully planned their time together. If it wasn't going to work with Alex, then this was goodbye.

"You painted such a vivid description of racing on those boats," she said instead, leaning against the railing. "So that's our afternoon. Tonight we're having dinner at a very exclusive restaurant in Malibu. We have reservations for a surf-side table, followed by dancing at a club in Santa Monica. Tomorrow—"

He threw her off by moving close and resting his free hand on top of hers. There was the cool brass railing beneath her fingers and his warm skin on top.

"What about after dinner and dancing?" he asked. "Where will I spend the night?"

Her mind chose that moment to seize up. Fortunately fate was smiling, and she was saved from answering by the appearance of a pod of gray whales directly in front of the boat.

"Aren't they beautiful?" she murmured as one whale blew water into the air.

Alex leaned close. "If you're not going to tell me, you're going to have to show me eventually."

They settled on chairs on the warm deck. Alex stretched out his legs and studied Deena. What kind of a woman arranged for an afternoon like this, then blushed when he asked where he would spend the night? Two days ago, if someone had asked him what he knew about his assistant, he would have claimed complete knowledge of every part of her. Now he realized he knew nothing.

"Tell me about your family," he said.

She sipped her champagne. "There's not much to tell. I have an older sister, Jenny. My parents died when I was sixteen."

He frowned. "I'm sorry. I didn't know that. What happened afterwards? Did you go to live with your sister?"

"My aunt. Her children were already grown. She used to say she and my uncle rattled around in their big house, and that having me around kept them young." Her mouth softened into a tender smile. "She's the best."

"What about your sister?"

"She was already in college. She graduated with a nursing degree, then got married. Now she has two little girls and another baby on the way."

"Everyone close?"

She looked surprised by the question. "Of course."

No doubt in her world, families stayed together, cared about one another. His world was very different.

"How old are you?" he asked.

"Twenty-seven."

"Why aren't you married?"

Humor darkened her eyes. "Perversity. The one I wanted to ask didn't, and the one I didn't want to ask did."

Which made him want to know who had been refused and who had been foolish enough not to inquire.

The boat docked at five-thirty. As Deena unlocked the sleek convertible, she glanced at him across the low cloth top.

"I had your tux dry-cleaned last week," she said. "It's hanging in your closet."

"Will I need it for the restaurant?"

"Yes. Dinner will be formal."

"What will you be wearing?"

"A dress."

"Long?"

She nodded.

"Low-cut?"

She swallowed, then nodded a second time.

He couldn't wait.

She'd said dinner followed by dancing. He had a feeling there was going to be a change in plans. After dinner he would take her for a walk along the beach. It would be quiet, romantic and private. There under the stars, he would get to know the very intriguing young woman who had suddenly appeared in his world. Or had she been there all along, and had he simply not noticed?

She slide onto the driver's seat, then inserted the key. But before she started the engine, her cell phone rang. She reached for her bag.

"Hello?"

Alex watched the play of light and shadows on her face. Before today he'd never taken the time to notice the creamy perfection of her skin, or the dozen or so freckles across her nose. He liked the tiny line that formed between her eyebrows as she spoke and the fullness of her lips. How had he never seen any of this before? How had—

He realized Deena had tensed as she spoke. Her eyes widened with what he would have sworn was panic.

"Are you all right?" she asked, her voice low and strained. She listened before responding. "Of course. No, don't worry about it. I'll be right there."

She hung up and turned to him. "My sister has gone into labor about four weeks early. My aunt and uncle are out of town on vacation, and she doesn't have anyone else to look after her two girls. I'm sorry, but I need to take you home right away, then get to her house so they can leave for the hospital."

He took in her pinched mouth and the white knuckles where she gripped the steering wheel.

"Don't worry about me," he said. "Drive to your sister's. I'll find my own way from there."

CHAPTER FOUR

WORRY DOGGED Deena for the entire drive to her sister's house. She barely remembered to put on the parking brake before jumping out of the car and racing up to the front door.

"Jenny? Are you all right?" she called as she stepped inside.

She found her sister leaning against the wall by the stairs and panting heavily. The twins huddled close; John, their father, crouched beside them.

Jenny looked up and waved slightly, even as she winced, then sighed.

"That one was strong. Look, girls, Auntie Deena is here."

The twins smiled, but didn't let go of their father. It took the promise of baking cookies, along with *two* Disney movies to get them to loosen their grip.

"I'll be fine," Jenny said as she briefly hugged Deena. "Thanks for coming over. I appreciate it."

Deena clung to her for a second. Her sister might be calm on the inside, but Deena felt her worry as if it were her own. "Have John call me as soon as you know something."

"I promise."

Jenny waddled toward the door. She paused when she saw Alex. "Okay, I'm sure there's a story here, but it's going to have to wait."

Alex watched the very pregnant woman being gently escorted out to the car by her husband, then he turned back to look at Deena sitting on the bottom step. She had a child on either side. The young girls were small, red-haired with big, blue eyes. They were identical, right down to the brown-and-red stains on the front of their kitten-covered T-shirts.

"Who are you?" one of the girls asked.

Deena smiled at him. "Sorry. I haven't done introductions. Alex, these are my nieces, Kari and Lucy."

She touched each child's head as she said her name, but he knew there was no way he was going to keep them straight.

The girl on the left eyed him. "You've very tall," she said.

Not sure if that was a compliment or a complaint, he shoved his hands into his jeans and decided not to answer.

"I'm going to be stuck here for a while," Deena said. "I'll get in touch with my aunt and uncle, but they won't be able to get home for a couple of days. Until then, the twins only have me." She tried to smile, but it wobbled a bit at the corners. "I guess this means you're off the hook. For our date, I mean."

She was saying he could go.

"Aunt Deena, are we really gonna make cookies?" one of the girls asked.

"You bet. We'll make the batter and let it get cold overnight. In the morning we'll cut the cookies into shapes. When they're finished baking, we're going to decorate them. You'll have a good time."

She turned her attention back to him. "I can't fit the girls into the convertible. It doesn't have a back seat. So I can't drive you home. Would you mind calling a cab?"

He didn't know much about children. He'd been one once, but he did his best to forget those days. He didn't know much about pregnancy, either, but he could read the worry in Deena's eyes. She'd said Jenny had gone into labor a few weeks early. Did that mean something could go wrong?

"You paid for twenty-four hours," he said, pulling his

hands from him pockets and rolling up the sleeves. "So you're stuck with me. Besides, I've never made cookies. Maybe you could teach me."

He addressed that last bit to the two girls. They both grinned at him. "Makin' cookies is really fun," one of them told him. "You gonna like it."

Making cookies wasn't just fun, it was also messy. By the time they'd made the batter and wrapped it in plastic so it could refrigerate overnight, there was enough flour, sugar and butter smeared over the kitchen to qualify it for demolition. Deena's cheeks were streaked with the mixture, as were the twins', and Alex didn't want to know what he looked like.

After cookies, they'd settled in to watch two cartoon movies, by the end of which both girls had fallen asleep. Somehow having a small warm child draped across his chest and shoulder did something odd to his heart, he thought as he picked up Lucy and followed Deena upstairs.

She carried Kari and led the way into the twins' bedroom.

"I'm not going to bother putting them in their pj's," she said quietly. "There's no point in waking them up just to change their clothes."

Alex put Lucy in her bed, while Deena took care of her sister. She'd barely pulled up the blanket when the phone rang.

As Deena raced down the hall, Alex stayed in the girls' room. He checked that the night-light was on and then glanced around at the toys, books and clothes covering every surface. It was little more than controlled chaos, but homey. He could feel the love that filled this house.

He'd never thought of having a family. His goals had all been about business. For the first time, he wondered if he'd been missing something.

He heard Deena in the hallway and went out to greet her.

"That was John," she said as she sagged against the wall.

"Jenny's fine. They had a boy and he's doing really well. His lungs are working; he's okay. They're all okay."

She looked at him, smiled, covered her face with her hands and burst into tears.

Started, Alex moved toward her. "What's wrong?" he asked. "Isn't this what you wanted to hear?"

She nodded. "I'm happy," she said between sobs. "I l-love my s-sister, and I was so w-worried. It's just everything else is ruined."

He pulled her close, meaning to offer comfort. So he didn't let himself notice the heat of her body or how good she felt in his arms. "What's ruined?"

"Our day. I wanted to go to d-dinner with you and be beautiful. I wanted you to see me as a w-woman, not just a piece of office equipment. I spent all my savings on the boat and the dress and b-buying you at the auction, and now it's all ruined."

"What happened to you buying me because I needed a break from work?"

She dropped her hands to her sides and looked at him. Tears dampened her lashes and ran down her cheeks. She sniffed.

"I lied."

"Then you will have to be dealt with most severely."

Her breath caught, but before she could speak, he lowered his head and kissed her.

CHAPTER FIVE

DEENA COULDN'T believe it. Alex was *kissing* her. His warm, tender lips teased hers with a sensual gentleness that made her want to melt against him. He tilted his head slightly, then brushed her lower lip with his tongue. Instantly she parted for him.

He claimed her—passionately. There was no mistaking his need, or his desire. He wanted her.

"You want me?" she asked when he drew back.

He gave her a smile that spoke of male confidence. "Yes, and I mean to have you."

She supposed she should have bristled at his assumption, but she'd waited too long to be anything but happy.

"Only not tonight," he said, rubbing her lower lip with his thumb. "We have other priorities."

He glanced toward the twins' bedroom. "But soon."

He put his arm around her and led her downstairs. When they were settled on the sofa, he pulled her close. Her head was spinning. This was all happening too fast.

"I don't understand," she said. "When did you figure out I was more than just office equipment?"

He shrugged. "I think I've always known, but I never allowed myself to acknowledge the information. It would have interfered with business."

"And now?"

He grinned. "Business be damned."

His smile faded. "I'm not like you, Deena," he said as he took her hand in his. "I didn't grow up surrounded by a loving family. I never knew my father. My mother…" He dropped her hand. "She preferred partying with her friends to taking care of a child."

Her heart tightened as she sensed his pain. "Oh, Alex."

He looked at her. "I was taken away by the State when I was eight. Maybe it was better. My foster parents believed in education and hard work. They taught me about goals. There wasn't a lot of affection, but I didn't care about that—or so I told myself. They had a small business, which I bought from them when I turned twenty."

She knew the rest of the story. "You grew it into Thornton Industries."

He nodded. "There wasn't much time for anything but

work. I was engaged once, but I found out she was only in it for the money."

She ached for him. "I'm sorry."

"I'm not. She reinforced my belief that women don't care enough to stay."

Deena filled in the rest of the pieces: That he didn't matter enough to make them want to stay.

"You matter to me," she said. "More than you can imagine."

"I know." He leaned close. "Did you really empty out your savings just to arrange for our day together?"

"I have about eight dollars left."

"You didn't have to impress me. You could have simply told me the truth."

"When? Where? At the office between our international sales meeting and the regional summit? You would have thought I was crazy."

Alex considered her words, then nodded. "You're right. I needed to get out of the office to really see you."

The phone rang. Deena jumped up. "That will be Aunt Amanda. John said he was going to phone her next."

"Amanda?" He considered the possibility, then dismissed it. Too coincidental.

But Deena knew him well. Perhaps too well. She grinned.

"Yes, that Amanda. Your former assistant. When she decided to retire, she suggested I apply for her job. She said we would be well matched. Funny, at the time I thought she was talking about a working relationship, but now I have a feeling she meant something else entirely."

He followed Deena to the phone and waited until she'd spoken with her aunt. Once they'd discussed Jenny and the new baby, he took the phone.

"It's Alex," he said.

"Hello, dear. John told me you were with Deena."

He heard the humor and pleasure in her voice. "You planned this all along," he said. "You *wanted* me to fall for your niece."

"I had high hopes. I knew you were perfectly matched, but I also knew how focused you were on your work. I wasn't sure Deena would be able to get through."

He glanced at the beautiful woman standing next to him. "I would have been a fool not to see her."

"It has taken you over nine months to notice, Alex. That doesn't make you clever."

He laughed and returned the phone to Deena.

Later, when they had talked for hours and kissed and talked some more, Alex stared into her eyes. "Your aunt is right. I was a fool."

"Not anymore."

"I don't want to lose you," he said.

"I don't want to be lost." She kissed him. "I'm not leaving, Alex. I'm right where I belong."

* * * * *